W

THE HOLIDAY

THE HOLIDAY

GUY BELLAMY

SIMON & SCHUSTER

LONDON · SYDNEY · NEW YORK · TOKYO · SINGAPORE · TORONTO

First published in Great Britain by Simon & Schuster
Ltd, 1995
A Paramount Communications Company

Simon & Schuster Ltd
West Garden Place
Kendal Street
London W2 2AQ

Simon & Schuster of Australia Pty Ltd
Sydney

A CIP catalogue record for this book is available from the
British Library

ISBN 0-671-71899-1

Typeset in 12/15pt Garamond by
Hewer Text Composition Services, Edinburgh
Printed and bound in Great Britain by
Butler & Tanner, Frome, Somerset

For KATE BELLAMY

I am indebted to Elaine Lewis, who sacrificed valuable holiday time in the higher cause of literary research. And my thanks to Tessa Grellier and Sir Cyril Pitts who told me things I needed to know but didn't.

G. B.

WEEK 1

Travel, in the younger sort, is a part of education;
in the elder, a part of experience.

Francis Bacon

1

High over the Languedoc, a Boeing 737 belonging to Air France is scorching a solitary path through a sky that has become, in the last ten miles, completely cloudless. The view from the windows is no longer of endless white fluff but of the Cévennes, old granite mountains thickly wooded with oaks and pines and interspersed with steep-sided valleys and clear mountain streams. As the pilot makes a slight adjustment directing the aircraft to the south-east, those on the left of the plane find themselves gazing down at the wildest and least-explored region of France.

It is a view which holds no interest for one man in the first-class compartment whose immediate needs are adequately catered for. He has a large gin on the tray in front of him, a copy of *The Times*, and a beautiful girl in the next seat. It is the opinion of some of his fellow passengers in this privileged corner of the plane that the girl is too young to be his wife, and too old to be his daughter. It is possible that she is his secretary, but this is not an option that appeals to the bored passengers in the first-class compartment who did not get where they are today without exercising a little imagination. As the plane heads south, the bare brown hills below are replaced by olive and cypress trees, but this transition passes unnoticed by the first-class customers of Air France who, with the arrival of smoked salmon, have more immediate consolations to attend to.

Andrew Marner is sipping his gin and wondering what else he has to do to get a knighthood. The path to honours and recognition had always seemed clear enough: an exemplary life, a little charity work and copious donation to the Conservative Party. Andrew Marner has not only completed this hat-trick, but he is also a magazine publisher, and frightened politicians traditionally shower publishers with honours in the hope of sympathetic publicity. That Andrew Marner has so far been ignored by the mysterious men in Whitehall is a continuing source of grievance in a world which has usually bent to his will. He picks up *The Times* again and studies a new explanation of the economic malaise which afflicts Western civilisation.

The ambitions of Andrew Marner are but idle whims compared with the demons which drive the girl who sits beside him. Kimberley Neal, a tall, leggy blonde of thirty, is twenty years younger than her handsome, silver-haired travelling companion. She has never paid for a first-class air ticket in her life but is evidently at home here.

There is no gin on the tray in front of her, which she is using as a desk. On an unruled A4 pad she is scribbling sentence after sentence with a gold Cross biro. Occasionally she pauses and looks thoughtfully at the other passengers but mostly the words are pouring out as if this is a conversation which she is monopolising.

Kimberley Neal writes a page in one of the weekly magazines owned by Andrew Marner. She is hoping that someone from a national newspaper will spot her column and offer her far more money than she now earns to write for them, so that she will be read by millions instead of thousands, and earn thousands instead of hundreds. It is a column of comment, hyperbole and venom, but what Kimberley is really selling is her opinion. She has opinions on everything – Princess Di, children's television, Salman Rushdie, the modern man, designer clothes, the morals of politicians and the politics of morality. No subject has drifted into her sights that she couldn't pass a 200-word judgement on within half an hour.

She picks her pad off the tray, sits back in her seat and reads what she has written: *'The arrival of the ten-year-old murderer is a chastening moment for the so-called civilised community known as Great Britain. What do you do with a ten-year-old murderer?*

'But the real question is: who has created this monster? Who has produced it, moulded it, trained it? Whose handiwork is it?

'And the answer, naturally, is the parents. The dismal phenomenon of juvenile evil will continue until we deal with its root cause.

'I'd have the parents in the dock along with their poorly-reared offspring. And if a child is convicted of murder, I'd give Mummy and Daddy not less than five years each.'

Kimberley Neal reads over these words with a satisfied smile. Bringing up children is not a dilemma that she has faced, having meticulously avoided the horrors of motherhood while cheerfully pursuing a sex-life that makes a rabbit seem ascetic. She offers the pad to Andrew Marner who lowers his newspaper to take it.

'Splendid, Kim,' he says, fondling her knee. 'It takes you four paragraphs to say something that would take anyone else four pages.'

'Any ideas?' she asks. 'I've got to fax this column by tomorrow.'

Andrew Marner drinks his gin. He pays other people to have ideas and often wonders where they get them from.

'Why don't you wait until we arrive?' he says eventually. 'I should have thought that the south of France will provide you with plenty of material. The food, the *mores*, the Gallic charm.'

'Don't be silly, darling,' says Kimberley Neal. 'If I dateline it "the Côte d'Azur", everybody will know that I'm here with you.'

The remark gives Andrew Marner a jolt. He is so comfortably ensconced here with this girl that he has completely forgotten that deceit is built into the programme. He glances round the first-class compartment, half-expecting to see a familiar face gleefully recognising him.

He is flying to Nice for a series of business meetings with a French publisher; wrapping a three-week holiday around these tedious discussions was not difficult. Nor was it hard to persuade Kimberley Neal to accompany him, or to convince his wife that she would be less bored at home. In fact, everything has been so easy that he has forgotten the dangers. He beckons a stewardess and asks for another gin, and then reaches between his knees for his code-locked executive briefcase. The documents that he draws from this wrinkle his brow. Too many words are in French, and his staff have failed to provide him with a translation. He stares at the sheaf of papers but, making no sense to him, they fail to hold his attention.

Instead he contemplates life in a five-star hotel with Kimberley Neal. The sexual athletics which had once been a central part of his life have been circumscribed by recent depressing developments, and he wistfully recalls the magic years that began with the acceptance of the Pill and skidded to a panic-stricken halt with the arrival of Aids – twenty years of spontaneous sex without fear of descendants or disease. Caution was now the fashion, but when he met Kimberley Neal on a felucca on the Nile, she volunteered the information quite early on that she had been tested for Aids (for an article that she was writing, she said) and suddenly it was just like the sexy Seventies again.

He returns the documents to his case and picks up his *Times*. He reads about transputer microprocessors, fibre optic telephone systems and video CDs. He marvels at the progress the human race is making, but what really grabs his attention as he turns the pages of his newspaper is the high proportion of knighthoods that have been awarded to the people mentioned in it.

Twenty rows behind him where the knee-room is harder to find and the cutlery is white plastic, sit a silent couple who are immersed in such literature as they can find in the seat pocket in front. They ignore the occasional information that the pilot feels obliged to pass along about the progress of the flight, and decline the offer of duty-free baubles from the hyperactive cabin staff.

Bruce Kerwin, forty, freshly redundant and confronting a future that horrifies him, finds it impossible to relax on a plane. His routine is to stay belted in his

7

seat, never visit the toilets or stand up, and to listen with a morbid intensity to the sound of the aircraft's engines, monitoring and worrying over every change of tone. He is aware that this concern would make him an object of ridicule among today's hordes who use planes as carelessly as their parents once used buses, and so he suffers in silence, holding himself in a state of nervous tension until that delicious moment when he will feel the wheels bump on to the reassuring concrete of an endless runway. Only then will he allow himself the indulgence of a smile, as if the triumph of this safe arrival is all his.

A neurosis like this is infectious, and beside him his wife Frances betrays few signs that she is enjoying the journey. She is reading an article about Italian fashion designers in an airline magazine but is distracted by her husband's laconic précis of the realities of air travel, delivered tactlessly at the airport.

'You've got a machine that's seventy metres long,' he had said, 'and you pour two hundred thousand litres of flammable liquid into it, sit four hundred people on top, light the fuel in several places and go rocketing into the air at over two hundred miles an hour. Does that seem sensible to you?'

This close to take-off her response is less confident than it might have been.

'People do it,' she said.

'People climb mountains,' he had said. 'Their bleached bones are everywhere.'

Bruce Kerwin is a man who has run into a mid-life crisis rather earlier than he had expected. The career which was supposed to carry him in comparative comfort until retirement or death has evaporated in the recession. It was a double blow because of the surprise. He wasn't working in one of those vulnerable jobs like building or manufacturing, where the first winds of economic disturbance blow thousands into the dole queue. He was the manager of a Legal & General branch office, dealing in insurance and mortgages; it was a job where you could smell the money. But one morning there was no job and he left the firm their car and walked home.

In the days that follow, he discovers that all those stories about the shortage of jobs is not just stuff they used to fill up the news bulletins on television. It turns out to be an accurate picture of how things are today. Nobody wants to employ anybody.

This is not a setback that Bruce Kerwin is temperamentally equipped to handle, and as he sits tensely in the sky over France he wonders whether he is genetically gloomy, whether pessimism is bred in his bones. He has watched other men throw themselves into the demands of four-children families while doing nightwork and earning little, and yet managing to offer the rest of the world a smile and a joke. Bruce Kerwin cannot do that. Even when the times are good he seems to bring a depressed expression to the party.

He spots this flaw in himself but he can't explain it except by heredity. Like begats like. Footballers have sons who play football, actors have sons who act, politicians have sons who go into politics. His father was not a happy man.

Frances Kerwin, at thirty-eight, is an attractive woman, with black shoulder-length hair and sparkling eyes. She is wearing a sleeveless red dress and white cotton jacket bought, on one of her many shopping trips, specially for this holiday, which was her idea.

'You're out of work, you can't get a job, we'll have a holiday,' she had told her husband. 'Think of all the times when you couldn't take a holiday because of the demands of the job. Well, now you can. It'll give you a chance to consider your future.'

'I haven't got a future,' said Bruce Kerwin, but his wife ignored this and headed for the nearest travel agent.

Now, as the Boeing edges them ever nearer to the red rocks, the golden sand and the blue sea of the Riviera, she is determined to forget the uncertain prospects of the Kerwin family and make this a holiday to remember.

She turns to her husband who is staring expressionlessly through a window. With his short hair and his little moustache, he reminds her of the ailing star of an Aids documentary, but his manifold vices do not run to sodomy, a solace she clings to in these difficult times.

'What was the name of the girl who sang "Little Things Mean A Lot"?' she asks. 'Do you remember the record?'

'Was it Brenda Lee?'

'No,' she says impatiently. 'Not Brenda Lee.'

Bruce Kerwin turns back to the window and looks down at wild mountain terrain and hilltop villages. Why do they call this a crowded planet? he wonders. There seems to be room in France for another billion people.

Frances Kerwin hums the tune to herself but the singer's name won't come. She must either remember the singer or forget the problem, or it will nag at her for days. She picks up her magazine and tries to concentrate on Italian designers.

Sunlight pours into the cabin, hitting their faces at an unnatural angle. An aged couple struggle up the aisle in the direction of the toilets and Bruce Kerwin frowns at them as if their selfish journey will interfere with the equilibrium of the plane. He glances at his watch and then remembers to wind it on one hour. This seems to bring his arrival time much nearer and he sits back feeling that his ordeal is almost over.

'What are we going to do on this holiday, anyway?' he asks.

Frances Kerwin puts down her magazine with its pictures of chiffon tops and satin trouser suits, and says: 'Think of it as a second honeymoon.'

'A second honeymoon?' says her husband. The idea disturbs him. Recent setbacks have mysteriously drained his energy.

'Think of appetites,' says Frances, smiling flirtatiously. 'Food, drink, love. We're going to satisfy 'em.'

'What about sunbathing and sightseeing?' asks her husband. 'Any time for that?'

'We'll try to fit it in,' says Frances, 'but we've got to concentrate on the essentials first.'

Bruce Kerwin tries to remember his first honeymoon, twenty years ago when marriage was still fashionable. A cheap hotel beneath a grey Cornish sky, a windy beach. Life was full of promise, laughter and hope because he didn't realise then how hard it could become. Food, drink and love? There had been fish and chips, beer and sex, and they had never been so happy. It seemed inconceivable that all that lovemaking should not have produced a baby, but no child appeared then or later. It was the first blemish on their life plan.

The years have sobered him now – the years with their dashed hopes, unfulfilled ambitions and sorry disappointments. He has learned to adjust, to water down his hopes, to lower his expectations. Until the bombshell of redundancy came flying through the window, he had learned to accept – but now he is beginning to wonder whether the world has been entirely fair with him. A sense of grievance is beginning to gnaw.

Thirty thousand feet beneath them, threading its way between olive groves and fields of lavender, a grey Ford Granada is doggedly heading south. It has forsaken the autoroute in search of wild, untamed countryside – wooden mountains and limestone gorges – but is slowing now in the hope of enjoying the more certain pleasures of French liquor.

At the wheel, contemplating a rare spell of leisure, is Roger Blake, a lean man of about thirty whose handsome features are beginning to look a little worn. He has calculated that it is just under 800 miles from Calais to Toulon and he is wondering where he is going to break this journey and spend the night. He follows a small Italian car off the main road and drives behind it into a village. A notice in the back window of the Italian car says BIMBO A BORDO, and there is, indeed, a small child in the back waving a soft toy that has one arm.

The Ford Granada pulls into a brown, tree-filled square where a man on stilts is playing a violin.

'What we want,' says Roger Blake, 'is a proper French bar with a zinc counter.'

The girl to whom this remark is addressed is studying a Michelin map of southern France which, so far as she can tell, they have not yet reached. She is a slim, pretty girl with short, brown, wavy hair. For the purpose of reading the map she is wearing a pair of cheap, wire-framed glasses.

'Oh yes?' she says. 'And what's the French for breathalyser?'

Roger Blake ignores this and parks the car in front of a small bar next to a patisserie. He climbs out and stretches his long legs and then he looks up at the cloudless sky in which a lonely Boeing 737 seems, from this distance, to be hardly moving at all.

'Abroad's better,' he says. 'The climate, the food, the wine, the scenery. Also, people don't talk to you.'

'You like that, do you?' asks the girl, whose name is Esme. 'People not talking to you?'

'Reticence is a much undervalued quality,' says Roger Blake, pushing the bar's door open. 'Think of the nonsense that people talk when they do open their mouths.'

Only two old men occupy the bar. They are sitting at a table playing cards and drinking pastis, and they look up briefly at the two English visitors, both wearing pale blue jeans and white shirts, who go up to the bar and order beer.

'I've got to get with this money,' says Roger Blake, studying French notes that he has pulled from his back pocket.

'It's seven point eight to the pound,' Esme tells him, picking up her beer.

'My God, it used to be ten. We're the paupers of Europe.'

'Paupers is what we are,' says Esme, and laughs. She worries about the wounded planet, the polluted water and the poisoned air, but she doesn't worry about money. She cries at the Hovis commercial but bills leave her cold.

Roger Blake looks at his French francs and wonders how long they will last. He cannot understand how financial success has eluded him. He has kept his eye on the target, ignored the distractions no matter how tempting, and put in the hours. This, he had read, was the recipe for prosperity and happiness and as his twenties ticked past he had looked to the looming milestone of his thirtieth birthday as being the date when he would be able to sit back for a moment and admire his perseverance, his achievements and his bank balance.

The discovery that at thirty he is marginally less well off than he had been at twenty angers and confuses him. His income has increased at a speed equalled only by his bills. He has formulated his own law to explain this mystery: expenditure rises to swallow available income. At twenty he had not had a house and a car and a lady like Esme. The demands had grown like plants in fertile soil, but the supply's slower improvement suggested that it was rooted in stonier ground.

Roger's work experience has been so widespread and disparate that he feels he should qualify for an award – Master of None, perhaps. If a job did not require five or six stultifying years in a training college he had thrown himself into it, collecting the basics, as it were, on the wing. The only demand that he made about the employment he had chosen was that, in doing the job, he was working for himself and not for somebody else who would cream off the rewards of his labour and pocket some money that should rightfully have belonged to Roger. This proviso had necessarily placed many activities beyond his reach, but he had in his time sold pine furniture, painted the inside and outside of large houses, laid both bricks and carpets, driven a taxi, opened a boarding kennel for cats and dogs and given driving lessons. The prohibition on being employed – a fundamental requisite for himself – did not seem so important when applied to other less demanding men, and he had in more than one of these projects hired three or four people who worked so conscientiously that he hadn't actually had to do any work himself.

From all of these experiences he had evolved into an unofficial one-man employment agency, introducing jobs that urgently needed to be done to men who were desperately seeking work. If a firm needed thirty men at Waterloo Station at six o'clock on a Sunday morning they saved time, money and sanity by phoning Roger Blake who promptly provided them. His total reliability at producing hired hands gave him a reputation among those who needed that sort of service, and no advertising was necessary. At this very moment, ten members of his unofficial team were working on a petrol station in Germany.

Roger Blake always paid the men promptly in cash, which was why there were so many who were willing to respond to his call, and he subsequently billed the firm for slightly more than he had paid out in used notes. He always knew that there were dangers in this system and he had recently found one. Having paid out £600 to each of twenty-five men for work on a new housing estate, he discovered that his bill to the firm for £20,000 arrived on the day after it went into liquidation.

The hole that this has kicked in his nest egg causes a drastic reorganisation of the three-week holiday that he had promised Esme in the sun. They are driving, not flying. And in the boot of the Ford Granada is a tent.

This modification to their arrangements does not attract the disappointment that he has expected. The prospect of life in a tent seems to lift Esme's spirits in a way that he has not anticipated. She talks about being closer to nature and refers lewdly to 'the alfresco bonk'. Lyrical references to fresh air and flowers fill her conversation.

Roger Blake, who had thought that camping sites had been mercifully consigned to the past, is less enthusiastic about life under canvas. He has grown to appreciate the comforts of a modern hotel with amiable chambermaids and obedient waiters, service at all hours and an *en suite* bathroom. This lurch into the impoverished customs of his youth alarms him, reinforcing the feeling that has come to obsess him lately, that for every step forward in his life there has been at least one step back.

He picks up his bottle of beer and reads the label. *Bière d'Alsace*, it says. *25cl*. It is certainly small and something of an insult to a man who is accustomed to drinking pints of lager; he orders another bottle.

'They sell it by the mouthful here,' he complains. 'It'll be hard work getting tired and emotional.'

'We don't want you to get drunk, darling,' says Esme. 'We want you fit, brown and sexy.'

'Couldn't I be fit, brown, sexy and drunk?' he asks. 'I've always been versatile.' He pours the new bottle into his empty glass.

'It depends what you want from this holiday,' Esme says, watching him.

'Good ale and a comely wench,' he replies promptly.

'No, that's what you get at home,' she tells him. 'Here the options are broader.'

'In fact,' he says, ignoring her, 'if you could get lager out of women's breasts life would be almost perfect.'

'Sometimes I think you don't take life seriously enough, Roger,' she says.

'I take it too seriously. That's my trouble.'

And he does look serious as he gazes into his beer, contemplating the austerity of life in a tent. He is wondering whether he should have borrowed some money to finance a more luxurious holiday, but he knows that the world is full of organisations that want to lend you money – unless you actually need it. They don't like it if you're poor.

He looks at his watch, which he has wound on one hour, and ponders aloud where they should spend the night. 'We don't want to get the tent out and then have to pack it away in the morning,' he says. 'We've got to find a room.'

'The open-air holiday didn't last very long,' says Esme.

'We'll camp when we get there,' he decides. 'Tonight it's going to be the luxury of a warm double bed.'

'Are you trying to tell me something,' she asks, 'in your shy, evasive way?'

2

Kimberley Neal checks her face in a small silver mirror she has pulled from her Gucci handbag. What she sees reassures her; she replaces it and turns to kiss Andrew Marner's cheek. She wants to believe that it is a lucky man who is allowed to enjoy what she thinks of as her charms, but admits privately that there have been so many that luck can hardly have been a factor.

The peck on the cheek barely interrupts Andrew Marner's reading, and Kimberley returns to her pad and the column that she is trying to write. The misguided aspirations of the demented royals seem to merit a vituperative blast, but too many other journalists have already trodden that path. She runs through likely targets in her head but nothing suitable occurs to her. The distractions of air travel – noisy children, chatty pilots, importunate cabin staff – don't help her concentration, and she watches a mother and baby on a seat to her right. Sometimes she thinks that she ought to get something organised in the mother-and-baby department before she is mugged by age, although in these days of cosmetic surgery and liposuction clinics, she should be able to put off the evil day for a while. One trip up the aisle and her career could shoot from obscurity to total oblivion – unless she married the right man.

The right man is sitting beside her, although she hadn't immediately recognised this when he approached her on the Nile. Andrew Marner, silver hair and head-to-toe Armani, seemed a little too distinguished for a struggling hackette with a sub-career in dating and mating, but the man turned out to be a walking hard-on and after extensive rumpy-pumpy, as he called it, in a Cairo hotel, she decided that it was a poor *quid* that didn't have its own *quo*. A month later she was writing the main column in one of his magazines. There were better jobs within his gift.

Women became editors now and not just of women's magazines. They edited national newspapers. They ran MI5 and the prosecution service. They became judges. They became Prime Minister.

The men were getting tired.

Kimberley feels that a high-profile editorship would be a suitable development in her career at this moment, and that a little holiday with the great man is her best chance of ensuring that it happens. Thirty is a nasty age, surrounded by ominous signposts. Either you are on your way up, or you are already heading for the glue factory.

A headline in Andrew Marner's newspaper catches her eye: DROPPED FOOD KILLS STARVING REFUGEES. There ought to be a point she could make there, she thinks, about the inefficiency of charities and whether the money ever reaches the destination that the donor intends. Problems that have baffled bureaucrats and stumped statesmen hold no terrors for her. She always has her answer ready. Ireland? Pay off the Protestants. Yugoslavia? Bomb Belgrade. She pulls out her pad again and starts to write.

Bored now and anxious to land, Andrew Marner is counting the knights on one page of *The Times*. He is beginning to feel that in the world in which he moves, 'misters' are a despised minority, pariahs without a handle.

'You work like a dog, and for what?' he mutters when he has finished counting.

'A lousy fortune?' suggests Kimberley Neal.

'Money!' says Andrew Marner reproachfully. 'What's money?'

'It's what makes people get out of bed,' she says. 'Unless they're in bed with you, of course.'

He smiles at her and touches her knee again. The thought of being in bed with this sex machine distracts him, but only temporarily. 'Any fool can make money and plenty have,' he says. 'A man needs more than money.'

'Are we talking sex here, Andrew?' she asks hopefully.

'Recognition, Kimberley. A just reward for a lifetime of service. My God, even that boss-eyed plank David Frost has got a knighthood.'

'I see,' says Kimberley. 'I didn't realise that you wanted a knighthood.' She is familiar with these sudden surges of fury that produce a red face and a cruel tongue. She loves him when he is angry.

'It would be nice to know that your efforts have been appreciated and not ignored,' he says. 'It's the way the system works.'

Kimberley Neal finds this revelation so interesting

that she puts down her gold Cross biro and considers it. Sir Andrew Marner. His name, she realises, is screaming out for a knighthood, unlike some others who had received the Queen's approval. Sir Alf Ramsey had never sounded right.

'When might this happen?' she asks.

'It doesn't look as if it *is* going to happen. That's the whole point,' says Andrew Marner irritably. 'They'll knight dozens of dozy backbenchers to compensate them for the fact that they're too thick for office, but the people who are out there in the real world, providing jobs, making things happen, paying taxes and achieving something, get ignored by the bastards.' His face is red again.

'It's not right,' says Kimberley soothingly. 'I could do a column about it.'

Andrew Marner shakes his head. 'Could be counter-productive.'

She leans back in her first-class seat and brushes a speck off her Versace psychedelic-print stretch jeans. Having an *inamorato* who had been knighted by the Queen would be a quantum leap for a poor girl from Bexley, and she allows herself the secret pleasure of imagining what it would do for her prestige. But soon she has abandoned the reviled role of mistress and replaced Bertha, the first Mrs Andrew Marner, who toils loyally at home and so generously shares her husband with a younger woman. Lady Marner ('*seen here at Ascot with Lord Doubleday and the Earl of Hereford*').

She closes her eyes and begins to think seriously about her holiday. She isn't sure that it's going to be hot enough. In an ideal world she would live in Spain and fly to France for the meals.

*   *   *

Frances Kerwin is reciting the words of 'Little Things Mean A Lot' to herself in the hope that the name of the singer will arrive with them. *Honestly honey, I don't want mon-eee*. She is strongly tempted to consult the man across the aisle who looks old enough to remember the song, but it would be embarrassing if he didn't know what she was talking about, and he would probably think that she was trying to pick him up. She remembers another line: *Say I look nice when I'm not*. She can see that this line should have ended 'I don't' but it has to rhyme with the song's title. She tries to picture the singer's face but the hit must have been pre-television because no picture appears.

She glances at her husband who is staring watchfully through the plane's windows, presumably thinking about all those litres of flammable liquid that he is sitting on.

She asks, in an inspired moment: 'What's it like being you?'

He turns from the window. 'What's that supposed to mean?'

'You take your pleasures so sadly, Bruce. Why don't you have a large gin?' She has read and enjoyed among the graffiti at the airport: *If they can put one man on the moon, why can't they put them all there?*

Her husband says: 'I find no pleasure in air travel, Frances. Still, we're nearly there.'

'And then you'll cheer up?'

'So long as I can forget what it's costing.'

The prospect of him fretting over every bill takes some of the shine off the holiday for Frances. Shopping is her favourite pastime and she has boasted more than once that she can find her way round Harrods blindfolded. This holiday is bringing her to some of the most exotic

23

and expensive shops in Europe. Her husband is not the person she would choose to have at her side when she hits them.

'Cost?' she says. 'It's no good taking a holiday if you are going to worry about money all the time.'

'I can hardly forget our new situation, much as I'd like to.'

'Well, try to while we're on holiday,' she pleads, 'for my sake.'

Bruce Kerwin is thinking about his father who hanged himself in the potting shed on his fiftieth birthday. The resultant trauma was not helped by his farewell note which simply said 'Bollocks'. He had named Bruce after the post-war heavyweight boxing champion Bruce Woodcock, but had lost the will to fight himself. Bruce was twenty when his father died and now he was only ten years away from that momentous birthday when he had decided that the struggle was too large for the prize. He didn't think about his father much now, finding it safer to direct his thoughts elsewhere, but he remembers him on the plane and he remembers his sadness and where he probably got it from. His grandfather was a joyless Methodist preacher whose idea of hospitality was to offer his guests booze-free vegetarian dinners. Bruce recalls bleak family gatherings in chilly rooms and sees gloom and melancholy as his only inheritance.

The cabin staff are making a final effort now to unload some duty-frees. The heavy silver trolley fills the aisle between the seats. Frances has her eye on a Longines watch, but the earlier conversation discourages her from suggesting that she buy it. She picks it up and admires it, hoping that her husband will show some interest, but he has turned away.

Bruce Kerwin is watching the plane's wing as it inches along against land that has now turned green, and then he sees to his alarm that they are crossing a coastline and are flying out over water. This seems wrong and he has the momentary sensation that he has sometimes had on trains, boarded too quickly in the rush hour and perhaps not going to the destination that he wants. If they are over the sea and heading south they could end up in Corsica or Sardinia or even, God help him, Africa. He looks round to see whether any of the other passengers are aware of this development but no surprise or concern is being registered by the other customers of Air France who smoke, drink, chat and snore, happily oblivious to this dramatic shift in their arrangements.

Bruce Kerwin stares down at small boats stoically painting white paths in a dark blue sea and wonders whom he should tell. At the front of the plane where experienced pilots are guiding this monster through the sky (or, more likely, phoning home to remind their wives that the plumber is due) there is obviously now a mad hijacker who has decided that they are all going somewhere else. Kerwin's hands begin to sweat.

The plane is turning so that sea fills his entire window. When he looks across to the window on the other side of the plane he can see only sky. He clings to his seat and bitterly regrets agreeing to this foreign holiday. He reminds himself of the charm of Chagford and the beauty of Bognor, and then notices that the plane has levelled off and is beginning to judder. It seems to be descending in a series of uncomfortable bumps and there is only water beneath them. He looks out of the window and tries to gauge their altitude. We're going down, he thinks, and nobody realises it.

He watches with a dry mouth as the sea approaches and tries to remember where he has been told his life-jacket is hidden. The descent is swift; a collision between plane and water now seems inevitable and he braces himself for the impact. But at the last moment, as he waits rigidly for the turmoil and the noise, land appears beneath the aircraft's wheels. They are on the runway at Nice.

Esme Rutherford in her granny glasses is poring over a map.

'We're on the N7,' she says. 'N stands for national highway.'

'But are we where we're supposed to be?' asks Roger Blake. 'Don't we want the autoroute? It goes east all the way to Italy.'

'We're not going to Italy,' says Esme. 'This is prettier and cheaper. No tolls. Over there are the Luberon mountains.'

'And what is this big place looming up ahead of us?'

'Aix-en-Provence.'

'Do they have cheap hotels there?'

'Let's see, shall we?'

Extensive suburbs have marred the approach to this place which is the old capital of Provence, but once they have manoeuvred their way to its stylish heart they begin to feel, after the endless miles, that they have arrived somewhere and their holiday has really begun. Within half an hour they have booked a room in a cheap backstreet hotel and set off on foot in search of dinner.

But before they can eat it is necessary for Esme to look at this elegant city that she has never seen before and will probably, life being what it is, never see again. With its wide avenues, squares and fountains it is everything that she has expected to discover on holiday, and Roger Blake finds himself loitering beneath rows of plane trees while she pauses to admire the bookshops and the balconies, Baroque hotels and Romanesque cloisters. Students from all over the world are studying at the university, and now on a summer evening are heading for the museum in the Mazarin quarter. There is something reassuring, she thinks, about their seriousness.

'I wish I was a student again,' she says, taking Roger's hand. 'I'm not sure I used the time properly.'

'Or the taxpayer's money,' says Roger, whose own education ended so early that Prime Minister is the only job for which he is properly qualified.

'They really got value for money out of you,' says Esme, hitting back. 'The day you left school you could have written everything you knew on the back of a stamp.'

'I picked up the important things,' says Roger, 'like how to undo a bra with one hand, use a condom and recite "Eskimo Nell".'

'A well-rounded person,' nods Esme. 'A real Renaissance man.'

She is dragging him towards Cézanne's studio, left just as it was when he died in 1906. It is not the destination he had in mind, but Esme was an art student, *is* an artist, and he feels obliged to accompany her on this unwelcome cultural diversion. While Esme looks at still lifes, landscapes and portraits, he begins to wonder why he learned so little at school and why the path that he has chosen since has been so unconventional.

'Who is this Suzanne, anyway?' he asks. 'Didn't she have a surname?'

'He's probably the greatest figure in modern French

painting,' says Esme. 'See how he raised the horizon to increase the impression of depth?'

'It's a con,' says Roger. 'Your paintings are much better than his.'

He wanders out into the bright evening. The afternoon beers have left him with more thirst than appetite, but what he wants most of all now is to stop travelling and lie mindlessly on a beach. He has not had many holidays in his life, and is only taking this one to calm the rumblings of discontent that were beginning to emanate from his loving partner. But now that they are almost there he can begin to see its promise and its possibilities, and he is impatient for it to begin.

Esme emerges with a virtuous glow. Proximity to great art places an expression on her face – satisfied, sated, superior – that Roger, in his Philistine way, associates with a protracted bout of sex. But it is difficult to feel jealous about a man who has not only been dead for almost ninety years but was also, when he was alive, French – and so he takes her hand and leads her in the evening sunshine towards food.

The little restaurant that he finds refuses to be isolated from the cultural influences that permeate this town: oil paintings cover the walls, and a concoction by W. A. Mozart leaks from secret orifices in the ceiling. They sit in a corner and eat charcoal-broiled steaks, listening to half a dozen different languages at the adjoining tables.

At the hotel, a small brown building that hides away from the crowds as if shamed by the modesty of its facilities, Esme has booked in under the name of Esme Blake. It is a surname that she has increasingly used during the year they have lived together, finding that people expect it and ask fewer questions. The trend is away from marriage, one in three children is now illegitimate, but it still occasionally smooths her passage through life to pretend that she is Roger's wife.

And yet, true to the trend, marriage is never mentioned by either of them. Roger suspects that you can get more enjoyment into your life if you are single, although his monogamous relationship with Esme is indistinguishable from the condition that he avoids. Esme is far from certain at twenty-eight that she wants to be married anyway, fearing that domestic duties which may then become obligatory will swamp her progress as a painter. She, too, has freedom to lose. But at the same time her heart tells her not to let Roger go.

'An unlikely liaison,' said her mother uneasily after she had taken him round to meet her parents. 'Do you know that he's never heard of Kafka?'

But Esme relishes the contrast between them, admiring his physical prowess and practical efficiency more than her own vaunted cerebral qualities. He is her man of action who can actually *do* things instead of discussing them languidly in elegant soliloquies that are rich with political overtones and philosophical *culs-de-sac*. She has known enough male artists and they couldn't change a plug. Her own subversive opinion about the conventional picture of two artists starving in a garret is that neither knows how to mend the cooker.

It is Roger's great virtue, no matter what her mother might think, that he has no precious gift to nurture or hide behind. He is, quite simply, impossibly talented. If the car needs mending, or the roof needs repairing, or a tree needs felling, or a wall needs building . . . he goes out and does it. The results

of his work, unlike her own, are immediate and useful.

He is also good in bed, a thought that returns to
cheer her as they climb the narrow stairs of their
cut-price hotel.

3

On the third floor of the luxurious Carlton Hotel on the Croisette at Cannes, Andrew Marner is unpacking. He had intended to hang up his clothes, but the wardrobe is now being filled by Kimberley Neal, who is unveiling a breathtaking collection of dresses from a succession of Vuitton suitcases and lovingly installing them in a capacious wardrobe at one end of their large bedroom.

So instead Andrew Marner opens a smaller case in which he has brought the latest issues of all his publications, issues that he has not yet had time to read. There are women's magazines, children's magazines, games magazines and television magazines, but the one that he picks up first is his newest and most prized possession.

His latest publication, out now for a month and slowly finding the discerning readership that its survival demands, is called *World Review*. Despite its portentous name, with hints of assiduous writers scattered around the globe filing perceptive reports on the passions and predicaments of distant republics, it is a political and literary weekly whose words are provided by desk-bound literati who would regard a day trip to Southend as a major adventure. With this publication, Andrew Marner hopes in one double hit to kick the stanchions from beneath the Marxist loonies at the *New Statesman* while at the same time delivering a mortal wound to the self-regarding clique at the *Spectator*. *World Review* is intended to become Britain's compulsory weekend reading, and is his present pride and joy.

He reads it in wonderment and finds that the standard of the writing has raised his expectations about the prose that he is now disseminating to hundreds of thousands of readers in his other magazines. Although he prefers numbers to letters, he has become an editor *manqué*, irritably monitoring his many employees' choice of words.

While Kimberley Neal proudly unwraps and hangs up her designer-label dresses, sexy little numbers for the summer and gowns that flow, he looks at the other magazines and scribbles messages to their various editors to let them know that their work is under continual scrutiny and that he, too, has occasionally used the English language.

To the editor of a children's magazine he writes a snarling fax: *'Why head-butt? Do we say fist-punch or foot-kick?'*

To the editor of one of his women's magazines he uses a gentler approach: *'Do we have to use daft phrases like "received wisdom", "window of opportunity", "state of the art" and "quality time"? What did people write before these ludicrous neologisms came along?'*

To the young and trendy editor of one of his television magazines the rebuke is magisterial: *'America speaks*

English – not the other way round. Please avoid the following imports: "head up, meet with, working out, sliced salami".'

While he goes downstairs to dispatch these little bullets to his neurotic and insecure staff, some of whom are not even aware that their proprietor is literate, Kimberley Neal is phoning room service for champagne. It arrives before his return and she pours herself a glass and drinks silently to the success of her holiday.

From her window she can see other women who have made it, or appear to have made it, strolling elegantly along the Croisette. A high proportion are escorted by white poodles and she ponders this conjunction, suspecting that there is a sexual explanation at the root of it waiting to be exposed. But her inventive mind, so adept at plumbing and exploring depths from which most women would shrink, fails to find a connection and she goes over to the large table in the middle of the room and gets out her pad and pen.

She is writing fluently when Andrew returns, feeling all the better for the verbal artillery that he has discharged.

'Champagne!' he says, rubbing his hands. 'Is it opening time?'

'*Mais oui,*' says Kimberley, getting up to pour him a glass. '*À votre santé.*'

'I hope you haven't been learning French,' he says suspiciously. 'I need someone round here who will talk to me in English. What have you been writing, my love?'

She hands him a sheet that is already half-covered with her hastily scribbled sentences. 'I'm trying to finish this column,' she says.

He stands in the middle of the room, the pad in one hand and champagne in the other.

'I don't like "hidden agenda" much,' he says. 'It's one of these newfangled phrases, isn't it? What does it mean?'

'I suppose it means secret objective,' says Kimberley, looking slightly put out.

'Why don't you say "secret objective", then?' he asks. 'I know what that means.'

'Andrew, you're the proprietor, not the editor. You'll be wheeling the tea trolley round next.'

'You're quite right,' he says, softening. He hasn't brought her to this celebrated hotel to quibble about semantics. He takes his cases across to the wardrobe and starts to hang up his own clothes in what little space there is left. The suits, the jackets and the shirts have been carefully chosen to make him appear younger than he is. Andrew Marner doesn't like to hurry the years: they are moving quickly enough. He goes into the bathroom for a routine face check: food on teeth, egg around mouth, bogies up nose, any of a myriad of foreign bodies lodged cosily in the corner of his eyes. He is looking at a handsome man who seems a little younger than fifty, despite the silver hair. At one time he had toyed briefly with the idea of postponing the change of hair colour with a cosmetic aid from his chemist, but was deterred by the bizarre sight of ageing American politicians gracefully turning red instead of grey.

'Let's case the joint,' he says when he has finished.

'Case the joint?' echoes Kimberley. 'I thought you had appointed yourself guardian of the language?'

'I'm on holiday,' says Andrew, opening the door. 'Let's give this dive the once-over.'

The Carlton Hotel – or 'the Carlton Inter-Continental'

as it calls itself – has 354 rooms, some of them suites which resemble lavish apartments. It has a grand salon that is classified as an historic monument because of its fresco ceiling and marble columns, eleven other conference rooms, a health club with swimming pool, jacuzzi, hammam, sauna and solarium, its own casino, a club reserved for dancing until dawn, many bars and restaurants and its own segment of the beach across the road. Kimberley Neal wanders among this world of Brazilian marble and solid mahogany and feels a sense of achievement that makes her want to shout.

'Let's take a walk,' says Andrew Marner.

The warm air greets them as they go out to the Croisette, the pink promenade that skirts the bay for three kilometres. Walking arm in arm beneath the palm trees, Kimberley Neal is able to convince herself for a short time that she is Mrs Andrew Marner and not his mistress. Being a mistress has never worried her. In fact she has always felt that she is enjoying a better deal than the housewife, becalmed in bills and nappies, and tied to the relationship for twenty-four hours a day. The wife who gets a feeling of superiority from the possession of a wedding ring has always seemed a rather sad creature to her. She prefers her independence and her freedom, interrupted by short, passionate assignations which would be wearying if they became a full-time occupation that demanded all her attention.

But now that she sees where Andrew Marner is driving himself – to Buckingham Palace for a brief but significant meeting with the Queen – the picture has changed a little and the emphasis has shifted. 'Lady Marner,' she says to herself, and keeps on repeating it as a warm breeze ruffles her hair.

*　　*　　*

The Kerwins emerge from Aéroport Nice Côte d'Azur in the care of a harassed woman courier who bundles them and their luggage past orange trees and palm trees into a large black taxi which roars off as if this is the start of a Grand Prix. But the driver's taste for speed is swiftly quashed when they reach the Promenade des Anglais, a three-mile, eight-track traffic jam that runs along the front at Nice. From here they gaze out at the bay while they sit immobilised in a welter of traffic fumes and angry car horns.

This halt in their progress irritates Bruce Kerwin, who has travelled enough and is now anxious to arrive somewhere. The tiny picture of their hotel in the brochure does not fill him with enthusiasm, but Frances has chosen it for its price and he is not able to argue. As the taxi moves again they pass gleaming white hotels that face the sea and suggest, with their stylish exteriors, luxurious interiors, but they are not where the Kerwins are heading. Presently the taxi escapes from the seafront congestion by heading inland into the town. The sunlight is reduced by half as tall, ornate buildings throw their shadows across the streets and through the rear window Frances watches the sea recede.

'Where are we going?' she asks.

'Switzerland by the look of it,' says Bruce Kerwin, but the taxi turns left again and stops abruptly in a back street. The small, dark building alongside which they are now parked looks familiar and he realises that this is the hotel they chose from the brochure. It is smaller than he had imagined, smaller and darker. It stands in a street which the sun visits only briefly, overhead at midday.

The inside of the hotel is even gloomier, with dark

walls and few windows. At the small reception desk their documents are examined by a lean, balding man who stares at the papers in his hand as if they are barely comprehensible. But eventually he pushes a form across to each of them and breaks the silence with two words that are foreign to him: 'Sign, please.'

A surly youth appears from the shadows, picks up their cases and escorts them to a lift which shakes ominously as it hoists them to the fourth floor. They follow him along a narrow corridor which is lit by a solitary bulb.

'This place seems to be deficient in the window department,' Bruce Kerwin says as the youth unlocks the door of their room. It is a small room because part of it has been annexed for conversion into a tiny *en suite* bathroom. There is a double bed, a table and a chair. Frances gives the youth some francs and he slips wordlessly from the room.

'Well,' she says. 'La Belle France! Bring on the Bollinger.'

But her husband can see that she is disappointed with this accommodation. It is too small, too dark; it is the opposite of cheerful. She is trying to comfort herself by talking about champagne, but her eyes tell him that she had expected something better.

He sits on the bed, testing it for comfort while his wife unpacks. He fancies that the room has a musty smell and wants to get out into the sun. It is difficult to imagine that his only home for three weeks will be a room as small as this. He stands up to help with the unpacking and then says: 'Let's go for a walk.'

And when he gets outside something mysterious happens. His mood changes. He finds himself in a different world and the sights and the smells go to his head. The traffic is on the wrong side of the street, the shops have different names and the goods that they display are unfamiliar. Aubergines, courgettes and yellow peppers are piled high at the edge of the pavement, along with fruit that he has never seen. Gardens, fountains and Italianate arcades arrest their progress as they walk in the hot sunshine.

'I could live here,' he says. 'It's different.'

Frances, accustomed to his wistful dreams but more familiar herself with life's harsh realities, snorts dismissively.

'My God, Bruce,' she says, 'when are your people coming back to fetch you?'

The oblique implication, which she has made before, that he is some kind of alien, hopelessly unsuited to the company of human beings, doesn't rile him in the usual way. He laughs.

'I've spent my life on tracks,' he says. 'One track took me to the office and another track brought me home. I've trundled back and forth for twenty years like that, seeing the same things every day, thinking the same things every day most of the time. The same problems, the same solutions. Do you know, for instance, that I've never been to either Scotland or Wales?'

This is clearly not a deprivation that Frances recognises. 'Who would want to?' she asks.

'It's the principle,' says Bruce. 'One short stay on this earth and we hardly have time to look over the fence.'

'Blimey,' says Frances. 'Welcome to the male menopause.'

But nothing can dampen Bruce's spirits now. He is seized by a tremendous feeling of liberation. They have reached the flower market and are assailed by the scent of roses, tulips, dahlias and geraniums, an aromatic cocktail that Bruce finds almost intoxicating.

'Probably there are people working in a factory in Wigan at this very moment,' he says. 'Probably it's raining. And yet two hours away there is this and they'll never see it. A life to be lived but the doors are shut.'

'What we have here,' says Frances, 'is the fanaticism of the convert. You were never interested in holidays.' She has passed too many wonderful clothes shops already to be entirely happy but is making a mental note of their names and locations. To drag her husband into a shopping spree during the first hour of their holiday would be tactically inept. Instead she stops to buy postcards that will produce the desired amount of envy among her friends. One, that she doesn't buy, a picture taken in January 1985, shows the Promenade des Anglais under thirty centimetres of snow.

'Don't let's get too carried away,' she says. 'Winter reaches here, too.'

'That was a freak,' says Bruce cheerfully. 'That's why they've put it on a postcard.'

They leave the flower market and rejoin the street. Little white drawings of dogs on the edge of the pavement announce periodically where the animals are allowed to relieve themselves, but whether they heed these messages is not clear. Bruce pauses in front of a men's clothes shop that sells jeans and T-shirts. The trousers that he is wearing are part of a suit; his grey tie is still on. But the informal clothes in the shop window grip his attention. They seem to belong to this bright new world which he has come to reluctantly but is now desperately anxious to join.

'You're too old for jeans,' says Frances, but she laughs

as she says it. If her husband starts buying clothes, an important precedent will have been established.

'In China everybody wears jeans,' says Bruce.

'And since when have we followed China's example?' Frances asks but her husband is already walking into the shop. She watches through the window as he leads an assistant to a rack of jeans. She can't imagine what language they are using but some sort of understanding has evidently been forged because the shop assistant produces a tape measure and runs it round Bruce Kerwin's waist. She is torn by the rival attraction of a nearby shop window which displays a lot of the clothes that she covets, but the prospect of her husband in jeans is too good to miss and she waits as he vanishes into a cubicle with a pair of them. He reappears very quickly looking about twenty years younger, and walks across the shop to a pile of brightly coloured T-shirts. He picks up orange ones and yellow ones, holds them against his chest and studies the mirror.

When he comes out of the shop he is clutching two bags.

'I'm getting myself a new image,' he says.

'I see it,' says Frances. 'Now let's go and buy the pram.'

'You can slip into middle age too easily,' he tells her. 'Next thing you know you're waiting for the undertaker.'

'Forward into the past,' says Frances, but then she sees how serious he is. His eyes gleam.

'The moustache is coming off next,' he announces. 'When I wake up tomorrow I'm going to be a different man.'

*   *   *

The grey Ford Granada that heads east on the auto-route the following morning, plunging ever deeper into Provence, looks a little out of place among the Carrera Porsches and Lamborghinis that dart along the motorway, but the Ford is full of music. The stereo is giving full vent to a Genesis tape which is clearly welcome to the two people in the front seats who make the strange movements with fingers, feet and lips that you see from a person marooned in the private pleasures of a Sony Walkman.

Near Fréjus the road turns north to skirt coastal hills, but then it turns again and they see from a multitude of signs that they are on the outskirts of Cannes.

Esme Rutherford consults the map on her lap, turns down the music and says: 'We've got to get off this road somewhere. Antibes is over there.'

Roger Blake is more concerned about the lowering sky. 'It's going to rain,' he says. 'It's going to piddle down.'

Esme takes her eyes from the map and looks up at dark clouds that are drifting down from the north. 'You told me this place was sunny, "Come and get a tan," you said.'

'That's the second time I've been wrong,' says Roger. 'I thought Reagan would lose in 1980.'

'If you're only wrong once every twelve years that's good enough for me,' says Esme.

They spot the turn-off and head south to the camping site at Antibes where they have made a reservation. Camping in France is big business and there are 300 sites around here somewhere for tents and for caravans. The sites are awarded stars for merit, like hotels, and cost more the nearer they are to the sea.

But two hours later as he struggles with ridgepoles

41

and guy ropes, Roger looks at the sky again and yearns for the warmth and comfort of an hotel. It is many years since he put up a tent and he wishes that he had erected this one just once in his garden before leaving for the holiday. But it is brand new and as he pulls the pieces from their plastic bag he finds himself looking for the instruction sheet.

'Make sure you do a good job,' says Esme. 'With the wind that's blowing up it could vanish in the night.'

'Not with us in it,' says Roger. 'The floor is part of the tent. This isn't one of those old-fashioned numbers where you have to use a separate groundsheet.'

Presently something that resembles a tent is secured to the ground and Esme brings from the back of the car two flimsy camp beds that do not look comfortable.

'I don't think that one of those beds will take the weight of both of us,' says Roger.

'That's why there are two,' says Esme. 'One each.'

'Ah,' says Roger. 'I think we're overlooking something here.'

'Perhaps we should ditch the beds and sleep on the ground?' suggested Esme.

'Have you felt the ground?' asks Roger. 'It's like Tarmac.' He looks round at the site which is covered with tents and caravans. Some of the tents are so large that they have separate rooms within, and the small model that he has brought is a very poor relation in this company.

'Some of them look as if they've got double beds and television,' he says. 'I thought camping was supposed to be a rugged business?'

'It's not obligatory,' says Esme. 'Comfort is permitted.' She refuses to be depressed although she has just felt the first drop of rain. 'Let's go and eat.'

The site is set in an avenue of trees. It has three swimming pools and two bars. There is a shop that sells beach balls, lilos and general groceries, and two large wash blocks with toilets, showers and washing machines.

They walk past fellow campers who seem mainly to be German, some of them cheerfully cooking their own food on little stoves beside their tents.

'Is this the recession,' asks Roger, 'or are these people actually enjoying themselves?'

But the rain has started in earnest now and Esme is hurrying ahead to the shelter of the bar-restaurant. It is an idea that has occurred to many other campers and soon the place is crowded with a queue that reaches to the door. They stand in line flicking the rain from their clothes while people around them chatter in several languages, none of them English. Esme hears some Italian and wonders why they would leave their own sunshine and head north to spend time on this expensive coast. The Germans and the Scandinavians she can understand.

Armed with food on a tray and bottles of beer they make their way to one of the few vacant tables. A poster on the wall announces a Mr Camping Competition. Rain beats on the windows and more damp campers arrive to seek refuge in the bar. The veterans among them laugh noisily at the situation and proudly recall other rainswept holidays they have survived.

Roger Blake does not share the feeling of camaraderie which spreads among the sodden visitors. To find humour and pleasure in this situation strikes him as eccentricity which borders on outright loopiness, and the prospect of three weeks in that tent fills him with foreboding. They eat omelettes with chips, which is not the introduction to French cuisine they had intended. As compensation Roger fetches more beer and when they have finished eating they sit and drink while the sky continues to drench the camping site.

'It can't last,' says Esme.

'Who says so?' asks Roger. 'There's plenty more up there by the look of it.'

And appearances are not deceptive. The rain is now bouncing off the ground which it is slowly converting to mud. When they reach the tent they search for dry clothes but have no hope of drying the ones they take off. They lie on their camp beds, deafened by the sound of the rain on the tent.

But the worst moment comes in the middle of the night when the beer that they have drunk forces them to make a hundred-yard dash through torrential rain to the toilets.

4

When Frances Kerwin wakes up, her husband is doing press-ups on the floor. It is not something that she has ever seen him attempt and for a moment, still only partly awake, she imagines that a chambermaid is spreadeagled beneath him with a grateful smile on her face.

'What the hell are you doing?' she asks without raising her head. The bed is harder and smaller than she is used to and noises in the street have disturbed her sleep.

Bruce Kerwin jumps to his feet. His face is red and somehow different.

'Exercises,' he says, and smiles. 'Got to get in shape.'

'Into what shape do you wish to get, for God's sake?' his wife asks, looking at him in his blue underpants. 'What happened to your moustache?'

'This is the new me, kid,' says Bruce Kerwin. 'I've just got to do a little work on my waistline.'

Frances Kerwin sits up in bed. The loss of the moustache has mysteriously knocked a few years off her husband's age.

45

'You can't start getting fit,' she says. 'You're a hypo-chondriac. You're metabolically challenged.'

Bruce Kerwin sits on the bed. The beneficial effects of exercise are evidently not felt immediately.

'I'm not a hypochondriac,' he says. 'I just show an interest in my health.'

'Not a hypochondriac?' scoffs Frances. 'If you catch a cold you thinks it's Aids, every headache is a brain tumour and you only have to feel slightly tired to start talking about tsetse flies.'

'You can't be too careful,' says her husband. 'Now, if you'll excuse me I'm going to take a shower.'

'Ring for tea first,' says Frances. 'I want to know that I'm in an hotel.'

When Bruce Kerwin disappears into the small bath-room she gets out of bed and puts on a white dressing gown. She goes to the window but the view is of another building only a few feet away. There is a knock on the door and she opens it to admit a shy young girl with a tea tray.

Not long afterwards her husband emerges from the bathroom in new blue jeans, an orange T-shirt and white shoes. He is adorned with the bangles of youth – a chunky gold bracelet and a gold medallion that hangs on his chest like a medal.

'Jesus,' says Frances. 'People will think I've got a toy boy.'

'I'm putting my hand up to the advancing years and saying Stop,' says Bruce.

'That'll slow 'em down,' says Frances. 'That'll stop 'em in their tracks.'

'I'm a new man,' says Bruce. '*Nouveau homme.*'

'*Nouveau* wally, more like. Pour my tea.'

'You're as old as you feel, Frances, and I've begun to

feel young again. This is a fresh start for me and I'm going to grab the chance.'

She looks at him and realises that there has been some tampering with his hair; it is no longer combed back but encouraged to fall over his ears. This, too, has made him look younger. Words trip to her tongue but she bites them back. The possibility that her husband is cracking up in some way suddenly seems real. Perhaps the shock of redundancy has unhinged him. By the time they go down to breakfast she has decided to adopt a softer approach to this shift in her husband's personality, to play along with his strange flirtation with youth.

In the street afterwards she feels as if she is being escorted by a younger man. The striding figure in jeans at her elbow does not resemble the quiet and thoughtful office manager who has been her companion for twenty years. The metamorphosis takes her mind off the previous problem, which was that her husband is out of work. The new problem seems to be what toy to buy him.

They reach the seafront and walk along the promenade that overlooks a stony beach. Girls who are almost naked are lying in the sun on blue sunbeds, some of them with champagne in ice buckets. Beyond them speedboats cavort in the waves.

Bruce Kerwin glimpses a life of glamour and excitement that he has only imagined. When he recalls the zomboid existence that he has mutely endured for years he feels a surge of excitement at the revelations which confront him here. The world is full of delightful possibilities. Your future is not clamped on you by a malign deity or a suicidal father. You can shuck it off and choose another.

In this new mood of hope and enthusiasm he watches

as a beautiful girl approaches them on the promenade in a bikini. Her expression encourages him to believe that she finds him attractive but, stunning at a distance with her big brown eyes, she comes to resemble a frog as she moves closer and he averts his gaze as she glides past. But he recovers quickly, realising that not everything can be perfect. He suggests to Frances that they stop for a coffee.

'Well,' she says when they have found a table in the sun, 'for a man who didn't want to go on holiday you have adapted pretty well.'

'Haven't I?' says Bruce, smiling broadly. 'To tell you the truth it's been a bit of an eye-opener. What was I doing all those years sitting in an office?'

'Earning money,' says Frances. 'We used it to buy food and things like that.

'And after doing it for twenty years we still can't afford a decent hotel.' The hotel is worrying him; it is the only blemish on his holiday. Its gloomy corridors, dark rooms and back-street situation cloud the brightness of his mood.

Frances studies her bizarrely coiffed spouse and wonders whether he still has a full complement of marbles. 'The hotel is adequate, darling,' she says reassuringly. 'Anyway, with luck, we won't be spending too much time in it.'

'It is not adequate, Frances,' he says firmly. 'As a matter of fact it is singularly inadequate. It reminds me of one of those modern prisons.'

He drinks his coffee and stares out over the bay and then he has an idea. The idea cheers him up and he starts to sing.

'That's the song,' says Frances. '"Little Things Mean A Lot". Have you remembered who recorded it?'

'I've no idea,' says Bruce. 'Was it Brenda Lee?'

'No, it wasn't Brenda bloody Lee. You said that on the plane.'

But Bruce Kerwin's mind has moved on to more important matters. There are sumptuous hotels on the seafront here that he is not in, while other people, who are human beings just like him, have moved into their ritzy rooms as if nothing less would do. Why should he be consigned to a barrack-like edifice on the very rim of the fun? It didn't even have a swimming pool.

When the waiter comes out to collect their cups and their money he follows him back into the bar and asks for a telephone. The business of ringing Britain from here is more complicated than he had imagined but there is an Englishman at the counter who is happy to help him. He dials 19 and then 33 and then 44 before asking Bruce what number he wants. When he has finished he hands Bruce the phone and the voice of Dean Madgwick drifts out of it.

Madgwick is no doubt lounging in his office, grappling with the crossword and tampering with the temps. How he escaped the executive culling, Bruce Kerwin cannot imagine.

'It's Bruce here,' says Bruce.

'Where's here, Bruce?' asks Madgwick.

'Nice,' says Bruce.

'Nice is nice,' says Madgwick. 'I'm stuck in an office myself.'

'It must be awful,' says Bruce, 'having a well-paid job. You can guess why I'm ringing.'

'Indeed I can,' says Madgwick. 'You want to know what the decision is on your redundancy money.'

'I know it's optimistic of me to hope that anybody

in that office has made a decision about anything,' says Bruce.

'Well, as it happens they have,' says Madgwick. 'The figure I have here is thirty-five grand.'

This is rather more than Bruce Kerwin has been hoping for. 'I was hoping for forty,' he says.

'It started at thirty,' says Madgwick. 'I got it pushed up.'

'It's not so bad,' says Bruce. 'I accept.'

'I wish they'd make me redundant,' says Madgwick. 'I've never had thirty-five grand in one lump.'

'You're much too valuable to lose,' says Bruce, and smiling to himself he replaces the phone. He comes out of the bar whistling, the gold medallion bouncing on his chest.

'What are the toilets like?' asks Frances.

'Toilets?' says Bruce. 'I haven't been to the toilets. I phoned the office.

'You don't have to do that any more, Bruce. They removed you from the payroll.'

'We're moving into a better hotel,' says Bruce. 'We're going to mix with a better class of person.'

'We're what?' says Frances.

'I rang about my redundancy money. We're going to enjoy a taste of luxury.'

'Where are we going?' asks Frances, perplexed.

'Have you heard of a place called Cannes? They don't have pebble beaches there. It's golden sand.'

'How much is this redundancy money?' his wife asks suspiciously.

'Thirty-five thousand.'

'I'll pack immediately,' says Frances. 'Luxury I can handle.'

But instead of going back to their hotel they wander

up to the railway station at the top of the town and take a train along the coast to Cannes. The sky is clouding over and rain is threatened but nothing can spoil the pleasure of this exploratory visit. They make their way to the front and stroll in and out of all the best hotels. Finally, clutching a sheaf of brochures, they sit on the front and decide where they want to spend their holiday.

Across the road from the Kerwins, Andrew Marner is marching out of the Carlton Hotel and climbing into a taxi that he has ordered from his room. He is carrying his code-locked briefcase and looks like a man with his mind on work, someone not to be confused with the holidaymakers who surround him. He hands the driver a sheet of paper on which is written the Nice office address of Monsieur Alain Rocard and then sits back in the car and reflects that publishing today is all high tech and low cunning, recycled garbage dressed up as something fresh and interesting; half-truths, rumours and innuendoes (usually about the Royal Family), circulation figures that don't bear scrupulous examination, competitions that can't be won. Andrew Marner is above all this but he still feels that he is plying his trade in a murky marketplace.

The previous month, one of the serious Sunday papers had published a feature on Andrew Marner, his achievements and his ambitions. The caption to his photograph was *New boy on the block* and the writer had suggested, following the launch of *World Review*, that Marner's real ambition was to produce a daily newspaper and that Britain, which had meekly surrendered ownership of its newspapers to men from

Canada, Australia and Czechoslovakia, might be about to produce a home-grown Press baron.

The heading was: MINNOW OR PIRANHA?

Andrew Marner, who had never thought of starting a daily newspaper, has taken this article, written on the spur of the moment after a few pints of Ruddles, as a sign and a challenge. There is also the salient fact that people who own national newspapers don't bother with knighthoods; they slip smoothly into the House of Lords. The problem, as ever, is money.

And so Andrew Marner has a proposal for Monsieur Alain Rocard, with whom he once got on rather well at a publishers' jamboree in Bogotá. Monsieur Rocard publishes a string of newspapers from the Pyrenees to the Alps and is reputed to be one of the richest newspapermen in France. Andrew hopes to lure him into a joint venture, and as he sits in the back of his taxi he rehearses the lines that he will use to draw the Frenchman in.

Left on her own Kimberley Neal feels a rare wave of boredom. She is seldom bored, since to her, life is a series of interesting events whether work or play, but temporarily stranded in this luxury she is at a loss for a moment, not knowing which way to move. It is too early to sunbathe or swim, the television is in French, and a drink might blur the edges of her day. Behind the hotel and parallel to the Croisette, is the rue d'Antibes, a street with all the shops that she is planning to visit, but a shopping trip without Andrew would be folly indeed. He likes to buy her things.

Eventually she reaches for the phone, and in a matter of seconds her mother's voice is whispering cautiously in her ear: 'Hallo?'

'Hallo, Mum. It's me,' says Kimberley, lying back on

the bed now that contact has been established. 'Guess where I am?'

In her semi-detached in Bexley, Mrs Neal, a thin, grey-haired woman who always seems to have more work than time, considers the exotic destinations that she would like to visit herself. 'Brighton?' she suggests.

'I'll give you a clue,' says Kimberley. 'Everybody's talking French.'

'France?' says Mrs Neal.

'God, you're smart, Mum,' says Kimberley. 'There'll be no holding you once the world finds out.'

'I'm not as stupid as you think I am, Kimberley,' says Mrs Neal irritably. 'They talk French in a lot of places. Switzerland and Canada for a start.' She glances at her watch: there is a flower-arranging rota at church that she is due to fulfil.

'I'm in Cannes,' says Kimberley, brushing this aside. 'Cannes, France.'

'I know where Cannes is, young lady,' says Mrs Neal. 'I take it you're with a man?'

'As it happens I'm with Andrew Marner,' says Kimberley, but realises immediately that his burgeoning fame as a Press tycoon has not so far penetrated the sleepy suburbs of Bexley, and her little boast is wasted.

'Is that the character you met up the Nile?' asks her mother.

'That's right. The Publisher.'

'What happened to Boris?'

'The chop,' says Kimberley. 'First he had the snip and then he had the chop.'

This information about a German diplomat with whom she had languished briefly in Notting Hill is lost on her mother, who sighs and says: 'I don't know,

Kimberley. You're thirty, for goodness sake. Isn't it time you settled down with one man for good? You'll soon be too old to get one.'

'No problem so far, Mother,' says Kimberley, smiling to herself. 'Bees round a honeypot.'

The analogy, with its suggestion of numbers, depresses Mrs Neal who is unhappy anyway that most of her conversations with her daughter these days seem to take place on the telephone. She has always learned more from her face than from her words; the telephone removes Kimberley's vulnerability.

'I married your father when I was eighteen,' she says. 'I didn't, as you say these days, put myself about.'

Kimberley Neal, lying on her bed in the Carlton Hotel, sees a picture of her father on a bicycle, cycling to the allotment where he was a market gardener. It wasn't a job that was going to put him into a three-star hotel in Skegness, let alone a grand hotel in Cannes, and the picture that she has conjured up saddens her. She loved him, of course – he thought that she was wonderful – but it was always a love that was tinged with pity.

She tries a little laugh into the phone. 'They've brought sex out of the closet, Mum,' she says. 'People don't have sexual hang-ups any more.'

'Instead they have herpes, Aids and a million unwanted babies,' says Mrs Neal. 'How long will you be in France?'

'For every plus there's a minus,' says Kimberley. 'Three weeks is the plan. Andrew is doing some business with a French publisher.'

'And you?'

'I'm his assistant. And I'm writing my column from here so I'm working as well.'

'I'm glad to hear it,' says Mrs Neal.

'How are you keeping, Mum? Is everything all right?'

'I'm having a lot of trouble with my feet,' says Mrs Neal. 'I'll have to see the ventriloquist.'

'Chiropodist,' says Kimberley, examining her nails.

'Oh, you're the smart one,' says Mrs Neal. 'Well, I must get on with my work. Try to come down when you get home. I haven't seen you for weeks.'

Kimberley contemplates the prospect of a visit to Bexley with minimal enthusiasm. Her mother has raised the unspoken reproach to an art form, with a combination of disappointed expressions, ambiguous remarks which are only seen to have conveyed censure in retrospect, and mute gestures which signal, or seem to signal, disapproval of her daughter's lifestyle. When she puts down the phone she feels a topic for her column forming in her mind: the generation gap, the lack of comprehension, the placid acceptance of their fates by parents contrasted with the huge expectations of youth.

But when she sits down to write it the idea dies. Her mother will read the column and she doesn't want to hurt her unnecessarily. She tells herself that by not writing the piece she is contributing to the lack of understanding that she deplores, but a cutting falls out of her notebook, a cutting that she has stored away for future use, and soon her mind is filled with other thoughts. The cutting says that the World Health Organisation has calculated that more than one hundred million acts of sexual intercourse take place every day. She works out that if each lasts five minutes there are seven hundred thousand people at it, at any given moment.

She is on fruitful ground here. The material lends itself to the sort of wise and witty comment that is her column's hallmark, and she sits down at the table and waits for a comment, wise or witty, to arrive.

Midway between the Carlton Hotel in Cannes where Andrew Marner and Kimberley Neal are about to enjoy a life of luxury, and the back-street hotel in Nice which Bruce Kerwin is planning to vacate, Roger Blake and Esme Rutherford wake up the following morning in a tent in Antibes. It has been a very short sleep.

'I'll say this for it,' says Esme, sitting up. 'The tent's waterproof.'

'Pity it's not soundproof,' says Roger. 'It was like trying to sleep inside a drum that somebody's dropping peas on.'

When they get dressed and wander across to the restaurant in search of an egg for breakfast it is clear that the rain hasn't entirely finished with them. It is only a light rain now, one that they can almost ignore after last night, but the sky is showing that it has more in reserve. The mood in the restaurant is quite different from the previous evening. Instead of the cheerful Blitz mentality and a refusal to be cowed, the holidaymakers are now subdued. Other people have had sleepless nights, too.

'What I suggest is,' says Roger, 'that we get in the car and have a look at this coast. It's warm in cars and it can't rain on you.'

And when breakfast is over they get into the Ford Granada, which has a sticker on its rear window which says GOD GIVE ME PATIENCE – BUT HURRY and drive off the site in search of distractions. They head east, with the idea of visiting Italy, and are soon on the front at Nice.

'I want to look at Nice, but not in the rain,' says Esme, and so they drive on round the coastal road to Villefranche and Beaulieu and, as the rain stops at noon, they reach Monaco.

'I didn't know Monte Carlo was here,' says Roger. 'Let's have a look.'

'We know about your education,' says Esme. 'You obviously weren't listening during the geography lessons either.'

'Yes, I was,' says Roger, 'and all the old fart talked about was something called Equatorial Africa, climates and rainfall. He lost me quite early on.'

He parks the car in an underground car park and a lift brings them back to the street. They are immediately in another world of majestic buildings, clean streets, flowered terraces and rare plants. There is no rain.

'Wow!' says Esme. 'I'm beginning to see why we drove this far.'

Crammed into a square mile with scarcely an inch wasted, Monaco has managed to find room for beautiful gardens by building its car parks beneath them. Things are underground or ten storeys overhead or built on land that has been reclaimed from the sea. Tightly corsetted, Monaco swells where it can, finding room where no room had previously existed. The buildings suggest immeasurable prosperity, but the cars in the streets are surprisingly small, chosen for their manoeuvrability in the crowded Principality.

They walk for a while, round the port with its big yachts waiting for absentee owners, and through the tunnel from which Roger has annually watched racing cars appear at surprising speeds on his television. But today it is quiet and men fish for mullet from the low wall at the side of the road. At the end of the tunnel they climb a winding hill which brings them into the elegant Place du Casino. The casino itself is installed in the Opera House on one side of the square.

Roger stops. 'I played roulette once,' he says. 'I won thirty pounds.'

'Get thee behind me, Satan,' says Esme. 'That place caters for the richest gamblers in Europe. We live in a tent, remember?'

'To visit Monte Carlo and not go in the Casino is like going to Paris and not going up the Eiffel Tower.'

'I went to Paris and I didn't go up the Eiffel Tower,' says Esme.

'You're with a proper traveller this time,' and Roger takes her hand. 'Sights have to be seen: that's what they're there for.'

They cross the road and walk into the Casino. The immediate sight is of dozens of fruit machines, but once they have shown their passports and paid an entrance fee they are admitted to the *salon de roulette*.

'There is a limit to what we can afford to invest,' says Roger.

'You bet there is,' says Esme. 'Get me out of here.'

The gambling room is full of tables that have different ways of separating the visitor from his money: dice, cards, roulette. To Esme, the ornate décor, the golden pillars, the chandeliers and the painted nymphs on the ceiling are far more interesting than the prospect of gambling, an activity which her father had demonstrated often ends in tears. But Roger guides her to a roulette table, produces banknotes from the back pocket of his jeans and buys them both ten, 20-franc chips.

'It's only about twenty pounds each,' he says. 'If we lose it we're out of here.'

He places most of his chips on different numbers on the table and watches the croupier spin the wheel. There are only two other punters at this table and they watch as the ball settles in number 24.

'I'm ahead,' says Roger, and the croupier pushes a pile of chips towards him, but after that things start to go wrong. The ball lands in numbers that Roger hasn't covered. After ten minutes his money has gone.

Esme studies this financial débâcle impatiently.

'What are the odds on a number?' she asks.

'Thirty-five to one.'

'What are the odds on a colour?'

'Evens.'

'That's better, isn't it?'

She changes her ten, 20-franc chips into one 200-franc chip and puts it on red. The ball falls into a red number, 32, and the croupier pushes a second 200-franc chip in her direction.

'You see?' she says. 'I've doubled my money.'

'I noticed that,' says Roger.

She picks up one chip but leaves the other there. A black number comes up and she has lost.

'Now you've halved it,' says Roger. 'Life's a bitch, isn't it?'

Esme puts her last chip back on red. She wins and leaves both chips there and wins again. It wins a third time and now she has eight chips waiting on red

'It'll be black next,' says Roger. 'Pick 'em up.'

But Esme leaves the chips there, ready and even eager to lose so that they can go. But red comes up again.

'Now it will be black,' she says, and pushes her winnings across the table on to black. The ball jumps and spins and lands on 2, which is black.

'Roulette is an easy game,' says Esme, 'but you do need intuition.'

'For God's sake pick up some of the chips,' says Roger, becoming anxious. 'That's real money you're risking now.'

'It's called gambling, Roger,' says Esme. 'Let's wait for another black.'

And black comes up again. Roger tries to count the chips that are piled up over black. It looks to be at least fifty.

'How much is there?' he asks. 'Pick 'em up.'

And Esme is tempted now. She does not know how much money she has won, but having guessed right six times she is beginning to feel invincible.

'I'll put the lot on red and then we'll go,' she says. 'I'm an all-or-nothing person.'

As she slides the chips back to red Roger works out what she is risking. 'Six even-money bets. That's sixty-four chips. How much is that?'

'Sixty-four two hundreds,' says Esme. 'It's more than twelve thousand francs.'

They both feel the tension now but it is too late to withdraw: the wheel is spinning.

'My God,' says Roger. 'You're mad.'

'Who wanted to gamble?' asks Esme. 'Who brought us to this palace of sin?'

'Stop when you're ahead,' says Roger. 'That's the rule.'

'Not for you,' Esme objects. 'You stopped when you were behind.'

The ball seems to circle the wheel interminably before plummeting abruptly into 18, which is red. The croupier looks at Esme and smiles as he pushes the chips towards her. He wants her to stay because luck like this is always brief and soon the money will be back where it belongs. But Esme is picking up the chips and stuffing them in her pockets. Her heart is pounding. She hopes never to see a roulette wheel again.

They make their way across the gambling room between card schools and dice tables to the desk where they can cash their chips.

'It's getting on for three thousand quid,' says Roger, in awe as he watches the cashier counting out French notes.

Esme puts the money in her bag. 'And do you know what I am going to spend it on?' she asks.

'Me?' says Roger.

'Indirectly,' says Esme. 'I'm going to put us into the best hotel I can find.'

5

The four people who arrive almost simultaneously at the reception desk in the Carlton Hotel do not look like the rich guests who normally decant from limousines at its door. But the unconventional appearance of jeans and T-shirts passes unnoticed by the staff, who are distracted by fistfuls of francs.

Frances Kerwin, who expected to be embarrassed by her husband's new taste in clothes when he entered the beautiful hall of the Carlton Hotel, is encouraged to see that they have arrived at the same time as a man who is infinitely scruffier. The woman with him has hardly dressed up for the occasion – her jeans have holes at the knee. But it is she, Frances notices, who has the money. A huge pile of francs is counted out before the receptionist's greedy gaze.

Roger Blake glances round the marble hall with its golden columns and chandeliers and feels that his holiday starts here. He is not going to be intimidated by the alligator shoes and silk *foulards* that he sees on other guests, but he is quietly grateful that a hired lackey has mercifully removed his old car from their supercilious view.

'I bet we have to dress for dinner,' says Esme in a whisper.

'That ceremony has always been a complete mystery to me,' says Roger. 'A bit like Trooping the Colour.'

'Apparently people do it,' says Esme. 'They spend two hours getting ready to eat.'

Roger makes a face. He has renounced the tyranny of men's fashion and gone his own way. The ties that he receives at Christmas are like running shoes for a legless man. But as he gazes round the huge, cool reception hall where air conditioning has defeated the summer heat that has replaced the rain outside, he looks again at the stylish clothes of the other guests as they sweep past in search of pleasure and realises that he is surrounded by money. Even the middle-aged men in short trousers manage to look elegant. In showcases built into the walls he sees names that frighten him: Fabergé, Tiffany, Hermès, Boucheron.

'We'll eat out,' he says. 'They've got restaurants in Cannes, I believe.'

As a porter shows them to one of three lifts and takes them along wide, cheerful corridors to a large bedroom that has a sideview of the sea, Bruce Kerwin is still at the reception desk flourishing a couple of credit cards that he can now use without frowning. Life has opened a door to him and after one false start he is going to make sure that this is a holiday to remember. He orders champagne for their room.

When they reach it and see its handsome furniture, glass tables, concealed television and marble bathroom, the Kerwins laugh aloud at the dramatic contrast with the accommodation from which they have just escaped.

To Bruce Kerwin, who has decided to stop being a loser and to relaunch himself as one of life's winners, the de luxe room is proof that his new persona is working already.

'Who were those tramps who arrived here with us?' he asks as his wife starts to unpack.

'I was pleased to see them,' says Frances. 'I found it quite reassuring. I don't want to be overawed by the other guests.'

Her husband, with his orange T-shirt, gold bangles and hair over his ears, looks increasingly like a lonely hippie who has been dismissed from the pack and is now wandering aimlessly among people who place convention and etiquette above all else. Frances is a grammar-school girl and her background has defined her expectations: a home that is neither a castle nor a slum; enough money for the reasonable demands of a reasonable person; a life undisturbed by the world's harsher developments and, most important of all, the amiable approval of the people she knows. In this benign scenario, eccentricity is as welcome as a sexually-transmitted disease, and she has arrived in this palace besieged by doubt. Husbands are supposed to wear subdued suits and murmur politely when spoken to, not ponce around in designer jeans saying, 'Hi!'

'You mean you were afraid I'd stand out,' he says.

'It did cross my mind that the average Carlton guest wouldn't look like a superannuated beatnik,' says Frances. 'Yes.'

'Darling, you're so hidebound,' says Bruce Kerwin. 'Immured in your middle class.'

'To which class are you planning to shift me, Bruce?' asks Frances, but before he can answer there is a discreet tap on the door. An immaculate young man in a bow tie carries a gold tray with champagne in an ice bucket and two fluted glasses.

Bruce Kerwin loses no time in tipping the boy and attacking the bottle.

'Here's to the rest of our life,' he says, passing a full glass to his wife.

'Let's just concentrate on enjoying the holiday,' says Frances. 'The rest of our life worries me to death.'

This remark worries Bruce Kerwin who wants his wife to enjoy this extravagance, and he sits down. 'We got this far,' he says.

'Legal and General were a help,' says Frances. 'They gave us money every month, if you remember.'

'*Gave* us?' says Bruce incredulously. 'What was I doing during this time? Picking my nose?'

'Probably,' says Frances, 'but it was pretty lucrative.'

'Lucrative?' he echoes. 'Twenty years of my life and at the end of it what have we got?'

'We're in a wonderful hotel.'

'Yes, because I'm not working,' says Bruce. 'We've left wage slavery behind.'

Frances Kerwin feels that she doesn't have the energy to deal with the flaws in this argument and returns to the task of unpacking. She wants to forget about the future and concentrate on the present.

'I'm going on the beach,' she says. 'Coming?'

'Presently,' says her husband. 'I want to examine the health club first. A man could get quite fit during a short stay here.'

'It's the fit people who keep dropping dead,' says Frances. 'All that training weakens the body's immune system. The first whiff of infection and they've gone.'

'Frances,' says Bruce, 'can I do anything right?'

Two hours later, Roger Blake is looking at a blonde woman who from the back appears to be completely naked. A thin gold band round her waist seems to be all that she is wearing. But when she turns he sees that what she actually has on is a thong with a golden triangle of shiny material covering her pubic hair. Lying on a sunbed beneath a blue and white parasol on the Carlton Hotel's private beach, Roger Blake studies her firm, full breasts, her long legs and her aerobically burnished body and blesses Esme's prescience at roulette. When the woman sits down and begins to arrange her belongings on the next bed he wonders why he has had to be talked into this holiday. He averts his gaze and adjusts his parasol so that the sun reaches his pale body. He is wearing a pair of white boxer shorts which he hopes will eventually emphasise the tan he aims to get.

The sky is cloudless now and it is hard to believe that it has rained in the last month. The girl on the next bed is not the only one who eschews clothes: breasts and bottoms hover in every direction. The question for Roger Blake now is not why he had to be persuaded to come here . . . but how he will ever bring himself to leave.

The girl – is she a girl or a woman? She must be thirty – turns on to her back to allow the sun to work on her front. 'The golden breast', he thinks to himself, and the phrase seems unbearably erotic. He lies back to allow the sun to do its work on his own body. Behind him, a boisterous group of Australian girls with names like Arlene, Darlene and Noelene are discussing the sexual possibilities of the French waiter who brings drinks to his horizontal customers from the beach bar. It is clear that a Frenchman is an essential part of their European tour.

Roger pulls himself on to an elbow and beckons the waiter himself. This is thirsty work. He orders a lemonade. When he sits up to drink it the girl on the next bed rolls on to her side and stares at him. He looks at her and looks away. Chatting inconsequentially to a strange woman who is stark naked requires a panache he may not possess. But the woman continues to look and, eventually, smile.

'Roger Blake,' she says. 'These are classy surroundings for you.'

He stares at her now and smiles. 'Have we met?' he asks.

'Evidently,' says the girl. 'How are you keeping?'

'I'm fine,' says Roger, trying to place the face. 'Where did we meet?'

'I hope you're not going to insult me by saying that you can't remember?' says the girl.

'Well,' says Roger.

'It was memorable. Well, it was memorable for me.'

'It was memorable for me too,' Roger assures her. 'It's just that I can't remember it.'

'You're a bit young for Alzheimer's Disease, I'd have thought,' says the girl. 'If you've forgotten me, you've got a serious problem.'

Roger thinks back to the women he has known. There are quite a lot of them and he had thought he remembered them all. His mind flits through transient liaisons.

'Miriam Toplin,' he says. 'A certain sexual familiarity on a clifftop in Devon?'

'That sounds like you,' says the girl. 'However I'm not Miriam Toplin.'

'What about the Devon bit?' asks Roger. 'Am I getting warm?'

She offers him a frozen smile and settles down on her back again. Clearly she is angry or disappointed that he doesn't remember her, and Roger lies back too, ransacking his past. But he used to drink a bit once and alcohol was never a great memory aid. If he has forgotten this blonde beauty, how many others have slipped from his mind? He pictures his past as a series of sensational sexual conquests that would make a formidable store of erotic recollections if only he could recollect them. He looks back at the girl but she seems to be asleep.

From this private segment of the beach a small jetty juts into the water. At the end where a high notice says *Carlton Inter-Continental*, speedboats arrive and depart, carving white circles in the sea, but nobody swims. In these health-conscious days, Roger decides, they probably use the hotel's indoor pool.

An attractive woman in her mid-thirties arrives on the beach alone and takes a sunbed three along from where he is lying. She smiles at him and he nods. For a moment alarm grips him. Is this another angel from his past, carrying secret memories of shared passions that he can't recall? But then he recognises her as being one half of the couple who arrived at the hotel with him and he smiles back.

'Did you get a nice room?' he asks.

'They're all nice,' says Frances Kerwin. 'It's quite an hotel, isn't it?'

She stretches out on her sunbed in a one-piece yellow bathing costume and starts to apply sun protection cream to her face and shoulders. The rain has worried her a little and she is determined not to waste the sun when it appears. Shopping she can do any time.

Half an hour later Roger wakes up feeling slightly burnt. It is a long time since the sun has seen his body and he decides that he mustn't overdo it. He sits up and slips on his jeans and then pulls a T-shirt over his head. His movements disturb the girl on the next bed; she opens her eyes and looks at him again.

'Give me a clue,' he says. 'You're not my sister, are you?'

'You're worried. I can tell,' says the girl. 'You think I hold some dark secret from your past.'

'I wish you did,' says Roger. 'My past could use a few dark secrets.'

'My name is Kimberley Neal,' says the girl. 'Does that mean anything to you?'

Roger looks at her blankly. It seems rude to tell her that it doesn't. He tries another route, hoping to hear something that will jog his memory. 'Are you here alone?'

Kimberley Neal closes her eyes again. 'As a matter of fact, no. I'm here with Andrew Marner.'

The use of the name suggests to Roger that he is supposed to have heard of this man. 'Not *the* Andrew Marner?' he asks.

'Do you know of him?'

Roger shakes his head. 'The Alzheimer's has got me again,' he says.

'He's a publishing tycoon,' says Kimberley Neal. 'Somewhat to the right of Genghis Khan.'

'How delightful,' says Roger, picking up his shoes. He is anxious to go now, embarrassed that he can't even remember her name. He takes a final look at her body, memorising curves, and then plods across the hot sand. He decides that what he needs is a cool shower.

In an art gallery off the rue d'Antibes, Esme Rutherford is immersed in pictures of the sea and the creatures which live in it. Sharks, whales, dolphins all seem to leap from the wall of the tiny room as half a dozen people shuffle round admiring the exhibition.

She is sorry that she has failed to persuade Roger to accompany her on this trip. Exposing him to periodic bursts of culture is a mission that she has to conduct tactfully. She doesn't want to frighten him away.

'I'll be on the beach,' he told her. 'I'll see you when you come back.'

'A suntanned skin is a damaged skin,' said Esme. His ideal holiday would probably involve bungy-jumping and white-water rafting, she thinks, and she doesn't want to spoil this one for him by dragging him too often into the silent, airless world of art.

So she is on her own, absorbed in a print of a baleen whale, when someone behind her says, 'Hallo.' She turns to find the man who arrived at the hotel with them. He is wearing the same orange T-shirt and is one of those middle-aged men who choose a hairstyle that prevents you from taking them seriously.

'Oh, hallo,' she says. 'I saw you in the hotel, didn't I?'

Bruce Kerwin has decided to have a look round Cannes before lying on the beach. He likes to get his bearings, to soak up the atmosphere, to make himself feel at home. An art gallery is not an obvious call for him, but he has spotted Esme in the street and followed her here. It is necessary to meet people on holiday and it would be natural to strike up a friendship with the English couple who arrived when they did. More importantly, their informal dress is in keeping with his new image and he hopes to be accepted as a sympathetic free spirit in a conformist, bourgeois world.

'What do you think of it?' he asks. 'My name's Bruce Kerwin, by the way.'

Esme tells him her name and they shake hands. 'What do I think of what?' she asks. 'The whale?'

'The hotel.'

'Out of my league,' says Esme briskly. 'We drove down here to camp but then we won some money in a casino and decided to see how the other half lives.'

'Really?' says Bruce Kerwin, encouraged. 'We moved up-market ourselves after a little windfall.'

'In a casino?'

'My redundancy money, actually.'

'Ah,' says Esme. 'You shouldn't have voted Conservative if you couldn't take a joke.'

'The hotel is full of them,' says Bruce.

'I noticed,' says Esme. 'A combination of egoism, greed and venality for the most part, but we're not going to let that spoil our holiday, are we?'

'Certainly not,' says Bruce. He admires his audacity at plunging himself into this milieu and is surprised to find himself chatting to this intelligent girl. The personality shift really seems to be working for him. He follows her gaze as she studies a new painting.

'Uphill gardener, wasn't he?' he says.

'What?' says Esme.

'The painter. A homosexual.'

'Among other things,' says Esme. 'The mystery of his sexual orientation wasn't helped by the fact that he occasionally buggered his Labrador.'

The cool way that Esme raps this out impresses Bruce

Kerwin. Here is how they talk in that other world that doesn't concern itself with salaries and incrementals and differentials and pensions. He feels that simply by talking to the girl he is being granted admission to it.

He gazes at a picture of a leaping porpoise and tries to conjure up a remark that will keep this conversation bubbling. But his mind has gone blank. He blames it on the life that he has led. It has been all work – in the office or at home where he is continually mending things or making things, fixing plugs or tampering with his car or even picking moss off the roof. He seems to have missed out on the social life that has enlivened other brains which effortlessly produce quick chat, instant opinions, jovial insults or sparkling repartee. He has, he sometimes thinks, grown up in a people-free environment.

His silence, at any rate, has allowed Esme to drift away and now there are several people between them. He scowls at the porpoise but doesn't move. To approach her again might verge on harassment.

Instead he slips out into the street and selects a route to the seafront. There is a relaxed atmosphere here which he feels in tune with. He plunges his hands into the pockets of his jeans and whistles quietly. He will no doubt meet up with Esme again in the hotel.

In a side street leading down to the front he buys a guidebook that promises to tell him all about Cannes. He prefers Cannes to Nice and not only because the beach is sand. Cannes is bright and cheerful; Nice is sombre. But its history is violent, he now discovers. It has been attacked by Romans, Saracens, Spanish, Arabs and Austrians. We tell ourselves we live in violent times, he thinks, but in the past all they ever did was fight.

The guidebook has evidently been translated by

someone whose French is better than his English. 'The sports and leisure facilities of the city enable one to calibrate its dynamism,' he reads. He frowns and puts the book in his pocket. He reaches the front with its sea and its sand, its flowers and its palm trees, and wonders why he took so long to come here.

Esme leaves the art gallery and makes her way slowly to the hotel. There is much that she wants to see but she has the luxury of time. When she reaches their room, Roger is taking a shower.

'How did you get on?' he shouts.

Esme sits on the bed and removes her shoes. 'I've been looking at an art exhibition of aquatic mammals,' she tells him. 'Drawings of sharks, paintings of dolphins, prints of whales.'

'I thought he was at Balmoral chatting to the delphiniums,' says Roger, emerging with a towel round his waist. 'I met a girl.'

'I bet you did,' says Esme. 'Was she French?'

'Non,' says Roger. 'She's English and she knows me. Apparently we met somewhere but unfortunately I didn't remember her.'

'That must have cheered her up,' says Esme. 'She obviously doesn't know you well enough to know that you have the memory of a goldfish.'

'She did seem a bit peeved,' says Roger. 'You're supposed to remember things like that.'

'It must be difficult,' says Esme, 'when there have been so many girls.'

'They kind of blur,' Roger agrees. 'You remember a left breast, but you can't put a name to it.'

Esme picks up a shoe that she has just taken off and throws it gently at his head.

*   *   *

Above them, in a luxurious suite that is more like an apartment, with a lounge, a large bedroom and huge windows that overlook the bay, Andrew Marner is hanging up his jacket in a wardrobe. The exercise reveals a pair of red braces that have cost him more than £100 in Nice.

'Negotiating with the French is like trying to nail jelly to the wall,' he says.

'Is Monsieur Rocard being difficult, darling?' asks Kimberley Neal, who is sitting in front of the dressing-table mirror checking the effects of the sun's harsh rays on her delicate skin.

'He's a barnacle on the backside of progress. I can't imagine how he got where he is.'

Kimberley turns from the mirror, satisfied that no harm has been done to her complexion. 'What are you offering him?' she asks.

'Forty-nine per cent of the new company. Joint ownership of a new British daily newspaper.'

'Perhaps he got where he is by not accepting forty-nine per cent,' says Kimberley. 'Your really ambitious bastard wants fifty-one.'

'Well, I'd be running the thing. I'd be in London while he's swanning around the Riviera. Naturally I need control. I wouldn't want him cluttering up the office anyway. He behaves like a bloody amateur.'

'Never despise the amateur, darling,' Kimberley says. 'Amateurs built the Ark, professionals built the *Titanic*.'

'Who says amateurs built the Ark?' asks Andrew irritably. 'I bet they were all on time and a half.' He heads for the bathroom, frustration engraved on his face.

Kimberley sees what she must do. Her mission here is to soothe, placate, comfort and seduce. She takes off her clothes and examines herself in a full-length mirror. The thong that she has worn on the beach has given her a complete tan with none of those unsightly white bits to mar the picture. She brushes her hair, pops a peppermint in her mouth and waits.

Andrew returns to the room so involved with the problem of Alain Rocard that at first he doesn't see that Kimberley has shed her clothes. She poses before him, a picture from a magazine.

'Get your trousers and your rocks off, Andrew,' she says. 'It'll do you good.'

'You have a taste for syllepsis, Kimberley,' says Andrew, but his concentration has started to waver and he walks across to her.

'Don't let Monsieur Rocard spoil things,' she says. 'You must make up your mind to enjoy this holiday.'

'You're certainly stiffening my resolve,' says Andrew, undoing his trousers.

She stands before him, carefully unbuttoning his Turnbull & Asser shirt which she slips on to a hanger and then hangs from a chair. *Lady Marner*. Her busy mind and her concupiscent heart thrill to the sound of the words. She can see the place in the country and the green acres sprawled around it. Mullioned windows, mulled wine, multiple orgasms . . . It's a pity she can't work phrases like that into her column.

Andrew Marner falls back naked on the bed and pulls Kimberley on top of him. Their lips meet briefly and then her mouth embarks on a downward tour, kissing his chest and his stomach and eventually his penis, which is growing enthusiastically.

'There are two things you don't get at home,' says

Andrew Marner, smiling. 'And one of them is Lobster Thermidor.'

Kimberley removes her mouth and smiles back. 'That depends on who you have at home, darling,' she tells him.

Andrew Marner is too agitated now to consider the significance of this remark, and he pulls Kimberley up the bed and assaults her breasts with his mouth. She lies back, smiling at the concealed lights in the ceiling, and wonders what Bertha does when she is in bed with him.

She has never seen Bertha but the name suggests something large and formidable. She can't imagine that someone who is petite and sexy would have a name like that. She tries to remember where she has heard it before, and decides that it is the name of a gun.

No action seems to be called for from her on the bed. Andrew Marner is busy enough for both of them. He seems to have two pairs of hands, neither of which can stay still. Kimberley murmurs noises that she judges appropriate but, beyond a certain breathlessness, Andrew Marner pursues his goal in silence.

Eventually he rolls on top of her. A straightforward missionary position job, thinks Kimberley. I must introduce him to something else sometime.

It does not last long. Andrew Marner subsides on to her and she lies there hugging him and then waiting for him to get off. But he doesn't. He is asleep.

'Can you move?' asks Kimberley. 'You're hurting me.'

6

Cocktails at the Carlton are served at a bar which adjoins the large open-air terrace overlooking the Croisette. Guests take their drinks out into the evening sun to contemplate menus and watch the less fortunate strolling along the seafront; and the strollers look back, hoping to spot a celebrity among the well-dressed crowd sitting complacently with their exotic drinks. Prosperity and satisfaction exude from these people: there is no better place for them to be seen. The menus that they study are packed with the inventive cuisine of Provence. The yachts that bob on the sea across the road are probably theirs. The men are in dinner jackets now; their women, who have prepared laboriously for this relaxation, wear colourful dresses that make some of them look like Australian fruitbats.

The exception among this sophisticated clientèle sits alone at the bar inside wearing Calvin Klein jeans, tasselled loafers and a new yellow T-shirt which says across the chest: LIFE. BE IN IT. He is drinking beer and has been for some time, although having only recently discovered its price his consumption has slowed. Bruce Kerwin is not planning to join the diners in the hotel and has no need to dress up, but he is determined to mix with the other guests over a drink. After all, he is paying to stay at the Carlton Hotel, too.

The Englishman who arrived with Esme comes into the bar and approaches the counter. He is a lean man with a good-looking face that has been burnt by today's sun. He is wearing jeans, too, but has put on a more conventional white shirt.

Bruce looks up and nods as the man comes alongside him. 'Settled in?' he asks.

Roger Blake looks at him. In this decorous setting the man's appearance is so incongruous that he can't suppress a certain curiosity. 'Yes,' he says. 'And you?'

'I should say,' says Bruce Kerwin. 'What a palace! I never thought I'd stay in a place like this but then the redundancy money came along and I thought what the hell – spoil yourself! I'm Bruce Kerwin, by the way.'

The man evidently requires company. It is a need that Roger Blake has seldom felt.

'Roger Blake,' he says, beckoning the barman. 'I like your shirt.' When the barman comes over he orders whisky. He really wants a draught lager but all the beer here is bottled.

'It's my new image,' says Bruce Kerwin. 'I used to be grey suits and ties. I used to be a wage slave. But I've given all that up. The way I see it, you can start again. Become a different person, find a new perspective.'

'By buying a T-shirt?' asks Roger. The man has clearly been at the elixir for some time.

Bruce Kerwin smiles as if he is dealing with a child. 'Well, there's more to it than that, of course. You're probably too young to understand. But wait until you hit forty. You're in the second half now and you can't count on extra time. The feeling is you're trapped. Worse than that, there's nothing else to do. You've achieved what you're going to achieve. There's nothing to look forward to. Another thirty years of the same and then death, probably a painful one. Is that what we're supposed to accept?'

'What do you want to do?' asks Roger, picking up his whisky. 'Sail round the world?' Bruce Kerwin, it seems, has an uncontrollable desire to talk about himself.

'Nothing as adventurous as that.' After the drinks that he has had, 'adventurous' is a difficult word but he meets the challenge bravely. 'I ran into your wife this afternoon, by the way.'

'Really?' says Roger. 'What did she look like?'

'You don't know what your wife looks like?' asks Bruce.

'I haven't got a wife. I thought you'd found one for me.'

'Esme,' says Bruce, remembering.

'My friend, my partner, my lover,' says Roger. 'But we never mention marriage I didn't realise people still did.'

'She's a stunning girl,' says Bruce. 'Is she an artist?'

'That's her game,' says Roger.

'My wife's a shopper. There are many hobbies that a wife might have but the most disastrous from a husband's point of view is shopping. Would you like a drink?'

'I would,' says Roger, emptying his glass. 'Is there anything else you feel obliged to impart?'

'I'm talking too much,' says Bruce. 'I'm not used to a lot of beer.'

Esme and Frances arrive at the same moment although

81

they are not together. Esme has discarded her jeans and put on a white dress that shows her shoulders and knees. Frances is dressed more discreetly – a dark blue two-piece with a white blouse. A pianist has started to play in a corner of the room.

'This is my wife,' says Bruce Kerwin, getting off his stool. 'Frances.'

'And this is Esme,' says Roger.

'I've met Esme,' says Bruce.

'But your wife hasn't,' says Roger.

When everybody has been introduced to everybody else, Esme looks round at the immaculate guests and says: 'This is some place, but I'm not going to let them make me feel inferior.'

'You're not inferior,' says Bruce Kerwin, with a sudden flash of anger. 'That's the whole point. You're a creative artist. You add to the world's pleasure and enjoyment. These people here – ' and he waves his hand at the other customers '– they're . . . nothing.'

This ringing endorsement embarrasses Esme, who smiles politely and says: 'Thank you, Mr Kerwin.'

'Bruce,' says Bruce. 'Don't be intimidated by these robots, Esme. They're not proper people.' He sits down again, rather heavily.

Roger Blake orders drinks for the two women and another beer for Bruce Kerwin. 'Your husband seems to be going through a mid-life thing,' he says to Frances.

Frances smiles. 'He's certainly going through something. He's become more animated on this holiday for some reason. Usually I expect to find dust on him.'

The barman is disappointed at another order for beer. He has more interesting skills to display but the stimulating components of his many cocktails are being ignored. He pushes the beer towards Bruce Kerwin disapprovingly and looks round in search of a guest with more extravagant tastes.

One appears. Andrew Marner approaches the bar with Kimberley Neal on his arm. He is not wearing a dinner jacket but is dressed instead in a six-button double-breasted Cerruti suit. 'Top *schmutter*,' Kimberley has assured him. 'Trendy but not too trendy.' She is wearing a purple off-the-shoulder dress that attracts glances from both sexes.

'This pianist reminds me of the Beau Rivage,' says Andrew. 'It's what you don't get nowadays.' He orders himself a planter's punch; Kimberley asks for a Bloody Mary. While she is waiting for it to appear she looks round and notices Roger Blake a few feet away.

'Hi,' she says.

He smiles and nods, synchronised gestures which he feels have wrapped up this exchange. But Kimberley comes over to him.

'Are you dining here?' she asks.

Roger shakes his head. 'We're going out to find somewhere cheaper. Wombat and pickle crisps is about our mark.'

'Well, that's a shame,' says Kimberley. 'To get this far and not try the menu.'

'We've read the menu,' says Esme. 'The cost of one dinner would feed an Ethiopian village.'

'This is politics and not poverty?' Kimberley asks, genuinely puzzled. She has had the idea these English guests should all dine together. She is ready for some company. When Andrew turns from the counter with her Bloody Mary she goes over and says: 'Why don't we invite those people to dinner?'

'Why would we want to do that?' Andrew asks.

'They're English,' says Kimberley.

'I meet the English,' says Andrew, 'in England.'

'I'm a journalist,' says Kimberley. 'I like to meet people. It's where my material comes from.'

'If you like,' says Andrew. 'I really don't mind.' After his absence with Monsieur Rocard he feels that he should try to please Kimberley, and he would quite like some company himself.

'You'll have to pay,' she warns him.

'It's happened,' says Andrew.

It proves to be surprisingly easy to arrange because although the men are less than enthusiastic, both Esme and Frances are keen to pay at least one visit to the hotel's gourmet restaurant. Twenty minutes later the six of them are comfortably established at a large table in the corner of La Côte, the hotel's poshest eaterie. To the surprise of some of them, the sartorial shortcomings of Bruce Kerwin and Roger Blake are politely ignored by the staff.

Introductions are made, much wine is ordered and served, and Andrew Marner is soon exercising his privilege as host by dominating the conversation with an amusing account of the character defects of the famous people he knows. He has, with the help of the wine, a pungent way with words. The literary and the ribald collide in lively conjunction. One Cabinet Minister is a patronising turd, another a pusillanimous shit. A man whose appearances on television suggest that he would be the conscience of the nation is a sanctimonious Welsh arsehole, and the Archbishop of Canterbury is left for dead beneath a pile of abuse which makes Frances blush. Approval is rare, praise non-existent.

'This is fun,' says Esme. 'What are these magazines that you publish?'

'There are one or two downmarket publications for

people who can't cut up their own food,' says Andrew, 'but the jewel in the crown is *World Review*.'

'I've seen it,' says Esme. 'It's very good.'

Andrew's pleasure at this verdict shines across the table. 'And what do you do, my dear?' he asks.

'I'm an artist,' says Esme. 'If you want your portrait painted, give me a ring.'

'I might take you up on that,' says Andrew. 'There's a gap on the boardroom wall.'

A waiter appears, shuffling menus.

'What's French for *coq-au-vin*?' asks Roger.

Frances Kerwin is both embarrassed and delighted to be here. The setting is exciting and the company interesting. She had feared that the holiday would pass without her visiting this gastronomic heaven. The embarrassment is caused by her unresponsive husband who has a glassy-eyed appearance which suggests brain death. The message on his T-shirt now seems ludicrously inapt. His wife's reproving gaze prompts him to attempt speech.

'God is what teetotallers have instead of alcohol,' he announces. He is a little behind with the con-versation, as drinkers often are, and is still thinking about the Archbishop of Canterbury. 'We all need props.'

'God doesn't give you cirrhosis of the liver,' replies Frances, and to the others she says: 'He hardly drank until he got here. I don't know what's got into him.'

'You sound like your mother,' says Bruce. He turns to the others. 'Frances has got this mother.'

'Your mother-in-law,' suggests Roger.

'By marriage,' agrees Bruce. 'I've found her upside down in the garden twice.'

'How do you mean?' asks Esme.

'Tipped over in a chair. Feet pointing towards the stars. Couldn't get up.'

People aren't sure how to react to this story. They glance at Frances who is not amused, but Bruce is laughing at the memory of his upside-down mother-in-law.

Kimberley Neal is listening to the conversation, reluctant to intervene. Sooner or later something will drift across the table which will give her an idea for a piece in her column. Kimberley's law states: *You don't learn anything when you're talking*.

Frances looks at her and wonders who she is. The introductions did not announce her as Mrs Marner and she looks too young. She sits there, cool and beautiful, watching everybody with an enigmatic smile.

Roger looks at her too, waiting for some word or gesture to spark the flash of recognition that will enable him to place her in his past.

When the food arrives – a variety of starters that range from sushi to smoked salmon – Andrew Marner resumes his role of host and seeks to entertain the guests round his table as he does several times a month in the course of his work. More wine arrives. His audience is receptive: a rich man's jokes, he knows, are always funny.

He beams round the table and his smile finally settles on Frances Kerwin. He is taken by her eyes which not only sparkle but also radiate intelligence. Tired of his wife and wearied by bimbos, he wonders whether the time has come to get himself a mature and beautiful woman like Mrs Kerwin, saddled, as she quite obviously is, with a disintegrating partner.

'I shouldn't be in business at all,' he tells her. 'Basically I'm a romantic – unpractical, quixotic, dreamy.'

'That's not the image you project,' says Frances. 'You don't sound like a man who is going to throw his teddy in the corner if he doesn't get his own way.'

He leans towards her and she sees that he is handsome. His eyes, set far apart, are surrounded by friendly wrinkles. 'I'm a romantic in every sense of the word, Frances. I never got over Edmund Purdom not marrying Ann Blyth in *The Student Prince*.'

Roger Blake is watching him with fascination. The man is presumably a tycoon, a person untouched by failure. Roger suspects that most people are dissatisfied with their lives but are sustained by an irrational optimism or a mad pride. Andrew Marner seems to have got it all and be thoroughly enjoying it. He has Kimberley Neal. He can buy four people to brighten his dinner table. He is a driven man.

'How did you do it, Andrew?' asks Esme in the new relaxed atmosphere created by the wine. 'How did you make all this money? It's a trick most people miss.'

'There's no trick, dear,' says Andrew, smiling benignly. 'First you borrow, then you work twenty-four hours a day. The borrowing is quite important because the bank then makes sure that you work twenty-four hours a day. A lot of people who start businesses with their own money lose it because they haven't got the bank behind them waving a big stick. They don't work hard enough.'

Roger Blake finishes his shrimp cocktail and dabs his mouth with a napkin. 'When I was young,' he says, 'I used to think that money and power would bring happiness.'

'Young man, you were right,' says Andrew, glancing round the table. 'What's the matter with Bruce? His body language looks very negative.'

'That's a polite way of putting it,' says Frances. 'He's actually unconscious.'

When she eventually gets him to their room, Frances has had a few drinks herself.

'Let's make it, man,' she says, snapping her fingers. But her ageing hippie, who has stirred enough to walk to the room, has lost his impetus. He lies fully dressed on a bed that seems to be lurching in a rough sea. His mouth finds sentences difficult.

Frances has removed her blue two-piece and hung up her blouse. She is now in pink bra and pants and feels somewhat drunk herself.

'You really disgraced us, Brucie,' she says, although no disapproval has been expressed about her husband's fall from grace. 'What's happening, man? Are you getting younger or older?' She sits beside him on the bed and undoes the belt on his jeans.

'Just dying,' says Bruce. 'Don't worry about it.'

'Perhaps you're too old to be an adolescent trendy. Embrace your senility, man.'

'Wine on beer, queer,' says Bruce, opening his eyes. He finds the bed stops moving if he keeps his eyes open and he lies there waiting for the symptoms of nausea to subside.

'I get myself a toy boy and he breaks,' says Frances, 'just like all the other toys I ever had.' She gets up and goes into the bathroom. When she returns in a blue nightdress she collects a couple of magazines that she has brought with her in case she needs something to read on holiday. She gets into the bed that her husband is still lying on, groaning slightly. He hoists himself to a sitting position and finds this makes him feel marginally better.

'Read me a story,' he says.

'Christ,' says Frances. 'You've plunged straight through adolescence to infancy.' But she opens her magazine and does find something. '"A doctor writes",' she reads. '"The mid-life crisis is a crisis of motivation or rather, the lack of it. The targets have suddenly vanished and there is a panicstricken feeling that time is not only passing too quickly but also being wasted".'

'What sort of story is that?' asks Bruce.

'It's a story about you.'

'What would you do,' asks Bruce, 'if I bought myself a motorbike?'

'Check the life insurance,' says Frances.

'Perhaps a sports car would do it.'

'Do what?' asks Frances, turning the pages of her magazine.

'Make me feel young again.'

'Why do you want to feel young again, anyway? You were a miserable sod the first time.'

'Youth is wasted on the young, Frances. I could handle it now.'

'It doesn't look like it,' says Frances, studying her husband's pale face. 'It looks as if it's not doing you any good at all.'

Bruce gets off the bed quickly. 'I think I'll go to the bathroom,' he says.

'Don't make any noise,' says Frances. 'This is a class hotel.'

Andrew Marner examines his face in the bathroom mirror, wondering how he looked to Frances Kerwin. He regularly studies this image for the signs of slow deterioration that the years tell him are overdue. But he sees bright eyes, a firm face, a face that is young for fifty.

The hair refuses to recede. He has read somewhere, probably in one of his magazines, that it takes 500 hairs to cover an inch of scalp and it seems to him that each inch has the full 500. But moving back from the mirror he knocks one of the hotel's little bottles of bath gel on to the floor and is reluctant to pick it up. The first sign of growing old, he tells himself, is when you don't want to pick up something that has fallen to the floor. He stoops to collect it.

Kimberley Neal is waiting for him in bed.

'Have you rung Bertha?' she asks when he comes into the room in a gold and brown silk dressing gown.

'Who?' says Andrew.

'Bertha,' says Kimberley. 'Your wife.'

'Why would I ring her?' asks Andrew.

'I don't know,' says Kimberley. 'To tell her that you arrived safely.'

'She'll know that,' says Andrew. 'Plane crashes are on the news.'

From the window he can see the special machines that each night clean, groom and oxygenate the beach. People still stroll along the Croisette, but they are lovers now, pairs that are closely entwined, and not the family outings of a few hours ago.

'I think I would want you to ring,' says Kimberley, 'if I were your wife.' She regrets this directly she has said it. She is warning him about the type of wife that she would become. But it is not a warning that Andrew notices because the thought of marrying Kimberley has not occurred to him.

'I'd have to obfuscate,' he says. 'I hate all that. All husbands become liars in the end. It's the only way they can preserve their sanity.'

'And you told that woman you were romantic,' says Kimberley.

He removes his dressing gown and gets into bed. His pyjamas are white silk and they remind Kimberley of a cricketer she used to sleep with. She remembers him fondly, angry with the way that Andrew has been talking. But her situation doesn't allow her to display anger and she decides shrewdly to change the subject.

'What did you think of them?' she asks. 'Our guests.'

'A rum bunch,' says Andrew. 'Where did you find them?'

'In the bar.'

'Not your typical Carlton guests,' says Andrew. 'But I liked the women. Both lumbered with a couple of losers, it seemed to me. Know anything about them?'

'The Kerwins are spending their redundancy money, and Roger Blake and his girlfriend are paying for the holiday out of a roulette win.'

'Poverty,' says Andrew. 'It's a terrible thing.'

Roger Blake and Esme Rutherford are making love in the shower. The atmosphere here is more cheerful than in some of the other rooms and appreciably noisier. The venue has not been chosen by either of them. Esme has gone in for a shower and Roger has followed her into the bathroom and one thing has led to another and now they are making love. Although there are two people in the shower there is only one pair of feet on its tiled floor. Esme's legs are wrapped round Roger's body and both bodies are moving slowly beneath the warm water that cascades over them. In this steamy environment passions soar. There is no room for inhibition in the tiny cubicle. Esme straddles him, rides him and goads him. Movement is freer, penetration deeper, and she moans at the unexpected pleasure of it. Finally Roger sinks to his knees and they slip apart as water pours on their heads.

The performance has taken rather more out of Roger than is customary; it has been an athletic feat of co-ordination and control, made more difficult by the ever-present danger of slipping on the wet tiles. He dries himself perfunctorily, wraps the towel round his waist and flops on the bed.

'Wow,' says Esme. 'When's the next shower?' She has one towel round her body and a smaller one wrapped turban-like round her head.

'Life is full of surprises,' says Roger. 'I only went in there to clean my teeth.' He lifts himself from the bed and goes to the mini-bar in the fridge in search of a drink. He finds two beers and hands Esme one.

'Was that the girl?' she asks.

'Was who what girl?' asks Roger.

'Kimberley Who's-it. The girl who said she had met you before.'

'That's her,' says Roger. 'What did you make of her?'

'Hard,' says Esme. 'Where did you meet her?'

'I've only got her word that I *did* meet her.'

'But she knew your name. And now, by the look of it, she's a rich man's mistress.'

'I trained her well,' says Roger, 'if I did train her.' He drinks some beer from the bottle. 'Andrew Marner! I've spent about eleven thousand days on this godforsaken planet and I haven't got a farthing to scratch my bum with. And that smooth bastard's got it all.'

'What did you think of the others?' Esme asks. 'They haven't got it all.'

'Bruce Kerwin looks like the twelfth man in a paedophile ring to me. What's he playing at?'

'He's trying to be young again, by the look of it. Time's winged chariot is nipping at his heels. Apparently the older you get, the faster it moves, but being

92

a youthful twenty-eight I wouldn't know about things like that.'

'You know an awful lot though,' says Roger, sitting on the bed. 'I wish you knew how I could make some money.'

'You know the important things,' says Esme, 'like how to make love in a shower.'

'A difficult talent to convert into readies.'

Roger walks to the window and looks at the stars over the bay. He feels slightly uneasy now about being in this hotel. He can't afford the luxury that surrounds him and has to keep his eye on the prices. The beers that he has taken from the fridge have cost four times more than they would in England, and the wonderful options outside, the fishing and the sailing, snorkelling and water-skiing, all have prices that discourage him. They are in the Carlton but can't afford the facilities it offers. He walks back to the bed and sits down again.

'You're tired,' says Esme. 'We'd better make love lying down.'

7

B ruce Kerwin walks along the seafront like a som-
nambulist. He is wearing a black baseball cap with
Festival du Film French Riviera in gold letters at the front.
The heat comes off the Croisette and seems to hit him
in the face. He has the bruised eyes of the seriously
hungover and his lungs gasp for the fresh air that his
body craves. He is not familiar with the consequences
of excessive drinking but imagines this mild régime of
exercise and fresh air will help to repair the damage,
restore some colour to his face and clear the cobwebs
from his brain. He is mistaken in this and after a few
hundred yards realises that he is mistaken. His problem
is dehydration.

He turns away from the seafront and wanders up
side streets that are busy with early-morning shoppers
and littered with deserted Yamaha scooters. The trade
here seems to concentrate on antiquarian bookshops
and furniture stores that cover the expensive tables in
their windows with china fruit. He reaches the Place
Gambetta, a small square at the back of the town where

a morning market is about to take place, and nearby he spots a bar. It is an establishment that beckons to him.

Bruce Kerwin goes in and slumps on a stool at the counter. A fan whirrs above his head. At this early hour, when the rest of the world is taking its breakfast, there are not many customers, but a few stools away, sitting on his own, is a man in his twenties who is wearing jeans and and T-shirt just like his own. His dark curly hair is brushed back and looks as if it might occasionally do duty in a ponytail, although this morning it just hangs down his back. The man looks at him and smiles.

'How's the old Stock Exchange then?' he asks.

Bruce Kerwin looks at the man, feeling piqued. He resents the fact that he is instantly identified as English, and is irritated further by the suggestion that his natural habitat is the City, with its bowler hats and brollies. After the efforts that he has made to revamp his image he doesn't expect a complete stranger to look at him and see a stockbroker. Indeed, this young man who is obviously following an unconventional lifestyle, is just the sort of person that Bruce Kerwin had hoped would see him as a co-equal and comrade.

'I've no idea,' he says reluctantly.

The man has a pleasant-enough face, but Bruce finds his tendency to smile all the time somewhat unnerving.

'The doctor said I can only drink ten pints a week so I've decided to have them this morning,' the man says, holding a mug that is full of beer.

'I'm a bit hungover myself,' Bruce admits, having nothing else to say.

'Ah, the mourning after the night before,' says the

man. 'That's mourning with a U. You'd better have a beer. It's the absence of alcohol that causes the hangover.' He calls to the young barman who is busily filling shelves and talks to him in French. A pint mug of beer is placed in front of Bruce Kerwin who greedily drinks an inch or two and immediately detects some improvement in his condition.

The man watches him drink it and says: 'Shaftoe.'

Bruce pauses, wondering whether this is a new fashionable greeting, linked perhaps to some modish religious cult, which has replaced 'Cheers' or 'Good health' in the lexicon of young drinkers, but the man immediately follows it up with the declaration: 'Poet.'

Bruce Kerwin's dysfunctional brain slowly absorbs this. The man's name is Shaftoe and he writes poetry.

'You must be some poet,' he says. 'This place isn't cheap.'

'There's an old saying,' says Shaftoe. 'Those who live by the water will never starve. I guess they weren't talking about the Côte d'Azur, but I survive. Too lazy to work, too proud to beg. If there was no such thing as suicide I'd have killed myself long ago.'

Information is reaching Bruce Kerwin faster than he can assimilate it. His desire to communicate with young people like Shaftoe, the bright-eyed generation that hasn't sold its soul for a pittance, is impeded by the crapulence that afflicts him.

'Suicide?' he says, catching the end of this monologue.

'Why not?' says Shaftoe. 'If suicide was as easy as turning off the light, undertakers would be the richest people in the country.'

'My father committed suicide,' says Bruce. 'I don't recommend it.'

'Terminal, is it?' Shaftoe asks.

'Oh, it's okay for you. It's the ones you leave behind,' says Bruce.

'I haven't got any ones to leave behind,' says Shaftoe. 'My departure would be followed by a deafening silence. "To that dark inn, the grave!"'

'Is that one of your poems?' asks Bruce.

'Walter Scott,' says Shaftoe, picking up his beer. He has a clear classless accent that sounds like the man on the radio who tells you where the traffic jams are. 'My poems haven't actually been published yet. The world isn't ready for them.' He drinks half a glass and belches loudly.

'So you pass the time in the South of France while the world prepares itself?' asks Bruce. He doesn't know how to talk to this man. He knows nothing about the pop music that young people admire, or acid house parties or the amphetamines that he reads about in the newspapers. The gap between the generations may only be a few years, but young people today seem to come from another century, another world.

'This place has its points,' says Shaftoe. 'The old darlings with their epileptic corgis. The knuckle-heads in their suits. But I don't know. As the taxi driver said to Bertrand Russell: "So what's it all about then, Bertrand?"' The recollection of this quotation makes him smile all the more. 'Publishers,' he says. 'Plethora of plonkers.'

Bruce Kerwin, waiting for his brain to start working, is somewhat overwhelmed by all these words. He looks round the room wishing that there was somebody to help him field them. It is a bar with mirrors on both the walls and the pillars and for a moment Bruce thinks that it is suddenly full of beautiful girls until he notices their resemblance and realises that it is the same girl endlessly repeated.

'Pretty girl,' he says, and Shaftoe turns to see who he is talking about.

'That one?' he says. 'Had her. Daft tart. Covers herself with oil. I slid off her twice.'

Bruce Kerwin is suffused with envy. Here is another glimpse of that magical world where pleasure is paramount and beautiful girls are casually available, a world that he has never penetrated and knows little about. He picks up his beer and wonders who is paying for it. Quite soon it is empty and he holds it aloft to catch the barman's eye. Once the business of refilling it has been put in motion, he turns to Shaftoe, feeling a lot better than he did half an hour ago.

'I would like to hear one of your poems,' he says.

'Would you?' says Shaftoe. 'Let me see. The last one I wrote was called "In The Souterrain Of My Mind There Is A Doubt".'

'Sock it to me,' says Bruce. These four words, which had sounded so appropriate to the company in his head, acquire the stale whiff of the Sixties as soon as they leave his mouth, but he smiles encouragingly as the poet braces himself for recitation.

'"In the souterrain of my mind there is a doubt. It freezes the potential of my dreams . . ." no, bollocks to it. It's too early in the morning.'

'I like it,' says Bruce. 'You should work "no, bollocks to it" into the poem. Art should shock.'

The second pint is relaxing him and he feels more at home. Art galleries, poetry readings – this is where it's really at. It's a million miles from an insurance office.

But after his last remark Shaftoe is looking at him strangely 'Are you on something?' he asks.

Bruce Kerwin is disappointed by this question. The language gap has opened up again and he is left with an enquiry that he doesn't understand.

'What?' he says.

'If so,' says Shaftoe, 'I'm your man.' He winks and touches the side of his nose in a mysterious fashion. Bruce stares at him; comprehension seems to be moving away from where he is sitting.

'Man for what?' he asks.

Shaftoe takes this question as a consumer enquiry. 'At the moment I've only got Moroccan, but I'm expecting some new stuff this afternoon.' He produces something from his pocket that he displays furtively. Bruce can only see a beige square that looks like a leather lump in his hand. 'Twenty quid for an eighth. Call it a hundred and eighty francs.'

'Got you,' says Bruce, as comprehension returns. 'We're talking cannabis here.'

Shaftoe puts a finger to his lips. 'Not too loudly, we're not,' he says. 'Tell you what – let's go down to the beach and see how you like it. I don't want a dissatisfied customer on my hands.'

'I'm your man,' says Bruce, touching the side of his nose. No invitation in recent years has pleased him more: smoking dope with a hippie poet in the South of France represents, now he thinks about it, the pinnacle of his social aspirations, the realisation of his dream to become a new man. He picks up his glass, anxious to see it empty. The adventure starts here.

'Where are you staying?' Shaftoe asks as he finishes his beer.

'The Carlton,' Bruce tells him.

'Boy, you must be loaded,' Shaftoe says admiringly.

'Not exactly,' says Bruce, feeling that he should

100

disabuse him of this perception. Shaftoe might see him as an easy touch. 'There is such a thing as a credit card,' he adds.

'Debt card is the correct term,' says Shaftoe. 'I never touch 'em.' He stands up. 'Ready?'

'What about the beer?' asks Bruce. 'Or do they give it away here?'

'It's on my tab,' says Shaftoe. 'Let's go.'

They walk out of the bar together and head for the beach. An English family block the pavement, waiting for their infant daughter to catch them up.

'Come on, Portia,' says the mother.

'Portia!' says Shaftoe. 'I bet they don't get many Portias in Benidorm.'

And Bruce can see that here is different. Stunning women get out of huge cars that he can't even name. Black men cruise by in Mercedes. Are black people more prosperous here, or are they chauffeurs?

They reach the *plage publique*, the part of the beach that is available to the general public. All the rest has been carved up by the big hotels, and Bruce wonders what Frances is paying for a sunbed on the Carlton's little acre. Presumably the sight of all that coastline not earning any money offended the French, who would charge a supplement for fresh air if they could get away with it. Early-morning sunseekers are already unrolling towels and applying cream to their faces and arms.

They can sit on the sand here and watch the sun glinting on small white yachts that barely move in the tideless Mediterranean. Shaftoe guides Bruce to the back of the beach where they can settle themselves against the wall and not be seen from the path above. He produces his precious cargo and proceeds to roll a joint with loose tobacco from a tin.

'Where do you get it?' Bruce asks, watching him.

'My main man,' says Shaftoe. 'A very together gentleman. He's got rocks of crack cocaine in his garage up in Grasse.'

'You're a sort of agent?'

'The bread has to come from somewhere, my friend,' says Shaftoe, searching each pocket in turn for a box of matches. When he finds them a mild wind extinguishes two. He doesn't have the worker's secret of cupping the flame and concealing the cigarette, but eventually ignition is achieved and he draws deeply on the joint and then passes it to Bruce Kerwin.

'Try that,' he says.

Bruce Kerwin struggles to overcome hygiene reservations about sharing this joint. New diseases have made him nervous. But he knows that this is the etiquette of dope because he saw it in a film on television, and so he puts the sweet-smelling joint between his lips and sucks hard.

Shaftoe watches him, looking for a sale.

'Hold it in,' he says.

Bruce Kerwin feels nothing. He looks at the boats and the sunbathers on the beach. Nothing has changed beyond the taste in his mouth.

'What am I supposed to feel?' he asks.

'Nothing yet,' says Shaftoe. 'Just relax, man.' He takes the joint back, draws heavily on it and exhales slowly through his nose. 'Tranquillity,' he murmurs. 'That's a nice word.'

Bruce Kerwin takes the joint back and tries again.

'If they could see me now,' he says, and laughs. A pressure seems to have lifted from behind his eyes.

'If who could see you now?' Shaftoe asks.

'Oh, the blokes in the office. Plethora of plonkers.'

The phrase sounds familiar to him as he sucks at the joint but he can't remember where he has heard it. Doors seem to be opening in his head.

'Man,' he breathes. 'Like wow.'

'Lebanese Gold is the stuff,' says Shaftoe. 'A beautiful fragrant taste. I can get some if you're interested.'

Bruce Kerwin is beginning to feel very relaxed. It wouldn't be difficult for him to fall asleep here on the beach. He looks at the boats on the water and finds that his eyes aren't focusing as quickly as usual.

'The eyes are the first thing to be affected,' says Shaftoe when he mentions this.

'What else happens?' asks Bruce, taking another drag. 'I don't think I feel quite normal.'

Shaftoe laughs, pleased.

'If you feel normal, man, there wouldn't be any point in taking it,' he says. 'You're not a nervous person, are you? If you're nervous dope can make you a bit paranoid, but basically what you've got in your hand is an antidote to tension.'

Bruce Kerwin is too relaxed to listen to this. He is looking round the beach and seeing things that he doesn't remember noticing a few minutes before. It is a colourful scene, and the heat and the bright light are contributing to the intensity of the picture.

'I'm stoned,' he says. 'Is that the right word?'

'Wrecked,' says Shaftoe. 'Blasted.'

'Like wow,' says Bruce.

Shaftoe has stopped smoking now and is content to leave the joint with Bruce. Occasionally he glances round to see whether anybody is watching them.

'Do you want to buy then, my friend?' he asks. 'I can let you have an eighth for two hundred francs.'

Bruce can't remember what price Shaftoe had mentioned earlier. He struggles to get his wallet from the back pocket of his jeans, and pulls out two, 100-franc notes. A topless woman brandishing a flag is pictured on them, something that he hasn't noticed before.

'What's an eighth?' he asks.

'Eighth of an ounce. You'll get half a dozen joints out of it.'

Bruce Kerwin wonders who he can smoke this stuff with. It is not the kind of activity that will interest his wife. He thinks of the girl in the hotel, the girl he met in the art gallery, but he can't remember her name.

'You'll need some Rips,' says Shaftoe, producing some paper. 'You fold them like this.' He takes the two banknotes that Bruce Kerwin is studying and stuffs them into his pocket, and then passes him the cannabis and the papers.

'The offence here is possession,' he says. 'Be discreet.'

'I'm blasted,' says Bruce, putting the stuff in the pocket of his jeans. The joint has gone out and there is not enough left to make it worth relighting.

'I've got to move,' says Shaftoe, standing up. 'What you want to do is go back to your hotel and have a little rest.'

'The question is,' says Bruce, 'which is my hotel?'

'The Carlton,' says Shaftoe, pointing. 'The big white job with the two cupolas. Good, aren't they? The architect based them on the breasts of a courtesan.'

Bruce struggles to his feet, ignoring this.

'I'm in that bar most mornings,' says Shaftoe, 'if you need fresh supplies. When I get the Lebanese Gold it'll blow your head off.'

Bruce starts to walk along the Croisette. Walking is

not difficult, he feels light, but he is beset by a terrible vagueness.

He has hardly begun his journey when he turns to the beach again, attracted by the roll of the waves which have begun to assume magical properties. Somewhere a ghetto-blaster is playing reggae music and when he reaches the water he tries some dancing steps as he paddles in his shoes. The blue sky, bisected by the vapour trail of a jet at 40,000 feet, seems to be the roof of an enormous tent.

As he turns from the sea he notices a slim young blonde lying alone on a towel and laughing at his antics. He laughs, too, and heads instinctively in her direction. At the age of forty, he tells himself, he finally knows enough to make a very adequate twenty-year-old.

He has almost reached the girl when he stops, distracted by a terrible thirst and a craving for chocolate. He is a seething mass of indecision now but his next move is made for him because he sits heavily and involuntarily on the sand with the girl in front of him. Her long, straight, blonde hair rests on her breasts as she lies on her back and it seems to him that she is topless. All inhibitions have been quenched and new, exciting ideas thrust their way to the front of his confused mind.

'Hi, babe,' he says equably. 'D'you do blow jobs?'

The girl looks at him coolly, recognising a problem she has seen many times before.

'You're stoned out of your box,' she says with an American accent. 'Gee, you're blasted.'

Bruce nods in agreement. Beads of sweat adorn his forehead.

'I've had a joint and blown my mind,' he says. 'I'm buggered with a capital F.'

'Was it good stuff?' asks the girl.

'It seems to have done the trick,' says Bruce. 'Now I want chocolate and a drink.'

'You've got the munchies,' says the girl. 'Go buy a choc ice.'

'You know about dope, do you?' says Bruce. 'I'm Bruce.'

'I'm Jodie,' says the girl, 'from Idaho. I only smoke the best. I recommend Royal Nepalese temple ball. Get yourself a choc ice is my advice.'

Bruce drags himself obediently to his feet and heads for an ice-cream stall on the Croisette. When he returns it is clear that his attempts to find his mouth with the ice cream have not been entirely successful. Chocolate is smeared across both cheeks. He sits down beside her looking like a blacked-up minstrel, his wet shoes covered in sand.

'I'm besotted by your beauty,' he tells her solemnly.

Jodie from Idaho laughs gaily. She has always been nice to old people, hoping for a slot in their wills, and Bruce seems very old to her. She produces a tissue and wipes his face.

'Where's your wife?' she asks. 'You look as if you've got one.'

'Oh, I have,' says Bruce. 'I'm maritally involved.' He frowns to himself. 'Marital is an anagram of martial. I can see that now.' He talks in the slow, intense way of dope-users, but it sounds all right to him. 'I don't make her happy.'

'It's not your job to make her happy,' says Jodie. 'It's not possible for one person to make another happy for the rest of their life. We're responsible for our own happiness.'

This is not a concept that Bruce can grasp.

'I don't make the money, you see. If I was an undertaker people would stop dying.'

He laughs immoderately at this and sees that Jodie is joining him.

'The first time I got stoned I fell into a swimming pool,' she tells him. 'When I got out I was wearing a see-through dress.'

Bruce laughs some more; the laughter does not seem to be proportionate to the joke.

'You have an adorable face, Jodie,' he says eventually. 'How old are you?'

'Eighteen,' says Jodie. 'Young enough to be your – '

'Mistress,' says Bruce, laughing again. He has spotted the gap in his life; an eighteen-year-old girlfriend, wise beyond her years, familiar with dope and delightfully pretty.

But streetwise Jodie from Idaho sees warning signs now. Game for a laugh, she hasn't come all this way to get laid by a geriatric limey, and what she has read about Englishmen hasn't encouraged her to consider it. They are apt to be found dead wearing stockings and suspenders, trussed with flex, a satsuma in their mouths containing tablets of amyl nitrate and a plastic bag over their heads. They couldn't even masturbate without making an MGM production out of it, and this particular Englishman is obviously several hormones short of a hard-on.

'You'd better get back to your hotel,' she says briskly. 'You're gonna end up in trouble if you stay here.'

'Why's that?' asks Bruce, who is not anxious to move.

'Your condition is recognisable,' says Jodie. 'Go get a snooze.'

Bruce finds that the drug has made him curiously

suggestible and he rises to his feet immediately and tests his balance.

'A walk will do me good,' he decides.

Jodie from Idaho lies back, happy to see him go. 'If God had meant us to walk He wouldn't have given us taxis,' she tells him but he has already stumbled off.

Frances Kerwin returns from a shopping spree in the rue d'Antibes to be told by the concierge in the hotel: 'Your husband has been arrested.'

She looks at him, thinking that there has been a mistake. He is wearing a cream jacket and a striped blue tie and he has beckoned to her as she walked in as if he is a customs officer and her bag contains expensive goods that she has failed to declare.

'He went out for a walk to clear his head,' she says, confused.

'Nevertheless he has been arrested, madam,' says the concierge in impeccable English. 'He is at the police station.' His tone suggests that the police station is not where the Carlton Hotel expects its guests to end up.

'Do you know why?' Frances asks. 'Do you know what's happened?'

The concierge shrugs. He is a busy man. Guests are waiting with their questions and requests. 'The police rang and asked us to tell you,' he says, and then turns to other guests who have more respectable problems.

Frances, uncertain what to do, walks across the gilded lobby with her shopping and sinks into one of the elegant red velvet chairs beside the hotel's Caviar Club. Blonde women with faces like brown leather glide imperiously past. Others, astonished to find themselves surrounded by such opulence, are constantly taking photographs so that they can remind themselves when they get home that it was all true.

Frances is still taken aback by it herself. Alone at breakfast that morning she had never seen so many women with full make-up on first thing in the day. They all looked like Joan Collins. Some, she suspected from the way they walked, had had a cosmetic surgeon at work on their bottoms. On the rue d'Antibes she had watched in the glamorous boutiques as French ladies, with their deep voices, deep tans and apparently deep pockets, spent hundreds of pounds on fashion accessories without batting a false eyelash. She had bought herself a skirt and pair of suede boots with a credit card and felt thoroughly guilty, a feeling that eases now with the news of her husband.

She stands up and walks across the beige marble floor to the reception desk.

'Have you a map of Cannes?' she asks the girl, who produces one instantly. There is a picture of Cannes, taken from the air, on the front, and the message: *Life is a festival*. Frances unfolds it so that it covers the desk.

'Could you mark the police station on it?' she asks. The girl smiles and draws with her biro a ring near a big junction called Place du 18 Juin. The French are big on dates and Frances wonders what happened on 18 June. Off the rue d'Antibes she has just seen a street called rue 24 Août.

She walks over to the lift to drop her shopping in her room, gets out her Yaletronic card doorkey that will be changed when the room has a new occupant, comes down again and sets off in the direction of the police station. Her initial reaction of embarrassment was replaced by anger quite quickly but her predominant emotion now is curiosity. What on earth could her husband possibly have done which was sufficiently interesting to get him arrested? He didn't steal, he wasn't violent, he was not likely to have succumbed to lust. And going out with a hangover he would hardly have been drunk.

Contemplating outlandish possibilities, Frances pursues an uphill journey away from the sea, through the town, up narrow streets where music booms from tiny Peugeots caught in the hardly-moving traffic. A series of pedestrian lights get her across a busy six-line highway and she finds herself in the Avenue de Grasse. This far from the seafront, the town has lost its glitter: broken shutters, peeling façades and copious graffito mar an area which tourists seldom see.

Cannes Central Police Station is a drab, five-storey concrete building with the French flag flying from an ugly second-floor balcony. The notice over the front door says SÛRETÉ NATIONALE. This is, thinks Frances, as far as you can get from the splendour of the Carlton Hotel.

She steps inside and is confronted by a large printed notice which seems to contain the names of the recently accused and the charges they will face in court. To her left is a small window through which she can see a policeman in a pale blue, short-sleeved shirt sitting at a desk. She taps on the window and waits.

The policeman looks at her curiously and eventually gets up. Frances has her French phrasebook with her, but it is full of such conversational thrusts as 'Have you any brothers or sisters?' and 'My suitcase is not here.' 'You appear to have incarcerated my spouse' is not, she sees, in the book's repertoire.

'Do you speak English?' she asks when the man slides open his little window.

The man looks at her. 'Moment,' he says, and goes away. It is at least five minutes before he reappears with another policeman, an older man with a moustache, who smiles and says: 'Can I help you, madam?'

Frances feels embarrassment now. She has never been involved in a conversation of this sort before.

'My name is Frances Kerwin,' she begins. 'I'm told you have arrested my husband.'

'Monsieur Kerwin?' says the man. 'He is asleep.'

'Asleep?' Frances is astonished. She had imagined her husband to be in a highly tense state, anxious, fidgety, on edge. To take a nap on his first appearance in a cell suggested that he was carrying his new laid-back personae to farcical extremes.

'It is the drugs, madam,' says the man.

'You've drugged him?' says Frances. 'What the hell's going on?'

The man smiles. 'No, we do not drug him. He drugs himself. He is – what do you call it? Zonked.'

'Zonked?' says Frances.

'He is in possession of the cannabis,' the man says. 'In France this is not allowed. We will charge him – when he wakes up.'

'Cannabis?' repeats Frances. 'He's never even *seen* cannabis!'

'It was in his pocket,' shrugs the policeman.

'Somebody put it there.'

'I think not,' says the policeman. 'He had been smoking it. We found him wandering. He was lost. He was *zonked*.'

'You said,' says Frances.

A week or two ago it would have been impossible for her to believe what she is hearing, but this morning she

111

can recognise the awful possibility that the policeman is telling the truth.

'I want to see him,' she says. 'Now.'

'It is not possible, he is asleep,' the policeman tells her. 'If you can come back later, perhaps at six o'clock, you can talk with him.'

'When will you let him out?'

'Let him out?' says the policeman frowning. 'It is up to the court. One year? Two years?'

'What?' says Frances, and she starts to cry.

'Possession of the cannabis is a serious matter, madam. You're not in Holland. In France we do not do it. Nor in England, I think?'

'I've no idea,' says Frances, wiping her eyes. 'It isn't something I know a lot about.'

'This is good,' says the policeman. 'You come back at six o'clock and you can talk with Monsieur Kerwin about his predicament.' He slides the window shut and she is left standing in the tiny hall. She wants to sit down but she wants to get out of the police station more.

In a daze she makes her way back through the crowds in the gloomy back streets and struggles towards the sun of the seafront and the comforts of the Carlton Hotel.

8

In the early evening, Roger Blake walks along the Croisette in search of a bar that sells draught beer. Esme is preparing herself for dinner in the port, which leaves an hour's hole in the evening that can be usefully filled by a search for liquor. The sun feeds his libido and he sees, in one of those flashes of insight that so frequently unravel mysteries and explain the insoluble, why there are so many Africans and so few Eskimos. The heat makes him rampant. Unseen in caverns beneath his feet, chefs who work for the restaurants on the beach are toiling in greater heat over the evening's menu.

When he finds a bar he ignores the tables on the pavement and goes inside into the shade. He sits up at a round counter in the middle of the room so that he is facing the Croisette and the sea. A mug of Heineken costs him forty-two francs. He drinks half straight away.

From this angle the sun turns the sea to a gleaming white and he settles down to study the view, a priceless panorama of brown thighs, expensive clothes, designer sunglasses, yellow Lamborghinis, drop-head Rolls-Royces and, beyond, the smooth white yachts in the bay. Wealth is flaunted and enjoyed; the people here seem to belong to an enchanted race.

Roger ponders a more mundane matter: do women in hot climates have bigger breasts, or is it just that they wear skimpier clothes? And he can't get over how brown they are. This isn't the normal two-week holiday tan, it's a deeply ingrained ebony that breaches racial boundaries. These two subjects combine to vindicate an old theory of his: where the prices are high the girls are prettier. The plain ones are nannies.

He sips his beer and sees a familiar face coming along the Croisette. Kimberley Neal, in a short white dress, seems to be all cleavage and thighs as she strides between the crowds who are taking an evening stroll on the seafront. She has put in a lot of hours on her tan and is by no means out of place among the bronzed locals although, Roger suspects, the white dress is helping to accentuate the effect. She comes into the bar, a white bag swinging from her shoulder, and orders a crème-de-menthe frappé.

'Roger Blake,' she says. 'You do get about.'

'Where's Andrew?' he asks.

'Andrew?' says Kimberley.

'Your mentor, your partner. The chap with the loot.'

'Ah, that one,' says Kimberley. 'He's in the bath – a fairly protracted business where Andrew is concerned, so I said I'd hop out for a quick slurp.'

'And here you are,' says Roger. 'Well, you can put me out of my misery. Where *did* we meet?'

'The Alzheimer's hasn't cleared up, then?' says Kimberley.

'It's getting worse.'

She looks out at the chunky palm trees that run down the middle of the Croisette, dividing one traffic lane from another and says: 'Ten years ago you made love to me in the back of a Standard Vanguard.'

Roger is astonished. He doesn't know how to react to this. 'It must have been a very old Standard Vanguard,' he says finally.

'It was,' says Kimberley. 'It was yours.'

'I can't believe that I would make love to someone like you and not remember it,' says Roger. 'However, I do remember the Standard Vanguard.'

'You remember the car but you don't remember me?' says Kimberley. 'That's nice.'

'I spent a lot of time servicing the Standard Vanguard,' says Roger.

'I take your point,' says Kimberley.

'Where did this unforgettable event take place?' asks Roger. He used to cover a lot of miles.

'Blakeney,' says Kimberley.

'Blakeney, Gloucester, or Blakeney, Norfolk?'

'Blakeney, Gloucester. You rogered me in Blakeney, Roger Blake. I always had a great sense of time and place. I even lost my virginity in Maidenhead. Now I'm getting canned in Cannes.'

He looks at her sixteen-tooth smile and her crème-de-menthe frappé and is overtaken by a lust that surprises him.

'Ten years ago . . .' he says. 'I must have been – '

'Twenty,' says Kimberley. 'Apparently you spent a lot of time at that age with a microphone stuck up your arse. Do you remember why?'

Roger nods, embarrassed. This is not the story from his past that he would choose to be aired at this moment. There are worthier anecdotes to burnish his image.

'It was a little idea I had that I thought might make money,' he says lamely.

'As I recall it, you were recording your farts. But I can't remember why.'

'I was going to cut up the tape and rearrange it so that it played "God Save The Queen",' says Roger. 'I even had a name for the group: The Wind Section.'

'What happened?'

'My backside didn't have the range.'

'I'm surprised you had the wind.'

'I ate a lot of beans,' says Roger. 'If the record had ever appeared, I was going to set them against tax.'

'With an imagination like that you ought to be rich,' says Kimberley. 'You're not rich, are you?'

'Don't seem to be,' says Roger. 'I've been watching those people out there and wondering where they got it from. It must cost thousands a day just to run a yacht, never mind buy it.'

'They sure as hell didn't get them by farting,' agrees Kimberley. 'You have to own companies so that thousands of people are working for you. They get wages, you get yachts.'

'It doesn't seem fair, does it?' says Roger.

'It seems completely fair to me,' Kimberley sounds brisk. 'Enterprise and initiative win the prizes. Lethargy and inertia don't. It's called life.'

'The most unlikely people are Conservatives these days,' says Roger, drinking his beer. 'What happened to the Socialist revolution?'

'It failed,' says Kimberley. 'It knew how to spend money on the right things, but it had no idea how to make it. And soon there wasn't any, so Socialism's dying and Communism's dead.'

'Is that the way it went?' says Roger. 'I often wondered.'

'Well, now you know,' says Kimberley. 'How's Esme? I didn't see you ending up with a serious little lady like that.'

'Much better than a frivolous big lady,' says Roger.

'I'm not frivolous,' says Kimberley, 'if you meant me.'

'I didn't,' says Roger, 'but how was it in the Vanguard?'

'On a scale of one to ten? About eight.'

'That's good, isn't it?' says Roger. 'It sounds good.'

'It was good,' says Kimberley. 'I just wish it had been a Mercedes.'

Frances Kerwin's mood as she re-enters the police station has undergone many changes since she last stepped this way and has now settled into a cold fury. She feels that she is dealing with stupidity, pure and unalloyed, and she has had time, during a long afternoon in her hotel room, to consider the inconvenience and embarrassment that her husband is going to cause her. His disappearance will have to be explained to the people they have met, the hotel will start wondering who is going to pay the bill, and she will be left like a widow to eat alone. If the policeman's prediction is correct, she will be left to fly home alone as well, when a fresh raft of embarrassments will be waiting for her, along with much expense. Frances Kerwin is not a happy woman.

Her tap on the window this time elicits a smile of recognition from the young policeman but he still doesn't speak English. He departs in search of his bilingual cohort who appears looking grave.

'Monsieur Kerwin wakes up,' he announces. 'He makes much trouble.'

'Tell me about it,' says Frances sourly. 'Can I see him?'

'Go through that door,' says the policeman.

Frances turns back from the window and sees a green door across the hall. When she walks over and opens it, the policeman she has been talking to is already on the other side, waiting to show her down a long corridor, at the end of which is a small, windowless room. Its only furniture is a bare wooden table with a chair on either side; the policeman invites her with a flowery hand gesture to sit in one of them. Mysteriously, a single shoe lies on the floor.

Frances waits for something to happen but nothing does. The policeman walks across the room and leans against a dark brown wall. He explores a nostril with a thumb. He pulls a notebook from his pocket and examines its pages.

Suddenly the door opens and a policeman Frances has not seen before, enters. With him, still wearing his black baseball cap, is Bruce Kerwin.

'Bruce,' says Frances, standing up.

'Hallo, darling,' says Bruce sheepishly. 'We've got a right farce on our hands here.'

The policeman leads Bruce to the other seat so that when the Kerwins sit down they are facing each other across the table. He then takes up a position by the door while the older policeman continues to look at his notebook.

'Are you sure it's not a tragedy?' asks Frances. 'Tell me what happened.'

'I wish I could remember,' says Bruce. 'I met a man who had some cannabis and we had a smoke on the beach.'

'What the hell for?' asks Frances.

'A new experience,' says Bruce. 'We can't go through life rejecting new experiences.'

'I think you'll want to reject the one that life has lined up for you now,' says Frances. 'So what happened then?'

'You tell me,' says Bruce. 'I came over a bit vague.'

'They found cannabis in your pocket.'

'They may have done.'

'It's an offence, Bruce. They're going to charge you with it. They said you could get two years.'

'Three, I was told,' he says. 'I'm sure a good lawyer will sort it out. The trouble is that in this country, you're guilty until proven innocent and a case can take a year to get to court. I've been demanding bail but it isn't a concept they can grasp.'

Frances looks at her husband. He doesn't seem to be as worried as he should be and she wonders whether he is still influenced by the drug. His eyes are a little strange, the pupils dilated, and his skin seems unnaturally pale in this town of brown faces. He smiles and shrugs.

'You're a real idiot, Bruce,' says Frances. 'What am I supposed to do?'

'Get me some soap,' says Bruce.

'Soap?' says Frances.

'They don't supply things like that here. They have to be provided from outside.'

'Bruce, soap is not at the top of my priority list at the moment. In fact, it's not on my list at all. What you need is a lawyer, and who's going to pay for that? I doubt whether they take Access.'

'Apparently there's a British consulate at Marseille,' says Bruce. 'They should be able to help.'

'Marseille? That's bloody miles away.'

119

Frances sits back exasperated and sees that the policeman against the wall is making notes. He looks at her and says: 'Your husband broke a chair. It is not helpful. Bail! Bail! What is this bail?'

'Jesus,' says Frances.

'What we want to know,' says the policeman, 'is who he got the drug from.'

'And I've told you I can't remember his name,' says Bruce. 'These people have been driving me mad with their questions when they know it's all a haze to me.' He takes off his baseball hat and puts it on the table. The novelty of this new experience is beginning to wear off. 'I suppose I'll have to stay here tonight?'

'And tomorrow night,' says Frances, 'and the night after.

'I can't believe it,' says Bruce. 'I'm a law-abiding man.'

'A law-abiding man with a pocketful of drugs,' says Frances. 'A born-again prat.'

'Don't be like that, Frances,' says Bruce. 'We'll sort it out all right.'

'With me as usual doing most of the work.' She looks at the policeman and asks: 'What can I do to help him?'

'He needs a lawyer,' says the policeman. 'They will give you names at the desk. In the meantime he needs money for things. Soap, toothpaste, shampoo. He needs a toothbrush.'

'He needs a head transplant,' mutters Frances, opening her bag. She puts a 100-franc note on the table. Her husband suddenly looks very depressed. 'Cheer up, kid,' she says. 'Think of it as a new experience.'

'Oh God, Frances – you can't leave me here.'

'Well,' says Frances, 'I can't take you with me.'

* · *   *

120

Walking along to the port at the western end of the Croisette, Roger Blake and Esme Rutherford see boys flying kites from the beach, artists who will draw your portrait while you wait, a gigantic carousel packed with children, youths on roller blades zig-zagging down a straight line of empty Coca-Cola cans, the Palais des Festivals where the annual Film Festival is held, and the ramparts of the old town Le Suquet, glowing with orange lights. In the port they look at the yachts that have arrived here from all over Europe: the *Orient Star* from Jersey, the *Aporo* from Amsterdam and the *Starlet* from Southampton, on which a man is making a phone call. The signs say VIEUXPORT.

Picking their way through the evening strollers, they head for one of the many restaurants at the side of the port and finally settle at an outdoor table of one of them so they can watch the people wandering by a few feet away. On the back of their canvas chairs it says *Cécile B. de Mille*.

Two men holding hands walk by. One wears one pink shoe and one green. Another man has a black jacket and a black tie but no shirt. His girl has a transparent bra. Others are dressed more extravagantly but all are young.

'The beautiful people,' says Roger.

'The privileged people,' says Esme.

'Don't let's have any politics,' says Roger. 'I'm told the Socialist revolution failed.'

'You don't think these people got here on their own money, do you? Most of them have hardly started work.' Esme looks over at a drop-head Rolls-Royce with white leather upholstery in which a young man sits. 'It's rather more than a well-adjusted person needs, unless their intention is to induce envy in everyone

121

else – in which case a premature disability would be an appropriate reward.'

'Phew!' says Roger. 'Less of this green-eyed carping, please. It's only a substitute for action. The thing is to make money yourself.'

'You'd have to make a lot to be able to buy a car like that,' says Esme.

'Well, somebody did,' Roger tells her.

'But not the wally in the front seat, and that's my point,' says Esme.

She has changed tonight and is wearing a pink and blue dress that clings to the edges of her shoulders. Roger likes her shoulders but finds tonight that when his mind moves in that direction he starts to think about Kimberley Neal and a ten-year-old sexual triumph that has shamefully been allowed to fade from his memory. What will there be for him to think about when he is old, if he can't hang on to stuff like that?

He looks at Esme and wonders whether she is enjoying this holiday. She is grumpy tonight and he checks dates in his head. Something is obviously worrying her. The problem, he thinks, is that the things he wants to do – like lie on the beach and have a beer or two – hold no interest for her. Instead, she has searched out art galleries and roamed through quaint back streets in the old town. She has visited sixteenth-century churches, fourteenth-century castles and towers built by monks. In the museums she has found pre-Columbian ceramics, Polynesian ethnography, Egyptian antiquities and pottery from Asia Minor and Rhodes, while Roger, in more leisurely mode, has studied the modern phenomenon of the topless woman. Some people, removed from their normal comforts, become bored and restless on holiday, he thinks, but he could settle anywhere.

When a waiter arrives with a menu, they lay it out on the table to study it.

'What's *pamplemousse*?' asks Roger. 'I see the word everywhere.'

'Grapefruit,' says Esme. 'I'll have lamb, or *agneau* as they call it.'

'You should eat fish here,' says Roger. 'Look, there's the sea.'

'I'll have lamb,' Esme insists.

When the waiter has taken their order away, Roger leans across the table and asks: 'What's worrying you, babe? You're supposed to be happy here.'

Esme produces a sheet of paper from her pocket. 'Money,' she says. 'I've been looking at our finances. This is all costing far more than we imagined. Our win wasn't enough.'

'I thought we were leading a frugal existence?' says Roger.

'Living in the Carlton Hotel?' says Esme. 'Get real! I ordered a chicken sandwich in the room when you were on the beach and it cost eight pounds!'

'I didn't eat midday,' says Roger smugly. 'I was saving money.'

'Saving money?' says Esme. 'Your sunbed, in case you haven't noticed, costs fifteen pounds a day. It's also costing fourteen pounds a day to park your car. That's an extra six hundred quid over three weeks before you eat a cooked breakfast or open the mini-bar in our room. We're spending bundles.'

Roger falls silent. He is enjoying watching how the rich live and doesn't want to be told that he can't afford it. That afternoon, lying on a sunbed that he now knows

123

cost fifteen pounds, he had watched a man in an Armani suit walk along the Carlton's jetty with a very expensive briefcase in his hand, and climb into a fast launch that whisked him out to one of the yachts. He had greatly enjoyed lying in the sun and imagining what sort of life that man led.

'Are we looking at what the economists call a deficit?' he asks.

'Let me explain it to you,' says Esme, consulting her sheet. 'I won just over twenty-five thousand francs at roulette. The room costs twelve hundred and fifty a night unless there's a supplement for sex in the shower. Twenty nights equals twenty-five thousand francs. That's without all the little extras I just mentioned, like car parks, sunbeds, drinks and breakfasts. Then there's the indoor pool in the Health Club upstairs which I would like to use if we could afford it.'

'You'd better get back to the roulette table,' says Roger. 'I don't want to end this holiday doing the washing up.'

'We ought to get back in the tent,' says Esme. 'We're living in a fool's paradise.'

'Pass me the dishcloth,' says Roger. 'I'm never sleeping in that tent again.'

'In that case we'll have to make some money. What are you good at?'

'I never work on holiday,' says Roger. 'It's against my principles.'

'The tent it is, then,' decides Esme, 'or we'll be on the Plat du Jour for forty-five francs before we've finished.'

'No tent,' Roger is firm. His poverty infuriates him. When the waiter brings their food he picks at it with less than his usual interest, but the wine disappears quickly. Esme eats, deep in thought, fretting over the money problem that she has created by choosing such an expensive hotel. Suddenly she relaxes.

'I've had an idea,' she says.

'We need it,' says Roger.

'I was thinking of all that portrait-painting on the Croisette. Suppose I offer to paint Andrew Marner's portrait? After all, he practically suggested it. He mentioned a gap on the boardroom wall.'

'What would he pay?'

'It isn't a question of what he would pay,' says Esme. 'It's a question of what I would charge.'

Andrew Marner steps on to the terrace of the Carlton Hotel with Kimberley Neal and they are shown to their table for dinner. Overhead, stars have replaced the sun now and lights twinkle on the yachts.

'This joint's full of third-world tarts,' says Andrew, gazing round at his fellow diners. Certainly they have come from all over the world. There are even Moslem wives with covered heads. Others look as if they might well fit Andrew Marner's description, but Kimberley baulks at the word 'tarts': she is conscious of her status.

'Perhaps they are executive women with high-powered jobs,' she suggests.

'Perhaps airborne pigs will provide the evening entertainment,' says Andrew. 'Half these women got here on their backs.'

As the waiter brings their menus, printed and carrying today's date, he spots Frances Kerwin emerge from the hotel and look uncertainly round for a table. She looks terrible. He stands up to beckon her and she walks gratefully in his direction.

'Will you join us?' he asks. 'We haven't ordered yet. Where's Bruce?'

'That's very kind,' says Frances. 'I'd love to. Bruce is not here tonight.'

'Well, sit down,' says Andrew Marner, pulling a chair out for her.

'Hallo,' says Kimberley Neal.

Another menu is brought. It says: *Prix par personne TTC: FF 360.* This is not a cheap place to eat, but after trekking up to the police station twice today, Frances is in no mood to embark on another journey in search of one of the cheaper restaurants. The main course is *daurade grille.* She looks to the translation underneath: it says *grilled daurade.* Luckily there is an alternative: roasted saddle of lamb with garlic and stuffed local vegetables, and she orders that.

'How are things?' asks Kimberley. 'Are you enjoying Cannes?'

'It's wonderful,' says Frances. 'I just wish I could afford it.'

Andrew Marner watches her, curious about her husband's absence. He guesses that there has been some sort of tiff which would make questions from him unwelcome. But Kimberley is a journalist and feels no such inhibitions.

'Where is your husband?' she asks. 'He isn't working down here, is he?'

'He's been detained,' says Frances.

'Detained,' repeats Kimberley, as if this reply is by no means adequate.

'He's been detained by the police,' says Frances. 'In fact, he's locked up in a cell.'

'Good God,' says Andrew. 'How exciting. What has he done?' He wants to add, 'Nothing trivial, I hope?'

but controls himself. The removal of Bruce Kerwin fills him with hope and pleasure.

'Apparently he had cannabis in his pocket, which is strange because he has never touched the stuff. He met a man in a bar.'

'Goodness,' says Kimberley. 'I didn't have him down as a dope-head.'

'He's certainly a dope,' says Frances. 'It's his head I'm not sure about. He's trying to be young again. He's neurotic.'

'Neurosis is the absence of self-confidence,' says Andrew. 'How old is he?'

'Forty going on twenty,' says Frances. 'I was going to book him into nursery school when we got home but now it doesn't look as if he will be coming with me. He could get two years, apparently.'

She looks at the others and they wonder if she is going to cry but the waiter intervenes with their food.

'Champagne,' Andrew tells him, and then turns to Frances. 'I realise this isn't a champagne occasion for you, but we enjoy it with our meals. Will you join us?'

'I certainly will,' says Frances. 'I've got to grab my pleasures where I find them.'

'Exactly,' says Andrew, smiling.

9

On Friday morning a parcel of magazines arrives from London for Andrew Marner. Like a child with his Christmas toys he takes them off to a corner of the terrace, pausing only to order a coffee from a hovering waiter. As always he brings a certain anxiety to the new issues, fearing that he is about to be confronted by a ghastly mistake, a grotesque libel or just a blank space where an expensive advertisement should have appeared. The business is full of pitfalls and the mistakes are always embarrassingly public.

He glances only fleetingly at the most popular of his magazines; the readers' tastes are not his. It is *World Review* that he really wants to see and he pulls it from the bundle and settles back in his seat. Usually he has some inkling about what will be appearing in its pages but because he is away he can come to this issue as a normal reader.

He flips through the pages first, studying the contents. The future of Hong Kong, the nightmare of Iraq, the ten most influential men in the twentieth century.

The air fare scandal, the teenage illiteracy scandal, the scandal of innocent men in jail. He makes a mental note to suggest to the editor that one scandal per issue should be sufficient, and reads on. A comprehensive demolition job on modern Britain – 'with its incompetent politicians, lazy and greedy industrialists, spavined sportsmen and demoralised workforce' – has the feel of an important piece which will probably be reprinted, at a fee, in one of the Sunday newspapers . . . but not everything pleases him. Somewhere on the staff is a man, or quite possibly a woman, who is in love with the punning headline. There is one every week and today's, over an attack on a Midlands MP, is LEICESTER BIGOT, which strikes him as particularly crass, detracting with its whimsical tone from the intended criticism.

Next he trawls through the pages in search of the errors that he dreads, the mistakes that will prevent the right people from taking his magazine seriously. He is looking here for the screaming literal, the upside-down cartoon, the misplaced headline, or the article that ends abruptly in mid-sentence. But his eyes alight on something much, much worse.

The goblins in the printing industry have managed to part a word in the middle so that a man who should have been described as 'therapist' is called 'the rapist'. Andrew Marner vacates his chair as if he has been sitting on hot coals, and leaves the other guests on the terrace pitching and reeling in a wave of imaginative obscenities.

'Garnett!' he shouts into the phone. The hotel's switchboard has connected him with surprising speed to the fourth-floor office in London where a bald young man sits at a table surrounded by the morning newspapers. Garnett has found the intellectual niche in journalism that he wanted – a quiet, thoughtful existence where quality counts for more than the ill-considered torrent of words that gushes from the daily papers.

'Andrew,' he says coolly. 'Hallo.'

'Have you seen this bloody cock-up on page twenty-six?'

The angry voice of the proprietor bellowing at him from the South of France disturbs Garnett. This is what happens in proper newspaper offices; it has no place among the urbane courtesies of *World Review*.

'I've seen it, Andrew. It is much to be regretted.'

'Regretted?' shouts Andrew Marner. 'It looks like half a million pounds' worth of damages to me. What did *The Sun* pay Elton John?'

'Their circulation would have been a factor.' He explains gently: '*The Sun* sells more copies than we do.'

'I can't think of anything worse than calling a man a rapist whatever the circulation,' says Andrew. 'The question is: what are you going to do about it?'

'Naturally we'll carry an explanation and an apology next week,' says Garnett smoothly. 'In the meantime, I've phoned him.'

'What did he say?'

'He wasn't available.'

'Why was that?'

'He was with his solicitor.'

'Shit!' says Andrew. 'We're sunk.'

'Relax,' says Garnett. 'It's a genuine mistake. There's nothing malicious about it.' Andrew Marner is so het up that Garnett can't bring himself to tell him that in the excitement of launching *World Review*, they have forgotten to get their libel insurance in place.

With the magazines under his arm Andrew heads for

131

the lift. It feels as if steam is coming off him and he tries to calm down in his little air-conditioned box as it hoists him smoothly to the third floor.

Upstairs, Kimberley Neal grabs the magazines from him, extracts her own and turns to the page that carries her column. KIMBERLEY NEAL it says in huge type across the top of the page. Her picture, with only the hint of a smile, is placed between the two names. The sight of the page gives her a warm glow every week, as if she had never seen it before. But today the pride is diluted. This magazine, selling about 90,000 copies doesn't seem to have been read by anybody she meets. It comes tearing off the presses every week, the final moment in an exhausting schedule, and is rushed to newsagents all over Britain, but nobody has heard of her. Invitations to appear on television don't arrive on her desk. Not one of the people she has met in Cannes has reacted to her name. She gazes at her page and wonders whether anybody actually reads it. She slaves over her provocative message every week, but is anyone out there receiving it?

She flops down on the bed. Next week's column lies half-written on the pad beside her.

'What I ought to write is a book,' she declares. 'People read books.'

'That's news to me,' says Andrew, loosening his tie. 'I thought they watched television. The kids today can't read, can they? They can't even find Britain on a map.'

'I'm not talking about kids,' says Kimberley. 'The average adult woman – she reads books: fat novels crammed with filth. They love it. You must have noticed. The bookstalls are full of them.'

Andrew Marner is fetching himself a drink. The libel

discovery has created a space inside him that needs to be filled. 'And that's what you're going to write, is it? A fat novel crammed with filth?'

'Why not?' shrugs Kimberley. 'Practically everyone else seems to be doing it. Who's heard of Kimberley Neal? Now if you were to start a national newspaper, darling, and give me a column in there it would be different. Or if you were to give me an editorship.'

'Patience, lady,' says Andrew. 'One step at a time.'

'My steps seem to take me backwards,' says Kimberley. 'I'll have to write a book then. Preferably one that makes Jackie Collins look like Jane Austen.'

Andrew Marner takes his whisky to the window. He is barely listening. After today's news, the idea of Kimberley Neal editing one of his magazines is not one that would help him sleep. If Garnett, with his double first, his prodigious knowledge and his meticulous mind can't tell *therapist* from *the rapist*, what hope would she have of saving him from the greedy demands of lawyers? And where would his knighthood be then?

He gulps back his whisky and puts the glass on the table. He hoped that the libel would recede in his mind, but it grows larger, pushing other matters to one side. He walks restlessly across to one of the pictures on the cream walls. It is the gardens at Versailles, with the grand palace rising in the distance. Luxury on this scale always unsettles him. It seems to be telling him that his pot is not bottomless.

'It's all right, Andrew, I didn't want a drink,' Kimberley says, opening her pad.

The remark gives him a jolt. Even those who dislike him praise his manners.

'I'm so sorry,' he says, fetching the bottle. 'I've got a problem on my mind.'

'No, really. I don't want one,' says Kimberley, holding up her hand. 'What's the problem?'

'A little libel. Well, rather a big libel actually.'

But Kimberley is not interested in the minutiae of office life. Tomorrow she has to fax another column and she has much to write. 'Don't forget that you're meeting Monsieur Rocard for lunch,' she says, picking up her pen.

'My God, I had,' says Andrew. 'I'm coming apart here.'

When he disappears to change, she flips through her stand-by notebooks for likely subjects. If she can get this column done in a couple of hours she can spend the afternoon on the beach thinking about her novel. She sees a note that she has made a week ago, and when Andrew has gone she begins to write in her pad: *'You can hardly turn on the television news these days without seeing a funeral. Every day coffins are carried across our screen. Sometimes it is the sequel to a terrorist outrage, sometimes a murdered child, sometimes the last farewell to a fallen star. But whatever it is, I am sick of it. It depresses the elderly and bores the young. Of course, it is easy television for the lazy people who put these programmes together. They might not know where the news is going to happen but they always have the date and place of funerals in their diaries. Instant, easy drama. And it's cheap.'*

She puts down the pad, another few inches of her column filled, and turns back to her notebook in search of another idea. She finds a gem. Lancashire men, she reads, make love more than any other men in Britain. They have sexual intercourse seventy-seven times a year. Kimberley frowns at the celibacy of it, but the figures are there in black and white. The national average is seventy-one times a year and bottom of the league table with sixty-seven couplings are the dour men of Yorkshire.

Kimberley studies these figures with incredulity. What on earth are these people doing with their spare time? Even Londoners, those vaunted pioneers of pleasure and gratification, only manage it sixty-nine times, one more than the staid and serious Scots. Here is something that she can really get enthusiastic about, lacing her column with lubricious jokes while at the same time taking a satisfying swing at the boring British male.

'It isn't our defeats in the sporting arenas of the world that shame Britain,' she writes. *'It's the leg-over league table.'* Three hundred scornful words appear in half an hour and she reads them through with a satisfied smile. This evening she will type the column and fax it to London.

But when she has gone into the bathroom to prepare for a visit to the beach, she misses the normal satisfaction that arrives with the completion of a column. Again she wonders: who is going to read it?

As she dabs sun cream on her face, her mind turns again to the idea of writing a sexy novel that would reach those millions who have never heard of her little magazine. Perhaps it could be based on the survey she has just read. It could even be called *The Leg-Over League Table*. It's a catchy title.

She stands naked before the bathroom mirror, admiring her gently tanning limbs and wonders what her own score would be. She estimates it conservatively at 150, but there have been years that would make that figure look like a vow of chastity. Certainly at twenty, when she kept a record of such things, she had topped two hundred, although that figure was artificially inflated by a rugby team from Bognor Regis.

Her standards are higher today. She is old enough to seek quality rather than quantity. Quality is Andrew Marner, with his position, his money and his power.

She picks up her thong and wonders whether she would be allowed to write pornographic novels if her name was Lady Marner.

For the first time in twenty years, Frances Kerwin wakes up alone. But her initial feeling of dismay, which threatens to develop into a mood that will define her day, is surprisingly shortlived. The bed, not now depressed on one side by a thirteen-stone man, responds buoyantly to her movements. No longer hemmed into one half, she stretches her legs and lies diagonally, discovering coolness and space that she has rarely known. It feels like a kind of luxury and she is reluctant to get up. She extends an arm, finds the remote control by her bedside, and turns on the television. More than fifty channels arrive here from France, Spain, Italy and a dozen spinning satellites that bounce junk back to earth as if, superior beings, they are rejecting it, but eventually she finds the English language with CNN which is showing a long interview with Monica Seles who is recovering from being stabbed on a tennis court. Frances lies in bed listening to this for a while, but when thoughts about her own predicament begin to expand there is no room in her head for those of Monica Seles, and she turns it off.

Yesterday her concern was for Bruce and what she should do for him, but today she finds that her thoughts keep returning to herself. Her problems are more immediate than her husband's and there is a limit to what she can do for him. He is in a cell for the time being, and maybe for a lot longer. She is abandoned. The thought that she should save money by quitting the hotel and flying home is the first idea to reach her. After all, what sort of holiday was left for her now? But then she sees that she needs to be here to arrange whatever can be arranged on her husband's behalf and she realises that she must stay.

She gets up late and goes to the bathroom. For the first time she senses not the loneliness that she had expected, but a delicious surge of freedom. Ignoring the cost, she rings room service and orders breakfast in her room, an extravagance that Bruce would never have condoned. By the time it appears on an elaborate trolley which, with raised flaps, converts in her room to a table, her thoughts have raced ahead and she finds, to her surprise, that pity and compassion are scarce and that anger is still in control.

It would be different, she tells herself, if he was wrongly accused, or had been hit by a car, or had suffered a heart attack, but the fact was that he had brought this absence on himself. She sits down and starts on a breakfast of scrambled eggs, bacon and tomatoes and resolves to think about herself for a change. If Bruce is locked up for two or three years she may never see him again. People change, circumstances alter.

She pours herself a cup of tea and imagines life without Bruce, and the feeling wells up in her that she has been held back for too long. She has always been bright but has never had the opportunity to show it; she has always been ready for a lot more than her restricted life offered. 'A woman's place is in the home' – she had almost believed it herself. But now she was beginning to realise that yesterday's setback was today's opportunity. Each thought spawned another. If every married woman was given a million pounds today, how many marriages would still be intact by tomorrow?

When she thinks back to the long wasted years that she has devoted to her marriage, Frances wonders whether she was in possession of all her faculties. She was letting her life slip by and doing nothing with it. They didn't even have children, the conventional anchor, and their sex life wasn't likely to inspire any poetry. Frances has always imagined that this is the way it is with most people. Sexual frustration is a central part of their lives. They daydream about partners and experiences that will never be available to them. They yearn and they sulk. They accept.

She gets up from her breakfast and smiles to herself. What had Bruce said? 'This is a fresh start for me and I'm going to grab the chance.'

She pushes the breakfast trolley out into the corridor for collection and settles down at her table with the phone. She wonders whether she should break the news to such friends as Bruce has, but decides that she ought to consult him first. With his current capacity for fantasy, he is probably going to promote the story that he is on an extended world cruise.

Instead, after many linguistic and technical difficulties, she manages to make contact with the British Consulate, where a man listens to her story with languid boredom. He explains: 'I hear this one three times a day.'

'That's little consolation to me,' says Frances, who feels appreciably brisker this morning, 'except that you presumably now know enough about the subject to give me some good advice.'

'There's not a lot I can give,' says the man. 'Get a lawyer. Be patient.'

'He wanted bail,' says Frances, 'but he says the French don't seem to understand it.'

'They understand it,' says the man, 'but they won't grant it to someone who doesn't have an address in France.'

'Does that mean he could be locked up for a year or more before he even gets to court?'

'It could well do,' agrees the man. 'The wheels of French justice grind exceedingly slow.'

'Thanks a lot.'

'Keep in touch, Mrs Kerwin. We maintain a record of such things.'

She replaces the phone and goes to the window. The sun, an occasional visitor in her own country, is a permanent resident here. It scorches down, bleaching whatever is in its path. In the street below, people are carrying parasols as the British would carry umbrellas.

Frances sits down and plans her day. A coffee on the rue d'Antibes with perhaps a little shopping would fill the morning nicely. Then a sandwich and an hour on the beach. And then, somewhere between the beach and dinner, she will have to visit Bruce and see how he has enjoyed his first night in a cell. This is the least attractive item on her itinerary.

As she considers it, the telephone rings in her room. A girl on the Carlton Hotel switchboard says: 'A call from Nice for you.'

She waits, mystified, and then Andrew Marner's voice says: 'Frances?'

'Hallo,' she says. 'What are you doing in Nice?'

'A business meeting, I'm afraid,' says Andrew. 'Listen, have you heard of the Bâteau Restaurant?'

'I think I've missed that,' says Frances.

'It's a boat you have dinner on. It sails up the coast. Excellent, I'm told. I wondered if you'd care to join me on it for dinner tonight?'

'With Kimberley?'

'No,' says Andrew.

'Well, I don't know,' says Frances. 'I'm tempted.'

'I distinctly heard you say last night that you've got to grab your pleasures where you find them.'

'I did say that, didn't I?' She smiles. 'What time?'

'Eight o'clock in the lobby,' says Andrew.

'I'll be the one not carrying a copy of *Le Figaro*,' says Frances.

She puts down the phone and goes into the bathroom to look in the mirror. It tells her that a useful addition to her day's programme would be an hour in a hair salon, and a day that was full of gaps is now beginning to feel somewhat crowded. The long walk to the police station has to be fitted in somewhere but, her residual loyalty eroded by the present attractions, it is difficult to see where.

Esme Rutherford returns from a visit to the Musée de la Castre where she has inspected an Egyptian mummy's hand, a Japanese warrior's costume and a South Pacific hut pole, and wonders whether she is devoting too much time on this holiday to culture. She seems to be missing out on the conventional pleasures that are satisfying everyone else, and she is seeing less and less of Roger.

But as she comes into the hotel's lobby she notices Andrew Marner standing alone and remembers that there are more artistic duties in store. She goes up to him.

'I want to talk business with you, Andrew,' she says blunty.

He looks round. He is obviously waiting for someone. 'Business?' he says. 'That's my language.'

He is wearing a smart suit that is almost silver and a deep brown shirt. The tie is pale blue. He looks round again but nobody is approaching.

'It's about a portrait,' says Esme, 'of you. If you were serious the other day, I'd like to do it. To be frank, we need the money.'

'Fine,' says Andrew. 'How about a first sitting on Monday afternoon? I'm out in the morning.'

'Shall we do it in your room?'

'If that suits you,' says Andrew. 'Are you expensive?'

Esme pauses, afraid that a price at this stage might put him off. Rich men are notoriously cautious with their money: that's why they're rich. 'Let's discuss that when you've seen the painting,' she says.

'Such confidence is rare,' says Andrew. He looks round again. Frances Kerwin is beside him in a flowery pink dress. She seems slightly embarrassed.

'Hallo,' she says to them both.

Andrew takes her arm. 'We're off,' he says. 'Monday afternoon, then?'

Esme watches the two of them walk out of the hotel and wonders what is going on. She heads for the lift and ascends with two fat Arabs who appraise her frankly and then discuss her and laugh. In her room is a note from Roger. *'I'm in the swimming pool in the Health Club. Seventh floor.'* She puts on her white swimming costume, covers herself with a bathrobe and goes up.

Roger and Kimberley Neal are frolicking in the pool.

141

She is trying to push his head under the water, and when she succeeds he grabs her legs.

'Well, hallo,' says Esme, wondering again what is going on. 'Is it warm?'

The pool is small, the size of a small room, and is obviously a late addition to an old hotel. Beyond it is the Health Club with exercise machines, saunas, floating relaxation tanks and massage facilities.

'I thought I'd have a swim while you were culture vulturing,' says Roger. 'Kimberley was honing her limbs in the Health Club.'

'You don't have to explain, Roger,' says Esme, dropping her bathrobe and slipping into the water. 'Do either of you know where Bruce Kerwin is?'

'Haven't you heard?' says Kimberley. 'He's been arrested. He's locked up. They found him with cannabis in his pocket.'

'Cannabis? Bruce Kerwin? He doesn't look the type. Where is he?'

'He's in Cannes police station at the moment, poor sod. Some holiday!'

Esme swims across the pool and back. It does not take long.

'What's Frances going to do,' asks Roger, 'left on her own like that?'

'I expect she'll be all right,' says Esme. 'Where's Andrew, Kimberley?'

'Working,' sighs Kimberley. 'He's always working.'

The Bâteau Restaurant is a smart, low-slung craft, 36 metres long, with a restaurant, dance floor and discothèque inside, and tables and chairs in the open air above for drinks before the meal. Andrew Marner and Frances Kerwin are sitting at one of them in the company of a bottle of Dom Perignon and Frances, amazed at her audacity, is listening to a cacophony of hooters as some boats try to edge their way into the port and others try to get out. As their own begins its journey she looks round at some of the other customers. A Middle Eastern gentleman, with a woman who has very heavy legs, is enjoying a cigar as if it is his last; a black couple in expensive clothes are drinking wine; a German family are trying to appease their small boy whose pale face scowls at a waiter who is attempting to serve him with a drink.

Andrew Marner is trying to obliterate all thoughts of libel from his mind and enjoy the company that he has so cleverly provided for himself. He enjoys women and understands them. Their eyes tell him all he needs to know long before they open their mouths, and Frances Kerwin's eyes are an invitation.

She looks at him now and asks: 'Does Kimberley know we're here?'

'I don't have to answer to Kimberley,' says Andrew. 'I employ her.' He refills their glasses and then fills them again as the bubbles subside.

'How do you mean, employ her?' Frances asks. She imagines Kimberley Neal's tall frame splayed naked across a bed.

'She writes a column in one of my magazines,' Andrew explains. 'She's a very ambitious girl.'

'I sort of got that impression,' says Frances. 'She's going to the top.'

'Well, it's the age of the woman,' says Andrew. 'What did Mrs Thatcher say? "The cock crows, but the hen lays the eggs".'

'In her case the hen crowed as well,' says Frances, drinking her champagne.

'How's Bruce bearing up?' asks Andrew, who is not keen to discuss Kimberley Neal's role in his life. 'Have you seen him today?'

Frances nods silently.

Her excursion that afternoon to the crepuscular entrails of Cannes Central Police Station has not been a success and she knows that she is to blame. In the mistaken belief that it would help to cheer him up, she had arrived all smiles, in the manner of a neighbour visiting a sick friend. To Bruce Kerwin, who had now established a snarling relationship with his guards and an even less friendly one with many much smaller creatures who had spent much of the night biting lumps out of his backside, her demeanour was inappropriate. He was dirty, knackered and frayed, and his grinning wife, fresh from a hair salon and wearing what looked suspiciously like a new pair of black suede boots, didn't seem to be on the right wavelength at all.

'What have you done?' he had asked when they were seated face to face again at the same small table.

'Done?' asked Frances. 'How do you mean?'

'Have you found a lawyer for a start?'

'Not yet, Bruce,' said Frances. 'Lawyers cost money. What I have done is phone the British Consulate.'

'What did they say?'

'They said they'd heard it all before. About three times a day, I think the man said.'

'Well, for Christ's sake,' exploded Bruce, 'what was their advice?'

'Patience, Bruce.'

'Patience,!' he shouted. 'Am I going to sit in that godforsaken cell for ever?'

'Not for ever, Bruce. Not for ever. Have they charged you yet?'

144

'Yes, they have. Possession of a forbidden drug.'

'And you'll have to plead guilty. What can a lawyer do?'

'Jesus, Frances, he can plead my case. If there's a prison sentence, he can make it smaller. If there's a chance of acquittal, he'll fight for it. Apart from anything else, I need someone in court on my side who can speak French.'

'The Consulate seems to think that it could be a year before your case comes up. Do you really need a lawyer until then? He'll probably charge us for a year's work when there's nothing for him to do.'

Bruce leaned across the table and gripped his wife's arm. 'Get with it, Frances. I need to be represented. There are dozens of things a lawyer could be doing for me now. My conditions, for a start. I'm covered with bites.'

'Bites?' said Frances. 'Bites from mites?'

'Are you finding this amusing?' Bruce asked coldly. 'I really enjoy being a source of entertainment.'

Frances was full of contrition. She found it difficult to put herself in her husband's position. She placed her hands on his hands which were clenched tightly together on the table.

'I'm sorry,' she said. 'I'm still a little bowled over by the novelty of having a husband in prison. I'll find a lawyer tomorrow. How do I pay him?'

'The redundancy money will have gone into the account. Use the Eurocheque card at a bank. You can draw out what you need. I think there's a daily limit, but you can go to the bank each day.'

Frances, who had resigned herself to the use of credit cards with their circumscriptions and swiftly approaching upper limits, was cheered by this news

145

which opened up a fresh source of money. She wasn't as poor as she had thought.

'Okay, kid,' she said. 'I'll get you a lawyer.'

'Did you bring any soap?'

'Oh God, I forgot. Sorry, Bruce.'

Now, sitting on the boat, she is stricken by guilt at the memory, but her guilt does not extend to her acceptance of Andrew Marner's invitation to dinner. When they have finished the champagne they make their way downstairs and are shown to a table next to a window through which they can watch the coast recede. When they have left the port they can see the seafront at Cannes, the Carlton Hotel, and the traffic moving along the Croisette. The food that they have ordered over drinks upstairs arrives immediately and Andrew pours them wine.

'What was your husband?' he asks, when he has completed these formalities.

'Before he became a time-warp hippie, do you mean?' asks Frances. 'I suppose "a neurotic android" describes him best.'

'You've got a sharp tongue,' says Andrew appreciatively. 'But I meant his job.'

'He was manager in an insurance office, I'm afraid,' says Frances. 'He spent twenty years sitting at a desk and the memory of it seems to have turned his head. Let's talk about you, Andrew. Bruce seems to depress me for some reason.'

'Me?' says Andrew. 'What is there to say about me?'

'Are you married?' asks Frances. 'Is there a wife somewhere?'

'There is indeed,' says Andrew. 'Bertha is at home.'

'Is she beautiful?'

'All women are beautiful once,' says Andrew evasively. 'Nature fixes it.'

'Is that true?' asks Francis, wondering.

'In your case nature made an exceptional job of it. You're a very beautiful woman, Frances.'

'It's kind of you to say that,' says Frances. 'I don't get many compliments.'

Andrew leans forward to drop his voice. 'I should very much like to make love to you, as a matter of fact.'

'Is that a compliment as well?' asks Frances, disconcerted. She has read about how very successful men go directly for what they want, having neither the time nor the inclination to prevaricate, but his forthright approach has still surprised her.

'Whether it's a compliment or not is a matter for you,' says Andrew, 'but I meant what I said and there's no point in disguising it. More wine?'

'I think I'd better,' says Frances, holding up her glass. 'I don't get propositions like this every day.'

The boat has moved away from the coast now and is circling islands in the bay. They see pine and eucalyptus woods and, rising from them, a monastery used by Cistercian monks.

'A group of people I have never envied,' says Andrew when Frances points it out. 'Missing this world in the forlorn hope that there's going to be another.'

'Well, I gathered that the monk-like virtues weren't up your alley,' says Frances. 'Putting you in a cowl would be like putting a g-string on a nun.'

'I'm a healthy man, Frances,' says Andrew seriously, 'with healthy appetites.'

'You're lucky,' says Frances.

'I'm hoping to get luckier,' he says softly.

The boat crosses Golfe Juan and heads for Cap d'Antibes and Eden-Roc. Plates are moved, coffee is served, and music breaks out at one end of the room where there is a small dance floor. Soon several couples are on their feet.

Frances watches from the window as the lights of Juan-les-Pins come into view.

'Jolly Pan,' says Andrew.

'Jolly Pan?' says Frances.

'That's how you pronounce it. I'm a bit of a linguist.'

'Not a cunning linguist?' asks Frances, buoyed by the drink.

'Whatever turns your motor, Mrs Kerwin.'

It is a long time since Frances has danced but she needs to now. She feels an exhilaration that has to be released. She stands up and leans across the table to take Andrew Marner's hands. They walk between the tables to the dance floor and launch into a waltz. The feeling is strange. Andrew Marner is taller, harder and stronger than Bruce; she yields to his lead and senses surrender. The pleasant smell of an expensive aftershave fills her nostrils. When the music changes they stay on the floor for two more dances.

'How about a Benedictine?' says Andrew.

'Are we back to monks again?' asks Frances.

'I was thinking more of a brandy liqueur.'

When they get back to their table he orders two.

'I thought aftershave lasted two hours,' says Frances. 'You haven't refuelled in mid-evening, have you?'

'My stuff lasts longer,' says Andrew.

'I'm glad to hear it,' says Frances.

The Croisette is on their right now as the boat heads back to port. Their floodlit hotel stands out among the lights on the front. When the bill appears, Frances expects to see a credit card but Andrew produces a wad of real money and counts out notes on the table.

There are so many boats in the port that reaching their berth is a difficult manoeuvre; diners bunch at the exit, waiting to disembark.

'It's been a most enjoyable evening,' says Andrew, putting his crocodile wallet into his pocket. 'What happens now?'

'It certainly has,' says Frances. 'Thank you for it. What happens now? I suppose the next trick is to get off this boat.'

'I meant after that,' says Andrew.

'Ah,' says Frances. 'Difficult, isn't it?'

'Is it?' asks Andrew.

'Not really,' says Frances. 'Why don't you come and have a drink in my room?'

10

It is no surprise to Esme Rutherford when her sleep is disturbed by thoughts of Bruce Kerwin, confined by the four walls of a dusty cell. Her concern for other people is something that she could do without, but she seems to be lumbered with it.

What she thinks of as her natural compassion seems at times to be, more accurately, a maudlin and unproductive tendency to focus on the sad and unfortunate at the expense of her own peace of mind; she would be a lot more cheerful if she could fill her head with pictures of success, affluence, brimming health and sunshine. But drawn to losers, she has always signed petitions, lobbied politicians, joined committees and voted Labour. The world's wrongs alight on her shoulders, demanding action.

The following morning, without giving it a second thought, she leaves Roger with his coffee and a newspaper on the terrace, and sets off for Cannes Central Police Station.

Her sympathy for the prisoner had started before she

caught sight of his wife slipping away for an evening with Andrew Marner. She had found his vain attempt to hold back the years and relaunch himself as a somewhat younger man rather poignant. Bruce Kerwin was clearly in need of help even before the French judicial system brusquely took him away and locked him up.

As she hurries along the rue d'Antibes she wonders what little gift he would appreciate. It is the busiest street in Cannes and yet so narrow that there is only room for one-way traffic heading west. The cars here seem to have been shrunk so that they can be accommodated in the cramped conditions: little white mokes, drophead Golfs, Fiat Pandas and Renault Clios. At a loss, she stops to buy him a box of chocolates.

She cannot imagine in what conditions the French detain their prisoners. She has read reports that suggest that the Dark Ages still exist in secret corners of the Republic. Whatever the circumstances, they must have come as a considerable shock to a respectable middle-aged Englishman who thought he was on holiday.

She reaches the Avenue de Grasse and spots the forbidding façade of the police station. When she steps inside, she feels a slight draining of her resolve. The building is presumably full of policemen and villains, and she has never been very fond of either. Her urge to help wanes a little and she acknowledges reluctantly that concern for other people can be taken too far. In America, the home of peculiar causes, they even have Pet Loss Support Groups.

A policeman slides open a window and says, *'Bonjour.'*

'Je suis anglaise,' Esme says. *'Je ne parle pas bien le français.'*

The policeman leaves the window and returns with another *flic*. 'Hallo,' he says.

'A friend of mine is detained here,' says Esme. 'I would like to see him.'

'His name?'

'Bruce Kerwin.'

'Ah, Monsieur Kerwin. All the beautiful women come to see Monsieur Kerwin.'

Two floors above, Bruce Kerwin is lying on a small bed in a tiny cell, staring at a grey ceiling which has a single light in it protected by a shield of bars. He has declined the breakfast he was offered – a breadstick and lukewarm coffee – and is regretting that petulance. Any food or liquid would be welcome now. He is lying on a single grey blanket which he reluctantly gets under at night when his dreams are uniformly hostile. Enemies lurk, violence threatens. Strange creatures thwart his wishes and walls that can talk restrict his freedom. The distant memory of a black desk in an insurance office which he had only recently convinced himself was a misguided martyrdom, has now, in his present situation, assumed the status of a pleasure centre for the uniquely fortunate.

He gets off the bed and looks down at his dirty clothes. He feels grimy all over. He pulls something from his nose which is so solid that when he drops it he hears it hit the floor. His fingernails are black. He is thinking that he would be doing exercises if he had eaten enough food to provide the energy, when footsteps approach. A policeman opens the door and beckons him out.

'*Visiteuse*,' he says.

The man walks behind him as they march along the corridor and down stone stairs. His wife, he imagines, has finally managed to find the time to buy him soap.

But when he is shown into the familiar room it is Esme Rutherford who is sitting on the other side of the table.

'Bruce,' she says. 'I thought I'd come and see how you are.' She is shocked by the appearance of this man. His face is white and unshaven, his hair is unkempt. His new jeans are creased and marked and he must have been sleeping in his T-shirt.

Bruce Kerwin sits down self-consciously. He is not dressed to greet anybody, let alone this girl.

'Kind of you,' he says. 'You heard what happened?'

'Kimberley Neal told me they found cannabis in your pocket,' says Esme. 'I can hardly believe it.'

'I met a man,' says Bruce.

'What sort of man?'

'A cool one.'

'Cool like a toad,' says Esme. 'What can I do to help? This is ridiculous!'

'If you're a miracle-worker you can get me out of here,' says Bruce, sounding as depressed as he looks. 'Short of that, there's not much you can do.'

'I brought you some chocolates,' Esme remembers, and pushes the box across the table. 'The gentleman in the uniform has had a look at them and says it's okay for me to give them to you.'

To her surprise Bruce Kerwin opens the box and eats three.

'Don't they feed you?' she asks.

'I've had nothing today,' says Bruce. 'I can't wash or shave and now I seem to have given up eating.' He munches the chocolates greedily. 'Have you seen Frances? How is she bearing up?'

'Quite well, I think,' says Esme. 'She seems to be handling it.'

'I worry about her,' says Bruce. 'You know what women are.'

'I've heard about them,' says Esme. 'Listen, what are your conditions like? I'm quite good at writing letters.'

'Letters?' says Bruce. 'To whom?'

'Oh, I don't know. Your MP? *The Times*?'

'I don't think their writ runs this far,' says Bruce. 'You've done enough for me just by coming up here. The chocolates were a bonus.'

'Have you had it before?' asks Esme.

'Chocolate?' asks Bruce, who is tired and confused.

'Cannabis,' says Esme.

'Good God, no. I'd never even seen it before.'

'And have you told the police that?'

'Several times,' says Bruce. 'Of course they don't believe me.' The chocolates, eaten hastily, have made him feel slightly sick. 'They think I'm at the centre of some drugs ring. I should have stayed in my insurance office.'

'You're beginning to think that middle age is safer after all? That's sad.'

'Well, isn't it? I hadn't spoken to a policeman for ten years until I came here.'

'I thought the way that you were fighting the years was rather wonderful,' says Esme. 'Most people of your age become reactionary bores who hate everyone under twenty-five. You were knocking down the fences.'

'Well, now they've put them up again,' says Bruce, 'and I can't get out.'

Esme smiles at him across the table. She has seldom seen anyone quite so pitiable. 'How can I help?' she asks.

'What I really want,' says Bruce, 'is soap.'

*   *   *

155

When Frances Kerwin gets out of bed that morning, she feels as if she has spent an uninhibited night with the Foreign Legion. As she walks cautiously to the bathroom, her body seems to vibrate. The physical demands of a shower ask too much and she sinks gratefully into a bath that she fills almost to the brim. It is half an hour before she can bring herself to look for soap.

Twenty years of marriage to Bruce Kerwin have not prepared her for the sexual banquet which she has enjoyed and she lies in the water with a mystical smile on her face, wondering whether it will be repeated.

Andrew Marner had arrived in her room with a bottle of Krug, a box of ice cream and a packet of ribbed condoms 'for heightened pleasure'. He is a man with protean talents, judicious discernment and the sexual proclivities of a Barbary ape on speed. The champagne is barely breached before Frances is spreadeagled naked across the bed with lumps of ice cream placed on various parts of her body, and it is an hour before Andrew feels the need to unpack his ribbed condoms. By the time he rolls one on to a granite-like erection, ice cream still on his mouth, Frances is beginning to wonder whether this is a wise way for a middle-aged, middle-class, middle-brow lady from the provinces to be passing the time on a Saturday night. It is a doubt that is instantly dispelled. There is something about Frances Kerwin that inspires Andrew Marner in a way that Kimberley Neal does not. Gasping beneath him, Frances doesn't know whether it is the ribbed condom or Andrew Marner or, possibly, the ice cream or champagne, but she has the definite feeling at one stage that she has become separated from her mind.

When the storm subsides and a lull descends on the

room, Andrew leans across the bed and refills their glasses with champagne. Frances lies there, hardly able to believe that she is participating in all this. When she first removed her clothes at his quiet request she had felt embarrassed to be with a strange man. She was never promiscuous before her marriage and has been faithful since. But the boat trip or the champagne or perhaps her displeasure at her husband has transformed her into another woman.

'What is Kimberley?' she asks.

'Available,' says Andrew. 'She should have a bar code on her forehead.'

'I meant to you.'

'I told you,' says Andrew. 'An employee. Why do you ask?'

'I don't want her knocking on my door with her nails out.'

'You won't have,' says Andrew, stroking her.

The champagne that he has poured, it emerges, is the equivalent of a rugby player's half-time lemon. Refreshed and quite obviously replenished, he replaces one condom with another. He has a hard, fit body that he clearly spends time on.

Now, lying in the warm water, Frances admires the way that she was able to walk from her bed to her bath without the use of a Zimmer frame. But the water has curative powers and when she climbs out of the bath she feels younger, not older. She studies herself in the full-length mirror and decides that she looks nearer twenty-eight than thirty-eight. And by the time that she has dried and dressed herself, some more decisions have followed that one.

An hour later she is sitting in a beauty salon on the rue d'Antibes having a facial. She has already had her hair cut much shorter, an event which she thinks has taken five years off her age, and now she is at work on her face. She is told that she has a nice skin and should wear less make-up, but the shape of her eyebrows could be improved. For the first time in her life she has a manicure.

The woman who comes out of the beauty salon later that morning bears little resemblance to the Frances Kerwin who arrived in Nice a week ago, and the way that men look at her tells her that the changes have been a success.

She steps into a boutique and is soon examining a row of dresses. No more loose clothes, she tells herself. Something chic, something figure-hugging, but not too short or tarty. She takes a long time in the boutique but it is worth it. There are three new dresses in the large fancy bags that she carries when she comes out and crosses the street in search of a shoe shop.

She is aware as she slips on a pair of Charles Jourdans that she is imitating the youthful dreams that she had criticised in her husband, but she feels that in her case there is sober justification. If she is about to spend two years alone she had better look the best she can.

Thinking about her husband, she remembers that she is supposed to be consulting a lawyer, but it is Saturday and the lawyers are not at work.

Week 2

Half our life is spent trying to find something to do with the time we have rushed through life trying to save.

Will Rogers

11

One of the little jobs that Andrew Marner has given himself on this holiday is to write his chairman's message for the annual report. The accountants have been quietly probing the finances of The Marner Press for some weeks and the figures that they have now produced look good in a recession and would not look bad in more congenial times. Andrew sits at the window, a large pad on his lap, and watches brown female bodies on the beach.

'Nobody ever gets anywhere standing still and the aim of The Marner Press in the months and years to come is expansion,' he writes. 'This is not commercial vanity but common sense. It is not so much that we want to become larger but that the world is getting smaller. Foreign money pours into Britain, especially from Europe, and alongside this competition we must grow to survive. Plans to launch a new national newspaper in Britain are proceeding smoothly. The Marner Press is in negotiation with a leading French publisher to see whether a joint venture is a practicable possibility. At the same time we intend to increase our list of titles. All our *publications except one are making money and there are gaps in the market which we are supremely equipped to fill. Our only loss-making title,* World Review *is, of course, in its infancy and not expected to show a profit before the end of next year. But it is establishing itself successfully in a difficult corner of the market and I am proud of the way in which it is developing. Our other publications are warmly received by the audiences that they are intended for, and advertising, the first casualty in a recession, has held up remarkably well. Our staff are to be congratulated on their efforts at a difficult time. My thanks to them all.'*

He puts down his pen and gazes at the beach. At the table a few feet away, Kimberley Neal is also writing although her prose resounds to a different beat.

'Belinda lay panting on the bed,' she writes, *'transfixed like a rabbit before a snake as she contemplated the glistening black giant's throbbing extremity. This was not what she had expected when she was sent to the Reform Club to interview the Mozambique ambassador.'*

Reading her words, Kimberley begins to chuckle; but she is annoyed that she is laughing. The sexy bits that are supposed to be at the heart of her novel should attract and arouse the readers, not reduce them to helpless giggles. She had always imagined that writing this porno stuff was easy. The only problem, she had always said, was actually finding the time to produce 300 pages. But now that she has launched herself on the genre, she finds it elusive and difficult to treat.

Belinda, with her dead parents (victims of a 'flu epidemic), her sadistic aunt, and her brutal and unhappy childhood, has not adapted to the sensual life that Kimberley has planned for her. The seismic shift from squalid schooldays to media success has left her aloof and reserved, impervious to love and affection. The liberating effect of sex, the theme of the novel, is failing to work for the ambitious orphan, and the story is more bathos than pathos. Hilarity, not heavy breathing, greets the removal of her pants.

Kimberley throws her pen on the table and swears.

'How's the filth coming along?' asks Andrew, curious about her anger.

'It's not as easy as you might think,' says Kimberley. 'Comedy keeps getting in the way of the copulation.'

'Well, sex was always funny,' says Andrew.

'Not in a pornographic novel it's not,' says Kimberley, shutting her notebook. 'It's supposed to be a serious business. What I'm writing won't arouse anybody.'

'You ought to be good at it,' says Andrew. 'You write well and you've got the mind of a cockroach.'

'But when I write it, it seems to get away from me,' Kimberley complains. 'It goes off and becomes something else. It doesn't correspond to life.'

'In what way doesn't it correspond to life?' asks Andrew.

'In real life I've always found a naked man an attractive proposition, but on the page he's a comic figure.'

'Well, make it comedy then,' says Andrew sensibly. 'What are you calling it?'

Kimberley has compiled a long list of titles, exotic, salacious, cryptic and marketable. But the one that she favours now, having studied advertisements for books and discovered a fashion for one-word titles, is *Belinda*. Belinda is Kimberley Neal with a few minor alterations to her history and antecedents. Writing about herself had seemed an easy introduction to the agreeable waters of fiction: she could hardly make her hero a nuclear scientist from Peru. But Belinda is failing to comply with her wishes.

'I'm calling it *Belinda*,' she tells Andrew. 'I can see her on the cover, all legs and cleavage, but I don't seem able to see her on the page.'

'*Belinda* is a good title,' says Andrew. 'Short, simple, sexy.'

'Unfortunately the book is none of those,' sighs Kimberley. 'Why don't we go down to the beach? It's Sunday.'

'You've finished with the filth for the day?'

'And you've finished with work. I take it you brought some bathing trunks along with the Armani suits?'

'I did,' says Andrew, 'for swimming, not lying in the sun.'

'Get them on, Mr Marner,' says Kimberley. 'It's time to relax.'

On the beach five bodies lie on a neat row of blue and white sunbeds close to the water's edge.

At one end, in a new white bikini, is Frances Kerwin. The one-piece costume has been discarded, along with several other items in her wardrobe, and she is lying in the sun now with her new short hairstyle and her very brief swimwear, feeling slightly self-conscious about the sudden and drastic changes she has made.

Next to her, in a pair of green boxer shorts, is Andrew Marner, whose sunbed is raised rather more than the others so that he can sit and watch the yachts. He has never been able to relax like other people and tells himself that it is because he has never had the time to get used to it.

In the middle of the five, with a man on either side of her, Kimberley Neal is reading the latest research into U-spot orgasms and coital alignment technique. It is information that a lot of people will miss, but if you are writing a novel like *Belinda* it could be useful.

Roger Blake is lying on one side, enraptured by the curve of her thighs. He is trying not to concentrate on them too much because he is wearing tight white swimming trunks today and his appreciation of Kimberley's body could be revealed to the world without him saying a word.

Next to him, at the end of the row, Esme is writing postcards home. It is not something that her busy week has allowed her to do until now, but it is Sunday, many places are closed, and she has always known that sooner or later she would have to join Roger for a spell on the beach even though she regards it as an uncomfortable waste of time.

These people have arrived on the beach separately but are now together. They listen to the cries of the children, the distant murmur of the boats, and the restless sea sloshing around the Carlton's jetty. The temperature is 29 or, as Andrew Marner still calls it, 84.

'The Côte d'Azur,' he says, 'where the sky is blue and the women are brown. Actually I prefer the Costa Smeralda myself, with all that white sand.'

'Is that Sardinia?' asks Frances. 'I've never been there.'

'Nor have I,' says Andrew. 'I saw it on my television receiving equipment.'

Kimberley asks: 'What is the news of Bruce?'

'Old Time Warp?' says Frances. 'They've charged him with possession. Things don't look good.'

'Nor does he,' says Esme, putting down her cards. 'I went round to see him yesterday and he looked awful.'

'You went round to see him?' says Frances. 'He didn't tell me that.'

'Esme is a naturally kind girl,' says Roger. 'Lame dogs. Stray cats. Injured birds. They all know where to go.'

'I'm sorry for him,' says Esme. 'The laws on cannabis are absurd. It's not addictive and it's less harmful than tobacco. It doesn't produce violent or anti-social behaviour, and if it was legalised the price would come down and youngsters wouldn't have to thieve to buy it. It would also save police thousands of hours and bring in tax revenue for the government from legal sales. The world's mad.'

'Can you say all that again?' asks Kimberley, producing a notebook from her bag. 'I've got the makings of a column here.'

'What did Bruce say?' asks Frances.

'He wanted soap so I went out and bought him some.'

'My God,' says Frances, 'I keep forgetting that bloody soap.'

'What will happen to him?' asks Roger.

'God knows. Two years, they say. To tell you the truth I'm so angry with him that I find it hard to feel sympathetic. If he gets out he'll be buying flares and platform soles and floppy scalloped collars. This might be the jolt he needs to stop him vanishing into the past.'

'I can't see that vanishing into a French jail is going to do him any good,' says Esme.

'You're right,' says Frances. 'But what can I do?'

'Stand by your man,' says Kimberley, 'in the words of the song.'

'I've heard a lot of songs in which boys sing about their girls and girls sing about their boys, but I've never heard one in which a wife sings about her husband,' says Andrew.

'What about "Little Things Mean A Lot"?' asks Frances. 'I've spent the last week trying to remember who sang it. Does anyone know?'

'Anita Harris?' says Andrew.

'No, not her,' says Frances. 'It's driving me mad.'

'A quiz!' says Andrew. 'That's a good idea. We can't just lie here doing nothing. It offends my puritan ethic.'

'Since when have you had a puritan ethic?' asks Kimberley, lighting a cigarette. The message on the packet says *nuit gravement à la santé*.

'Where work's concerned,' says Andrew. 'Now, here's a question. The person who gets it right asks the next question. What's the only sport you can't play left-handed?'

A long silence greets this question.

'Was it Petula Clark?' asks Roger. 'I can only handle one question at a time. I get synaptic overload.'

'I think it was an American singer,' says Frances. 'If anyone remembers, please let me know.'

'I have a question,' says Esme. 'It's one of those questions that nobody can ever answer.'

'Wanna bet?' says Andrew.

'Who was the only person to be leader of the Labour Party three times?'

'Some masochist,' says Andrew, annoyed that he doesn't know. 'Was it MacDonald?'

'Henderson,' says Esme. 'I was in the Labour Party when I was a student.'

'So was I,' says Andrew. 'I was all in favour of the redistribution of income until I realised that it was my income they wanted to redistribute.'

'Andrew thought Maggie was left-wing,' says Kimberley. 'His shift to the right has been a sight to behold.'

'Once I moved in that direction the money rolled in,' says Andrew, 'so let me buy you all drinks.'

A waiter is delivering fruit juices to a couple on nearby sunbeds and Andrew manages to attract his attention. When their drinks arrive they pull themselves up to sitting positions and blink at the searing sun. Only Kimberley is topless and gently applies sun cream to her breasts, a development that Roger tries not to watch. Instead he looks out to sea where people are water-skiing, weaving a careful path between the moored yachts. Andrew is trying not to look at Frances' new hairstyle which he finds very attractive. She looks younger than she did on the boat and has evidently been taking some trouble over her appearance. He is flattered by this and wants to tell her how good she looks, but with Kimberley lying on the other side of him he has to exercise a degree of tact that conflicts with his outspoken nature. What he would like to do is arrange to see Frances tonight but it is Sunday and he will not be able to convince Kimberley that he has a business meeting in Nice.

Frances finishes her drink and lies back with her eyes closed. She is thinking about what Esme said before Andrew tried to involve them in a quiz. Prison will not do Bruce any good. Both women had managed to imply that her attitude to her husband's situation was disgracefully casual. On the other hand, she tells herself, they are not married to Bruce. She tries to sleep.

Esme gets up, bored by inactivity. She steps down to the water to cool off and wades in until it reaches her thighs. Only a few people are swimming and she doesn't plan to join them. She has read about the Mediterranean and the noxious items that can be found bobbing among its waves.

Andrew watches her from his sunbed. She has a neat figure and a pretty face, a combination that he has never even tried to resist. She seems to be self-contained and probably brighter than the others, but he allows himself to wonder what might come of her visits to his room when she starts to paint his portrait.

He looks round at the others. To his annoyance, they appear to be asleep.

'Polo,' he says. 'They can't play it left-handed because the horses would collide.' But his answer goes unheard.

12

Bruce Kerwin rolls off his bed and counts the bites on his thighs. Yesterday there were forty-two; today there are forty-eight. After four nights the assault is diminishing. Perhaps there is less flesh left for the little carnivores to enjoy. His dream comes back to him as he stands up. Often they have gone before he can arrange them in his mind, but last night's is still here, appalling in its vividness.

It is the evening of his father's suicide. The body, with the head at an odd angle, hangs from the banisters upstairs. His mother doesn't cry. She says: 'We are a peculiarly blighted family.' A policeman arrives and regales them with a story about a man who has blown his head off and had to be identified by his socks. Bruce is twenty and old enough to help cut down the body. His father's eyes are open and protrude frog-like in a way they never did in life. 'At least we won't have to identify him by his socks,' says the policeman with a dry laugh.

Bruce takes his jeans off the floor of the cell and

puts them on. He smells, he decides, like a bowl of minestrone soup.

The dream was strange because he was at the cinema when his father died and he never saw the body. But his mother's remark haunts him. *We are a peculiarly blighted family.*

Bruce Kerwin feels blighted this morning as he waits for a policeman to bring him what passes for food in this place. The meal that he left last night did not seem to be dissimilar to hedgehog excrement and he is hungry now.

What occupies his mind today, when he has woken sufficiently to edge the memory of his dream to one side, is the dramatic change in the appearance of his wife. The new, rather sexy clothes have demoralised him in a way that he can hardly explain; the short hair, after a lifetime of allowing it to reach her shoulders, is a shock that has left him bitter and confused. What message is she trying to give him? She is certainly not showing the concern that he would have expected. He does not see misery and despair on her face. Occasionally on her visits she has come to resemble with her infuriating smile a lottery winner who has suddenly been awarded a different, brighter future. Bruce Kerwin looks to himself for an explanation of this. Perhaps his wife is one of the four million people in Britain who, a recent survey has shown, would not choose the same partner if they were given a second chance.

He sits on his little bed, overwhelmed by helplessness. Problems mount but he can do nothing about them, and without his intervention they fester and grow. Footsteps approach and his door is opened. He watches listlessly as a tray is placed on the chair, the only furniture in the cell apart from his bed. A cup of coffee and a piece of French bread are on the tray. Neither looks inviting. His mind moves from Frances to Esme, who had taken the trouble to fetch him soap. Perhaps, today, she will visit him again.

He looks up. The policeman is a new one.

'I've news for you,' he says. His English is better than any of the others'. 'You're moving to a proper prison.'

'Where am I going?' Bruce asks. The news dismays him. If he is moved too far away, he won't receive any visits at all.

'Marseille,' says the policeman. 'The cells here are only for short stays. No washrooms, no baths.' So far Bruce has been shown with his new soap to a small room where he has been able to wash his hands and face at a sink.

'When do I go?' he asks.

'One day this week,' the policeman says, and smiles. 'I tell you, my friend, Marseille is the worst dungeon in the world. Violence, rats and Aids.'

In the side streets away from the glitzy shops with their famous names, Esme Rutherford finds many places that cater for somebody who wants to paint a portrait. Separated from her own materials, she has made a list of what she requires and is surprised now by the quantity and fearful of its cost.

Her first call is to buy a board for the painting. Economy tempts her to opt for one of the cheaper embossed boards, but she resists and buys canvas; if she skimps now she won't be able to charge the price that she wants later. Next she goes to the oil paints for a set of earth colours – browns, yellow ochre, burnt sienna, raw umber – and she also buys flake white, alizarin crimson, violet, a lemon yellow and viridian green. Turpentine and linseed oil are added to this and then she turns to the brushes. She selects several of the largest, round hog-hair brushes in the shop, together with a few smaller, flat hog-hair ones. She also chooses a pointed sable brush for fine lines, and then she looks again at her list. She needs rags to wipe the brushes, a white plate for mixing paints, papers to cover the floor in case she ruins the carpet, but all these things, she hopes, can be found free in the hotel.

All she lacks now is an easel, which she is reluctant to buy as it will only be used once. The man in the shop, sombre, bearded, seriously artistic, surprises her by mentioning it.

'After all this buying we will lend you one,' he says. 'I take your address.'

Laden with goods she walks back slowly to the hotel, where she looks for a helpful chambermaid. By two o'clock all her purchases are standing neatly outside Andrew Marner's door, along with an old plate, a torn and discarded sheet and some old newspapers.

Andrew opens the door. He is wearing an expensive suit. 'I thought I'd keep this on for the painting,' he says. 'Let me help you with that stuff.'

'I bet you thought I wouldn't come,' says Esme.

'For money? I knew you'd come.'

They lay the newspapers on the floor and set up the easel.

'It's a question of light,' says Esme, 'on you and on my canvas.'

'Sit me where you like,' says Andrew. 'I've always wanted to have my portrait painted. You'll find me a most co-operative sitter. How long is it all going to take?'

174

'All being well, six hours,' says Esme. 'Could you fit in three sittings?'

'A pleasure,' says Andrew. 'How else am I going to get a pretty girl into my room?'

'Well,' says Esme, 'you don't seem to be doing too badly on that front.'

Andrew laughs. 'You caught me with Mrs Kerwin, didn't you? Frances is an exceptionally beautiful woman. I wish she was my wife.'

'Gosh,' says Esme. 'Things are getting serious. What about Bruce?'

'The man with a penchant for herbal cigarettes? He seems unfortunately to be absent at the moment.'

'Something about clouds and silver linings springs to mind here,' says Esme. 'Are you comfortable?'

She has seated him in an upright chair by a window so that the light is on his face, and is beginning to lay in the picture in thin blue lines. He sits motionless with a rather solemn expression on his face, an expression to quell a boardroom revolt.

'How long have you been doing this?' he asks.

'Painting? Since I was three. I used to do my own Christmas cards. They were full of angels. At the age of three I was already a skilled interpreter of modern theological imagery.'

'From angels to Andrew Marner,' says Andrew. 'It's a quantum leap.'

While her outline dries, Esme makes some sketches of Andrew's face, its structure and character. They will enable her to work on the painting when he is not available to sit. It is a good-looking face but there is a hardness below the surface – the secret, no doubt, of his success – that she hopes to bring out.

'You ought to publish an art magazine,' she suggests.

175

'There's a gap in the market.' Like an old-fashioned barber, she feels obliged to chat to her customers although she would prefer to work in silence.

'There may be a gap in the market,' Andrew says, 'but is there a market in the gap? My impression is that the products of our art colleges are not over-endowed with coin of the realm, and an art magazine would be an expensive production.'

Esme acknowledges the truth of this with a resigned silence.

'Tell me I'm wrong,' says Andrew.

'You're right,' says Esme. 'We're all skint. Talent never equalled money. Ask Van Gogh.'

'It's enough to make an honest tycoon feel ashamed,' says Andrew.

'I shall try to convey that in my painting,' says Esme.

Kimberley Neal phones Roger from the telephone in the lobby downstairs. 'Esme is painting Andrew's portrait. I think we've been thrown together in the cause of art. Fancy a little sunbathing?'

'How very sociable,' says Roger, who is about to leave for the beach.

'Something strange is happening,' says Kimberley when they are lying side by side on their sunbeds. 'Andrew doesn't want sex.'

'I've heard of people like that,' says Roger. 'They're called – '

'Hermaphrodites,' says Kimberley. 'Andrew, however, is not one. In fact, he was a raging stud until last Thursday.'

'Perhaps he's resting,' says Roger. 'It can be a very tiring business, I've heard.'

'His recuperative powers have always been extraordinary,' says Kimberley. 'In fact, sometimes he has started again before you realise that he has finished.'

'Oh, really?' says Roger, who doesn't care to hear about the sexual prowess of other men. 'Perhaps he could screw for Britain in the Olympics. Lane one, Marner, *Grande-Bretagne.*'

'It might be a joke to you, Roger, but where does it leave me?'

'Alone, I should think,' says Roger. 'Don't you welcome a bit of peace?'

'Not that sort of peace,' says Kimberley. 'I could have got married for that. No, something's wrong.'

'Wrong?' says Roger. 'It's only Monday.'

'He's missed three nights. Either he's ill, which he obviously isn't, or he's got somebody else.'

'You're reading a lot into three days' abstinence,' says Roger. 'I went a whole week once.'

'Well, normally he's like a rat up a drainpipe. He was in Tokyo last month lusting after some pubically-bald Jap. His sexual energy is mind-blowing. It took two women to service him in Miami, and when he was in Nairobi – '

'You're telling me more than I want to know,' says Roger. 'Do you think Esme's safe with him?'

'He's not a rapist,' says Kimberley. 'The ease with which he obtains consent makes rape unnecessary.'

'What is he?' asks Roger. 'Irresistible?'

'He has a certain *je ne sais quoi,*' Kimberley admits.

'What's that French for? Big penis? I doubt that Esme will succumb to his charms. She's a very discriminating lady.'

'How is your sex life, by the way? Given my current availability.'

'I see what you're driving at,' says Roger.

'I'm sure we could find a Standard Vanguard some-where, if that's the fillip you need,' says Kimberley. 'It must be a classic car by now so it'll be all the rage on the Riviera.'

Roger sits up on his sunbed and looks round for the waiter. 'Do you want a drink?' he asks.

'Lovely,' says Kimberley. 'I'll have a Tom Collins.'

When the waiter comes down the beach, Roger orders a Tom Collins and a shandy. He had felt himself drawn to Kimberley Neal but now that she has put it on a plate the prospect loses its appeal. He is also conscious at the back of his mind that Esme is working hard at this very moment to earn the money that will keep them in the hotel. His idleness is an offence, but sex would be a betrayal.

When the drinks arrive, Kimberley reaches across to take hers and narrowly misses him with her left breast, which is almost as brown as her face. A man on the next sunbed can't quite stop himself from watching her.

'It's fine, in answer to your question,' says Roger. 'I don't seem to have the voracious appetite of Andrew Marner.'

'No go, then?' asks Kimberley. 'You're rejecting my generous offer?' She sips her Tom Collins and looks at him over the rim of the glass.

'It makes me feel quite saintly,' says Roger. 'I would love to, but there are other considerations.'

'I don't see any,' says Kimberley.

'But you're not sitting where I'm sitting. The view from here is different.'

'Well, I'm not going to beg,' says Kimberley, putting down her drink. She lies back on her sunbed and closes her eyes. 'I just thought I was being friendly.'

'You were,' says Roger, feeling awkward. He seems to have managed to hurt her feelings and make himself appear a prig in one go.

'After all,' says Kimberley, 'I did have your baby.'

'You did what?' asks Roger, certain that he has misheard.

'Have your baby,' says Kimberley. 'He was a boy, by the way.'

'You're kidding,' says Roger.

'Insofar as I had a kid,' says Kimberley.

'Why didn't you tell me?'

'I didn't know where to find you. If you remember, our meeting was a one-off.'

Roger looks at her to see whether this is a joke. The impression he receives is that it's not. 'You had a baby? A boy? Where is he?'

'I've no idea,' says Kimberley, not opening her eyes. 'They're the rules of adoption.'

'I don't believe you,' says Roger, but he does.

'That's not very chivalrous, Roger,' says Kimberley.

'Chivalry shrivels me,' says Roger. 'I've got a son?'

'No,' says Kimberley. 'Somebody else has him.'

Roger picks up his shandy and empties it in two gulps. The world is not quite the same place that it was a few moments ago. The distinction of fatherhood has alighted on his shoulders but the new status has a hollow feeling to it. He looks at Kimberley again, but she has abandoned the subject and is trying to sleep. He lies back himself and tries to absorb the information that has arrived from the past a decade late. After a long time he asks: 'What's his name?' But Kimberley is asleep.

He lies on his sunbed watching a plane trailing an advert in the sky. It is in French and he can't decide what it is that they are plugging. With time to think he decides that Kimberley is lying but he can't see what her motive is. Perhaps deep in her female psyche the story of a baby has materialised as a stratagem for luring him into her bed. But why this should prove an attraction defeats him. It is news that could cause a man to flee. Confused but curiously elated he waits for her to wake up.

After a while she stirs and when he looks at her she opens her eyes. Her hands slide gently up her body and cup her breasts.

'What was his name?' Roger asks.

'What?' says Kimberley, waking up.

'Our son. What was he called?'

Kimberley pulls herself up to a sitting position and checks in the mirror for burns.

'I called him William but I gathered that his adoptive parents were going to give him a new name.'

The nature and delivery of this reply convince Roger more than anything else that she is telling the truth. William, he thinks. Bill. He wonders what name the boy has now, where he lives and what he is like. Is he good at sport?

But Kimberley is getting up and assembling her clothes. 'You have to be careful,' she says. 'Half an hour too much sun and your skin falls off. Coming for a swim to cool down?'

'I'll stay here for a minute,' says Roger. 'I think better lying down.'

Kimberley slips a long T-shirt over her head, puts on her shoes and her sunglasses, and then picks up her bag, leaving him there with his dreams of what might have been.

Frances Kerwin comes out of Cannes Central Police

Station and hails a passing taxi. She tells the driver: 'Nice.' It is an expensive way to travel but she is following instructions. When she arrives in the Place Massena, Andrew Marner will meet her and pay the man.

Duplicity is simple on this coast. A short journey removes you from knowing eyes. And so, as Andrew was already in Nice pursuing his Byzantine discussions with Alain Rocard, he has suggested that she join him there for dinner in one of the city's many fine restaurants. The logistics of their return, when they must arrive separately but end up together, have yet to be arranged.

As the taxi skirts the Baie des Anges and passes Nice Airport, Frances tries to shake off the fog of depression in which another visit to the police station has enveloped her. At the beginning of his incarceration Bruce had been merely angry. After two days he was depressed. Now, with the news of his impending move to Marseille, he seems to be in a state of mental collapse, not able to think coherently or talk rationally. His expectations are ludicrous, his demands absurd. Tonight he has suggested that he should be allowed to give an interview on British television. When Frances escapes from his claustrophobic world she is shaking.

That afternoon she had finally summoned up the courage to visit a lawyer but he had warned her correctly that Bruce Kerwin would not be detained long in Cannes. 'They will move him to Marseille or Avignon,' he said. 'You need a lawyer from there.'

Now, as she sits in the taxi, she can see herself traipsing round France for the next few weeks, attempting to organise her husband's defence and catering to his needs.

The Place Massena stands at the bottom of Nice, a huge square of red buildings with a large fountain in the middle that has four bronze horses rising from its basin. Andrew is standing, as he had promised, by the fountain. He gives her a platonic kiss on the cheek, the businessman in public view, but when they have left the square and are walking between tubs of flowers in narrow lanes he takes her hand.

'Frances,' he says, 'this makes me feel young again.'

'Christ,' says Frances, 'don't you start.'

'How is he?' asks Andrew.

'Terrible,' says Frances. 'They're moving him to the jail in Marseille.'

Andrew shakes his head and presses his lips together, exuding dismay. The news delights him. He guides her into an exotic restaurant beside the flower market and they get a table against the wall.

'It's impossible for me to imagine the two of you making love,' says Andrew. 'And there are no children to encourage the picture.'

'It didn't happen,' says Frances. 'How about you?'

'Having a child has always seemed to me a peculiarly selfish act,' says Andrew, 'but nature's retribution is swift. Selfishness is the last indulgence that new parents can enjoy for years afterwards.'

'But don't you regret it now?' asks Frances. 'You could have a boy of twenty who could inherit the business.'

'Have you met any people of twenty?' asks Andrew. 'They stumble round with their six-word vocabularies. First it was "really", as in "really nice". Now it's "basically". They test the words to destruction, having no others.'

'Sometimes you sound a mite reactionary,' says Frances.

'I met one the other day who had actually got a degree. Do you know what in? Three-dimensional packaging!' He laughs and shakes his head at the folly of it.

The restaurant, they realise, is Italian and they both order seafood cocktails and lasagne. When the wine appears, Andrew fills their glasses then produces a small, gift-wrapped package from his pocket.

'I wanted to buy you something,' he says, placing it on the table in front of her.

'Andrew!' says Frances, genuinely surprised. It is a long time since a man bought her a present; Bruce is so careful with money that he even re-uses the dental floss. She opens the packet and discovers a small, gold Patek Philippe watch.

'It's beautiful,' she says, wondering how she can wear it without alarming her husband. It could stand out in the tenebrous innards of Marseille prison.

'Put it on,' says Andrew, and she does. It feels like a thousand pounds' worth on her wrist and she looks at it with pride.

'I want you to have it,' says Andrew, 'and I would also like to talk about our future.'

'Our future?' she repeats. 'I haven't got that far, Andrew. I seem to have a rather crowded present at the moment.'

'But what are you going to do in England without a husband? What are you going to do about money?'

'I shall probably enjoy my independence,' says Frances doubtfully. 'As far as money is concerned, I shall get a job.'

Andrew leans across the table. 'I want to help, Frances. And I want to see you.'

'I see,' says Frances. The implication is clear. She

asks: 'How many mistresses have you got, dotted round London?'

Andrew laughs and holds up both hands in a gesture of innocence. 'Mistresses? I don't have time for mistresses. But I'd make time to see you.'

'It would be nice to see you,' says Frances, 'but let's leave money out of it.'

Andrew shrugs. 'Whatever you say. But if you need anything or have any problems, promise me you will ask.'

'It's kind of you,' says Frances, picking up her wine. 'But I'm not the sort to collapse in a tearful heap.'

'That's one of the reasons I admire you,' says Andrew soothingly. 'Are you going to have any pudding?'

'Are you?'

'I thought I might eat a little ice cream back in your room.'

13

Not much comes free in the Carlton Hotel, but every morning at breakfast the day's newspapers are laid out on a table for the guests. And every morning Andrew Marner picks up a copy of the *International Herald Tribune* and reads it over his cornflakes. He is a man accustomed to rising early and moving quickly, and is invariably halfway through his meal before he is joined by Kimberley Neal, whose early-morning preparations are a slow and methodical event that cannot be rushed.

He glances at the main headline this morning and feels a tremor of alarm. WAR COSTS AND HIGH LIVING ERODE THE SAUDI DREAM, it says. He ignores the cornflakes for a moment and reads four paragraphs.

WASHINGTON – Saudi Arabia, long seen as one of the world's wealthiest countries, has undermined its financial stability with a decade of unrestrained spending, huge military purchases and irregular banking practices.

The $121 billion in financial reserves amassed by Saudi

Arabia less than a decade ago have almost vanished, drained by expenditures for weapons, social programmes, foreign aid and the Gulf War.

The spending has far outstripped the tens of billions of dollars earned annually from the largest oil fields in the world, which the State owns.

Saudi Arabia began to feel the pinch in the mid-1980s when oil prices sharply fell. Since 1983 the Saudis have racked up 10 consecutive years of budget deficits.

Andrew Marner does not like to read stories like this; they undermine his confidence in himself. If Saudi Arabia, with its limitless billions, is feeling the pinch, what hope is there for people like him? He reads on.

As the Saudis have forged ahead with ambitious plans to build a well-armed modern state, they have spent their national savings, and are now beginning to buy on credit.

'The Saudis have been drawing down reserves for 10 years,' a US official said. 'They're a mere shadow of their former selves.'

There seems to be something ominous about this story. Andrew Marner's political philosophy demands wealth and largesse for as many people as possible. The more money there is around, the better it is for everybody, including him. The envy of the Left, rejoicing in the financial misfortunes of other people, is a mindless reaction which would create a wasteland in which no one would thrive. He puts the newspaper down and returns to his cornflakes. If wealth is ebbing away at the top, the effects will trickle down and one day hit him.

186

Kimberley Neal comes in looking ravishing but, exhausted by the sexual depredations of a few hours earlier, he is not physically equipped to appreciate her. She is wearing white jeans, a black cashmere polo neck sweater and is carrying a Chanel handbag.

'I thought I'd do some shopping this morning,' she says, sitting down. 'Do you want to come?'

'I wish I could,' says Andrew. 'I'm meeting Rocard.'

'You keep meeting Rocard but nothing seems to happen,' says Kimberley, who has her eye on a dress that she'd thought Andrew might buy.

'It's a poker game,' he says airily. 'The watchword is patience.'

'You're sure he really exists?' asks Kimberley. 'You haven't got some tart banged up in the Negresco?'

'What a disgusting suggestion, Kimberley,' says Andrew, wishing it were true. 'Alain Rocard not only exists, he's one of the most powerful men on this coast. I don't know whether it's the Camorra or the Cosa Nostra, but he is used to getting his own way. You get the impression that if he wanted to knock down the Carlton Hotel and replace it with a supermarket, you wouldn't be able to move round here next week for shopping trolleys. When one of his accountants was arrested and charged with fraud, Rocard had him out and cleared in four hours.'

'Really?' says Kimberley. 'He could get Bruce Kerwin out then.'

'What?' Andrew is momentarily confused. 'Yes, I expect he could.'

'Well, ask him then,' says Kimberley. 'Get the poor sod out.'

After the pleasures of the previous evening, this is not a suggestion that Andrew Marner welcomes. The last person he wants to see trotting into the Carlton's lobby is Bruce Kerwin, but this is not something he can explain to Kimberley.

'I suppose I could,' he says doubtfully.

'You must then,' Kimberley tells him.

Her persistence aggravates him and he sees that he must quash this proposal before it gains momentum. 'The delicate balance of my relationship with Monsieur Rocard would be grievously damaged if I started asking him for favours,' he says. 'I'm not approaching him as a supplicant.'

They are interrupted by the waiter, who asks whether Kimberley wants coffee or tea. When he has gone Andrew tries to change the subject. 'Saudi Arabia's going bust. Is no one safe?'

But the world of high finance is not to Kimberley's taste at any time, least of all over breakfast, and she picks a *brioche* from the basket on the table and starts to eat.

When Andrew stands to leave, a wave of guilt – about yet another absence, or the frolics of last night, or Bruce Kerwin – prompts him to pull his wallet from his pocket and lay some notes on the table.

'Buy yourself something nice,' he says.

'That's very kind of you, Andrew,' says Kimberley. 'I will.'

And an hour later, with an agility born of greed, she is nipping in and out of shops with names like Fabri, Kenzo, Garella and Malibu, trying on clothes and shoes that cost more than she can afford herself. Coming out of a shop called Chacok she bumps into Roger Blake.

'Hallo,' he says, touching her elbow. 'Coffee?'

'Sure,' says Kimberley. 'Why not?'

'Are you on some sort of spending spree?' he asks, looking at the elegant bags that she has already accumulated.

'It's conscience money,' says Kimberley. 'Andrew gave it to me. It's been four nights now.'

'Four nights?' Roger queries, not remembering.

They find a coffee bar and go in.

'You don't think he's impotent, do you?' asks Kimberley. 'Perhaps I've worn him out.'

'Oh, sex,' says Roger, finding a table. 'You obviously need more than one man.'

'I do,' says Kimberley. 'Where's Esme?'

'The Picasso Museum in Antibes. A rich collection, she tells me.'

'And you didn't fancy it?'

'I wanted to see you while she's away.'

'Ah,' says Kimberley. 'Things are looking up.'

'Not necessarily,' says Roger. 'I wanted to talk to you about our son.'

Kimberley places her valuable bags on the floor by her feet and waits while Roger fetches their coffee.

'You were saying?' she says when he sits down.

'Yes,' says Roger. 'Our son. I'd like to see him.'

'But you know that's not possible,' Kimberley tells him.

'I don't mean *meet* him,' says Roger. 'I understand that he has another life now.'

'He has another *father* now,' she says firmly, 'who isn't you.'

'I understand all that,' says Roger, 'but I would like to see him. To have a look at him – you know, from across the street.'

'No chance,' says Kimberley, lifting her coffee. 'I'm

not even allowed to know where he is. Later, when he's older, if he wants to see me the authorities can put us in touch. But not now. Not when he's – what is it? – nine.'

'So he's out there somewhere and we can't see him?'

'That's it,' says Kimberley. 'The penalty of neglectful parenthood.'

'My handicap was that I didn't know I *was* a parent,' says Roger. 'I'm delighted to have a son. I want to buy him things.'

'You probably can when he's twenty,' says Kimberley. 'He'll want a sports car that will cost about thirty thousand by then.'

'I would sooner see him now when he would settle for a train set,' says Roger.

'You were always a cheapskate,' says Kimberley. 'Too mean to buy a condom, as I recall.'

Roger drinks his coffee. He has been unable to get the idea that he has a son out of his mind.

'If you want a son I should have a serious conversation with Esme,' says Kimberley. 'You'll find that one thing leads to another.'

'I'm afraid that Esme's creative urges at the moment lie in a different direction,' says Roger.

'That's good.' Kimberley is brisk. 'You'll save a fortune on train sets. In the meantime, what am I going to do about Andrew, my dry husk with no seed to spill?'

'That wasn't how you described him yesterday,' says Roger. 'You suggested that he would be at it as long as he had a pulse.'

'Well, if he's still at it, who is he at it *with*?'

'I think I know the answer to that,' says Roger,

'but unfortunately, you don't have any information to trade.'

'You do?' says Kimberley, pushing her coffee to one side. 'What do I know that you want to know?'

'My son,' says Roger. 'Give me an area.'

'Scotland, I believe,' says Kimberley. 'I honestly can't be more precise because I don't know. Who is Mr Marner's present paramour?'

'The second floor,' says Roger. 'I can't be more precise.'

'Frances Kerwin?' says Kimberley. 'Of course it is! The new look. The absent husband. I must be going simple. Well, I know how to put a stop to *that*.'

She stands up, collects her bags from the floor, and sweeps out of the coffee bar, leaving Roger to wonder whether his son has a Scottish accent.

By the time she reaches the hotel, Kimberley Neal has calmed down. She has had time to recognise the truth of her own position in relation to Andrew Marner – an ambiguous role in which neither function entitles her to attack either Andrew Marner or Frances Kerwin if they are indeed temporarily sharing a bed. Her strategy will require subtlety and even charm.

She unpacks the wonderful clothes that she has bought and hangs them carefully in her crowded wardrobe, and then gravitates as usual to the mirror, wondering, as she studies her face, why Andrew would stray. Her tan is deep enough, she decides. Today she will give her skin a rest.

Instead she heads for the Health Club, for a little exercise and swimming. It is an ideal place to think and she will emerge fitter, leaner, sexier. Perhaps today she will use the ozone-sauna or try the hammam. A girl has to neutralise the fallout of modern life.

But when she reaches the Club she is astonished to find Frances Kerwin there, clad in a pink leotard and pedalling furiously on an exercise bike. Her exertions do not prevent her from offering a slightly embarrassed smile.

'I didn't know this was your sort of thing,' says Kimberley. 'Welcome to the world of lettuce leaves and carrot juice.'

'No thanks,' says Frances. 'I'm just trying to shed a few unwanted inches.'

'And very good you look,' says Kimberley. 'Bruce will never recognise you.'

'That's what I call motivation,' says Frances, pedalling faster.

Kimberley watches the effort that she is putting into it and marvels at the effect that a man of fifty can have on a sensible, mature woman. It is more effort than she wants to make herself this afternoon and she decides instead to spend a relaxing half hour in the pool. As she swims in leisurely fashion from one side to the other, she thinks about what she will say to Frances Kerwin when she comes out of the little gymnasium beside the pool. To a woman like Kimberley Neal, triumphant veteran of a dozen office power struggles and a savage winner in many other professional intrigues, it barely constitutes a problem at all. At a stroke, she can damage Andrew Marner in Frances Kerwin's eyes and simultaneously return her locked-up husband to the Carlton Hotel. If that doesn't derail the Marner-Kerwin adventure, she'll streak down the Croisette. She smiles to herself and floats and waits.

Frances Kerwin appears eventually in a new blue tracksuit. She has taken a shower and done her hair and looks, Kimberley has to admit, about twenty-six.

'That's an amazing machine,' Frances says. 'It does your arms as well as your legs and even tells you how many calories you're burning off while you're pedalling.'

'Sooner you than me,' says Kimberley, who prefers a more passive role in the health clubs she uses: underwater massage jets, blitz showers, G5 vibro stimulators and deep action agents. 'I'm glad you came in, though.'

Frances leans over the rail at the side of the pool and looks down at Kimberley Neal, who is floating on her back in a black and white one-piece costume. 'You're glad I came?' she says. 'Why's that?'

'It's about Andrew,' says Kimberley, paddling gently with both hands. She watches with interest as a flicker of concern appears and disappears on Frances Kerwin's face.

'Andrew?' says Frances. 'What about him?'

'Good news and bad news,' says Kimberley. 'But I think you ought to know it.'

'Give me the good news first,' says Frances. 'I've had enough bad news this week.'

'The good news is that he could get your husband out tomorrow. He has some powerful and sinister friends in Nice. It would be no problem.'

'Really?' says Frances. 'Get him out?'

'No problem,' repeats Kimberley. 'But the bad news – and I can't for the life of me understand this – is that he doesn't want to.'

Frances pulls herself back from the rail and puts her

hands on her hips. 'Are you pulling my leg?' she asks. 'He could do it, but he won't?'

'Exactly,' Kimberley nods. 'It doesn't seem very kind, does it?'

'It's outrageous,' says Frances, seething. Her attitude to Bruce is based on the conviction that, thanks to his stupidity, he is gone for a long time and there is no possibility of getting him out. But if freedom is attainable, the situation becomes quite different.

'I think I'd better talk to Andrew Marner,' she says.

'I would if I were you,' says Kimberley.

Frances Kerwin returns to her room and waits for Andrew Marner to call, but the phone doesn't ring. After a while she finds it necessary to lie on the bed. Her body has seen more physical activity in the last twenty-four hours than it would normally endure in a month at home, when pushing a trolley past the papaws and tayberries in Sainsbury's is the most strenuous demand that it meets. After a passionate session with Andrew Marner, half an hour on an exercise bike was probably asking too much. She lies on the bed gratefully and reflects that trying to become young again makes you feel old.

She can't remember whether Andrew Marner said he would ring or not. By the time they had finished last night, she was so confused she wasn't sure what year it was, but she is fairly certain that at some stage of the evening he had said that Kimberley Neal's presence meant that they couldn't meet every evening because she would stop believing that he was at work. Perhaps tonight was for Kimberley – although

194

if there was anything left for her, the man must be on pills.

But Frances has to talk to him, and it is not a conversation that can be conducted over the phone. She decides that she will wait in the lobby and intercept him when he returns to the hotel.

She sleeps briefly and dreams about Acapulco where she runs in the skimpiest bikini along golden sand, chased by handsome, laughing Mexicans who would die for her body. But as they reach her, Bruce appears. When she wakes, she climbs painfully into a bath and lies there for a long time.

At six o'clock by her new watch, she gets the lift to the ground floor in a new figure-hugging white dress and finds a seat in the marbled hall near the reception desk. She fancies the staff are talking about her, speculating on the fate of her husband and wondering whether she will be able to meet her hefty bill. But they are too polite to raise such questions, and one of them even smiles at her. She smiles confidently back.

At half past six, Andrew Marner strides in in his Armani suit, his briefcase clasped in his hand. He looks as if the day has not unfolded in the way that he had hoped.

'Frances,' he says, coming over. 'Are you waiting for someone?'

'Yes,' says Frances, standing up. 'You.'

'You know I can't see you tonight,' says Andrew, 'much as I would like to.'

'I understand that,' says Frances. 'Relax. I want a quick word with you. Drink?'

Andrew Marner looks at his watch and nods. They walk down the hall towards the bar and then go through it to the terrace outside. A waiter takes their order as they sit in the sun.

'You look very good tonight,' says Andrew, laying his briefcase on the table. 'What did you want to talk about?'

'A little bird tells me that you have some very influential friends down here.'

'And who would this garrulous feathered vertebrate be?' asks Andrew. 'As if I didn't know.'

'Andrew, if you can get Bruce out you've got to do it,' says Frances.

'Why would you want Bruce out when you've got me?' Andrew smiles at her.

'Well,' says Frances, 'he's my husband.'

'It's not easy, Frances,' says Andrew. 'If I go to this man asking favours, it weakens my position. The favour gets thrown into the financial equation. Nothing is for nothing when you're dealing with the sort of men I meet.'

'Do you mean it would cost money?'

'Indirectly.'

'Nothing compared to the money it's going to cost me in lawyer's fees, plane fares, hotel bills and God knows what.'

Andrew picks up the gin that has arrived. 'There are other considerations. How will I see you if he's out?'

'Well,' says Frances, 'you certainly won't see me if he stays in.'

'I see,' says Andrew, sipping gin. 'I seem to lose both ways.'

'Not necessarily,' says Frances, feeling it slip away. She takes his hand. 'There are times and places.'

'Are you promising me that?' Andrew asks, looking into her eyes. If he hadn't given Kimberley Neal his word that they would have dinner together tonight he would take Frances away now.

'I promise,' says Frances.

'In that case,' says Andrew, reluctantly, 'I'll see what I can do.'

14

A ndrew Marner sits motionless at the window in his room thinking about the pound that is convalescing in the foreign exchange market, the tottering franc and the buoyant Mark, the impenetrable intentions of Alain Rocard and the wavering prospects of locking him into an Anglo-French partnership.

'How's your sex life?' he asks.

Esme Rutherford, concentrating hard now on the precise line of Andrew Marner's nose, ignores the question for a while and applies herself to the delicate touches and accents that she is adding to her portrait with her pointed sable brush. She had expected overt flirtatiousness and would have been hurt if it had not appeared. Ten years ago she would probably have called it sexual harassment, but she is twenty-eight now and it is a long time since she felt out of her depth.

'Not as active as yours, by all accounts,' she finally replies when her work has satisfied her.

Andrew smiles briefly. 'Do you live each day as if it's your first or your last?' he asks.

'You don't have to talk on my account,' says Esme. 'I'm working.'

'Roger seems a strange partner for you. Are you going to marry him?'

'I've got to train him first,' says Esme. 'Can you stop moving your head?'

The sitter, rebuked, freezes in his chair, but he soon finds the silence oppressive.

'Have you any idea how I'm going to get this painting back to London?' he asks.

'I'm glad you asked me that,' says Esme. 'You'll need a thick plastic bag and you'll have to take it as hand luggage: it won't be safe in the hold. You mustn't take it off the frame, either. It'll need to be varnished eventually, but not for a year and then anyone can do it for you.'

The room telephone rings before Andrew can respond to this.

'I'm sorry,' he says, getting up. 'This is about the first call I've had.'

'Mr Marner?' says a girl's voice that he recognises instantly. It is his private secretary, Stella, the only person allowed to contact him. She is both clever and beautiful and he has never touched her. She runs his office, regulates his life, controls his diary, deflects distractions, arranges appointments and is the conduit through which all company news, important or unimportant, reaches him. And so, scared of losing someone who is irreplaceable, he has kept his eager hands off her, an effort of will that has been immeasurably strengthened not so much by the knowledge of her husband's amateur cruiserweight title, as by the prolonged spells in hospital that two of his opponents have sustained.

'Stella,' he says. 'What can I do for you?'

'Mr Marner, I've had Mr Garnett wanting to get in touch with you. He seems to be in a tizzy.'

'In a what?' says Andrew.

'Tizzy,' says Stella. 'It means in a state of nervous agitation.'

'Very good, Stella. I'm glad that somebody in our outfit knows what words really mean.'

'Anyway, he wants to talk to you. *Needs* to talk to you, he says.'

'I'll call him,' says Andrew. 'Any other news?'

'It's all quiet here,' says Stella. 'How is it down there? You're not shagging yourself stupid, I hope?'

'Not stupid, Stella,' says Andrew. 'No.'

He replaces the phone and turns to Esme.

'I'm sorry, I've got to make another call.'

'That's okay,' says Esme, who is still working on the painting. 'I've nearly finished anyway. I reckon one more sitting will do it.'

'It's a fine picture,' says Andrew. 'I'm very impressed.'

He sits down to dial the numerous digits that will connect him to Garnett's fourth-floor office in London. He imagines his bald little editor poring over the latest leader in *The Times* and wondering what quirky notions he can pinch. But evidently he is not too busy because he picks up the phone himself.

'Marner,' says Andrew Marner.

'Andrew,' says Garnett. 'We have a problem.'

'We have or you have?' asks Andrew.

'It's the libel,' says Garnett. 'There's bad news.'

Alain Rocard and Frances Kerwin have between them managed to drive all thought of the libellous printing mistake from Andrew Marner's mind. It floods back now, though.

'What is it?'

'His lawyers are seeking an immediate out-of-court settlement on the grounds that it's an open-and-shut case and we can all save the costs of a court hearing.'

'You said it wasn't malicious,' says Andrew, 'as if that was a factor in our favour?'

'That was how I interpreted it,' says Garnett, grateful for every one of the 700 miles that separate them. 'Our lawyers take a different view.'

'How much does he want?'

'Half a million pounds, I'm afraid.'

Andrew Marner's sharp intake of breath does not delay his reply. 'Listen to me, you follicularly challenged berk, they can stuff their writs up their backsides before we'll submit to that.'

But Garnett, who has heard this bluster before, continues with his doleful message. 'The lawyers say it will cost us that anyway, and possibly a lot more if we fight the case through two weeks in the Strand. And Andrew – listen. There's worse . . .'

'There can't be,' says Andrew.

'There is, I'm afraid,' Garnett says bravely. 'In the rush to launch *World Review*, we forgot to take out libel insurance. It's done now, but it doesn't cover the issue in question.'

Andrew Marner feels a rush of blood to the head that makes his ears ring. For a moment the power of speech deserts him.

'You should probably talk to the lawyers yourself, but I can tell you they are adamant that an out-of-court job is our best option. Libel juries today consist of madmen who have no idea what anything's worth and leaving it up to them is a high-risk business.' Garnett's voice drones on, his words laced with legal jargon, his tone one of resigned gloom.

When Andrew has recovered his speech and gathered his wits he breaks in: 'What you're telling me is that I've got to find the half million myself?'

'Well, the Marner Press,' says Garnett.

'I *am* the Marner Press,' thunders Andrew.

'Well, yes,' says Garnett. 'The funny thing is that the man wasn't a therapist, anyway. He was a masseur.'

'Oh, that really is very hilarious,' says Andrew. 'An absolute bloody scream. There was no need for you to be wrestling with this unusually difficult word that splits so disastrously, Garnett. I think you'd better start looking for a job.'

Driven from her room by the chatter between painter and sitter, Kimberley Neal has established herself and her notebook at a table on the terrace where the novel that is intended to propel her from obscurity to ubiquity is at last making some progress. It is no longer called *Belinda*. The new title is *The Baited Trap*, a revision that seems to have given the book potency and impetus, although it has not done much for Belinda, who has abandoned the foothills of journalism and sunk even lower. She now has an Asian boyfriend who runs a team of dark-skinned hookers on the South Coast.

Belinda is the secretary and telephonist for this organisation, which is known locally as 'The Black Whores Agency', but the question which lurks in the reader's mind is – *will Belinda become a hooker herself?* For Belinda, with her complexes and neuroses and her unresolved psychic tensions, is not the sure-footed

female who first appeared in this story. Kimberley Neal
has knocked her around a bit and now finds that she
is easier to handle, more amenable to the demands of
a pitiless author who will have no compunction about
sending her on to the streets if it will make the words
easier to produce.

Kimberley Neal beckons a waiter and orders a gin
and tonic. She knows that many writers have oiled
the works with such lubricants; they were all dead
at forty but at least they produced a book. She gazes
out to the Croisette where people who have not made
cruel demands like this on themselves wander freely
in the sunshine. She shuts them out and turns back
to her busy notebook. Belinda's decline began when
she made love to a tall, dark stranger in the back
of a Standard Vanguard, and found when she had
lost touch with him that she was pregnant. When
she ransacks her crowded past, Kimberley finds that
her problem isn't what to put into the book, but what
to leave out . . .

The chair next to hers is moved and she looks up to
see that Andrew Marner has joined her at the table.
He does not look his normally composed self, but
instead resembles a man who has recently been hit in
a vulnerable spot by something that lacked flexibility.
Uncharacteristically, he picks up Kimberley Neal's gin
and drinks the lot.

'I'll get you another,' he mutters.

'You'd better give up posing for pictures if it affects
you like this,' says Kimberley. 'What on earth's the
matter?'

'It's printers, not painters,' says Andrew, waving at
the waiter. 'I've just had some very bad news.'

'My God!' Kimberley goes cold. 'What?' She imagines

the collapse of the Marner Press, the disappearance of her column, a future without a salary cheque.

'That idiot Garnett has involved us in a libel action that is going to cost me personally half a million pounds – which is not a sum I can afford at the moment. We're stretched on all fronts. Almost as bad, it's not going to do anything for my credibility when the news gets out. It's not exactly going to endear me to Alain Rocard, is it?'

'Oh dear,' says Kimberley, who doesn't know what to say. 'What are you going to do?'

'Well, I've sacked Garnett for a start. Next I'm going to try to nail Rocard down to a deal before the news leaks. This is where you come in.'

The waiter arrives and Andrew orders two gins.

'Where I come in?' Kimberley prompts him.

'Yes. You're my ace in the hole. I want you to meet Rocard, be nice to him and win him over. I want him to get *very* enthusiastic about the Marner Press.'

'Do you mean flirt with him?' asks Kimberley doubtfully.

'That sort of thing. You're not busy, are you?'

'Oh no. I'm only writing my column and a hundred-thousand-word book.'

'Let me look at the column,' says Andrew. 'I'm not paying for the book.'

Kimberley hands him three sheets that she has written earlier that morning. It is a carefully argued piece, garnered from Esme Rutherford, on the laws about cannabis. While Andrew reads it the waiter brings their drinks.

'I've misjudged you, Kimberley,' says Andrew, picking up his glass. 'This is really very good. I thought you

205

specialised in the short, sharp comment, but this is – well, it's an essay.'

'I write for a living, Andrew,' says Kimberley. 'Show me a cheque and I'll churn out some poems.'

'I'm going to fax this to Garnett and tell him to use it in *World Review*. It's much too good for your little mag.'

'I thought you'd sacked Garnett?' says Kimberley, pleased.

'I've told him to find another job. He's not about to leave this morning.'

'Now you've pinched my column, I'll have to write another one.'

'But you'll be paid five hundred for the article in *World Review*, and you'll be reaching a whole new audience. Broaden your horizons, Kimberley. You could be the new Germaine Greer!'

'I don't want to be the new Germaine Greer, Andrew. I want to be an editor.'

'It could happen,' says Andrew, standing up. 'This is a hot piece. I'm going to fax it to Garnett right now. I'll see you in the room. Dress sexy – we're taking Monsieur Rocard to lunch at Villefranche.'

Kimberley remains at the table to finish her gin. The idea of lunch with Monsieur Rocard does not appeal to her; she would prefer to work on her novel and lie in the sun. But she knows that ignoring Andrew Marner's wishes would not help her career. It is easy to forget in these glorious surroundings that she is a hired hand. The people who are sitting at the other tables on the terrace, enjoying morning coffee or studying the lunch menu, don't have to answer to anyone. There is a leap that she is going to have to make before she will be free from the financial subservience which hampers her life. She doesn't know whether it is into an editor's chair or, permanently, into Andrew Marner's bed . . . but a move of some sort is necessary if she is not going to spend her time bowing to the whims of others.

Perhaps her best hope of independence lies with the novel. She opens the pad again and considers the fragile figure of Belinda, scrabbling down there in the dirt to earn a crust. Should she become a whore? Would this give the book that magic ingredient which would send it soaring into the stratosphere? And if this is the answer, is she capable of writing it? She tries to imagine the outlook of a prostitute, the things she would believe and the way she would behave. Could she pick one out in a supermarket? They were no longer caricature creatures with bum-high skirts and cigarettes drooping from their mouths. Unlikely souls laboured in their ranks. The Black Whores Agency included two teachers and a nurse.

Immersed in the complexities of her novel, Kimberley Neal assumes the veneer of a prostitute and thinks about lunch with Alain Rocard.

In his bar on the Croisette, Roger Blake is thinking about his son. His unexpected promotion to fatherhood has unsettled him, and whereas before he would stay out of bars until the evening, he now finds that a pint at lunchtime is a midday boost that he enjoys. He has taken to the brasserie-bar-restaurant idea, where a steak appears as easily as a pint, and wonders why his own country, with its grubby pubs and curling sandwiches, deludes itself that the world enjoys its hospitality.

A barmaid provides his Heineken today. She is one of those women who have huge breasts but a curiously drained face, as if all their vitality has been used up to provide this magnificent bosom. Roger Blake is only momentarily distracted. He sips his beer and watches the tourists parade on the Croisette, the flashily dressed with their Pentax zoom cameras, the kids with their roller skates, the old ladies with their dogs. This last partnership fascinates him. Is it that they have enough love left for a dog, but not quite enough any more for a human being, or are they finding comfort in the company of animals that no human relationship ever provided?

A man in jeans and T-shirt comes in and takes a stool two away from him at the bar. He has curly dark hair that has been pulled back into a ponytail. He looks at Roger Blake as if a conversation would be welcome, but Roger turns away, reluctant to get involved in the tedious small talk that such meetings usually produce.

He is wondering what sort of boy his son is and whether he is happy. Does he know that he is adopted, and does he think about his real father? Is there a physical resemblance? Does he have a similar character and disposition, or has he already been moulded by people who won't really understand him?

These questions have gone round in his head for a couple of days and he likes to sit and think about them, imagining answers, guessing at truths. One truth he does know is that this is a small crisis in his life, a rapidly developing obsession that is thrusting other things, even Esme, from his head. But he cannot shake it off.

He sits up, looks round and catches the eye of the

man with the ponytail, who grabs his chance for a chat.

'How's the old Stock Exchange then?' he asks.

In the taxi that takes them through Nice and then another six kilometres along the coast, Kimberley Neal imagines Alain Rocard as a tall and wistful Frenchman with dark eyes and native charm. He is, she decides hopefully, a man who, despite his wealth and power, has a gentle almost playful side that surfaces in the company of women. But the reality, as so often, is disappointing.

Villefranche is one of the most sheltered harbours on the coast. Yellow, pink and red stucco houses stand out on the hillside behind it, while men with drinks fish from the quayside. Monsieur Rocard sits at a table outside one of the restaurants on the front, and stands as they approach. He falls some way short of Kimberley's template, being short, fat and with receding grey hair that has been greased and ruthlessly brushed back.

'Alain,' says Andrew Marner, 'this is my personal assistant, Miss Kimberley Neal.'

The Frenchman takes her hand but does not let go. After a while Kimberley Neal realises that her hand is now being held by both of his, which have very hairy backs.

'I should have a personal assistant like this,' he says, in perfect English. 'Miss Neal, you are a tribute to English womanhood.'

'Call me Kimberley,' she says, attempting to retrieve her hand. 'What a nice place Villefranche is.'

Alain Rocard nods. 'It is full of history. Cocteau decorated the chapel.'

They sit at the table that Alain Rocard has chosen and a waiter appears immediately with three menus. While the men study them, Kimberley Neal studies their guest. If Andrew Marner imagines that she is going to introduce a little romance into this man's life in the interests of the Marner Press, he has made a serious misjudgement. Even at her most promiscuous she has never become involved with a man so short of sex appeal. The problem of her novel, the viewpoint of a prostitute, suddenly seems more difficult to comprehend. Being whoreish is one thing, but to actually be a whore requires qualities that she cannot imagine. She wonders how to approach this man, but when the waiter has taken their orders the other two ignore her and become involved in an animated discussion about the arcane mysteries of stockbroking which leaves her bored. When they start talking about running with the bulls she isn't concentrating enough to know whether they are discussing buying shares in a rising market or flying to Pamplona.

The food arrives, a unanimous choice of fish, and Andrew Marner attempts to steer the conversation towards the subject of the joint venture that he is seeking. Even now, after hours of discussions, he isn't sure whether Monsieur Rocard is genuinely interested or is just stringing him along for no apparent purpose. It seems to him sometimes that Rocard, bored, enjoys Andrew's company and is prolonging these talks for social reasons.

'Is it the greatest idea since the duvet or a recipe for disaster?' the Frenchman asks. 'You have many newspapers in Britain already, and some of them are cutting their prices. What does this tell us?'

'Production costs are our trump card,' says Andrew. 'I gave you the figures.

'Production costs in my experience are something which invariably go up,' says Alain Rocard. He turns to Kimberley Neal. 'What do you think, beautiful lady?'

'I think the Marner Press' record speaks for itself,' says Kimberley. 'Don't you?'

Alain Rocard winks at her. 'How do I know what I think till I see what I say? I think we are sitting here in a recession. What does everybody talk about? Green shoots and lights at end of tunnels. I see no lights. I see no green shoots. Each day is full of – what is the word? – tension.'

'If you are turning the idea down, Alain, I wish you would say so,' says Andrew Marner.

'Turning the idea down?' says Alain Rocard. 'I'm not turning the idea down. I'm going to discuss it with my board.'

'But you said yourself that the board do what you tell them!'

'However, I listen to their opinions. Sometimes I hear an intelligent one. I welcome their advice: occasionally, it's useful. This is the way of a successful company. It is how important decisions are reached. Power without consultation is the route to ruin. God gave us ears as well as mouths.'

Andrew Marner tries to interrupt some of this but Alain Rocard talks on. It is like trying to discuss something with the speaking clock.

Kimberley Neal, watching this man and curious about the nature of the power that he wields, is suddenly reminded of the plight of Bruce Kerwin. Andrew Marner has not raised the subject and she wonders whether he has forgotten or does not intend to. It seems quite wrong to her that a man could lie in prison because of an unspoken request.

'We have a friend, Monsieur Rocard,' she says, when a gap at last appears in the conversation. 'He is locked up in the police station at Cannes because he had some cannabis in his pocket.'

'Your friend had cannabis?' Alain Rocard shrugs. 'Big deal. Everybody has cannabis. Who is this friend?'

'He's an Englishman who was on holiday in our hotel. Is there any way of helping him? They're talking about jailing him for two years.'

'This is ridiculous,' says Alain Rocard. 'I will talk to my contacts. Give me the man's name.'

'Bruce Kerwin.'

'No, write it down.'

Kimberley Neal takes her notebook from her bag, tears out a sheet and writes Bruce Kerwin's name on it in capital letters.

'Write your name, too,' says Alain Rocard. 'I may call in a favour.' He gives her another wink.

'I wasn't going to mention this to you,' says Andrew Marner, looking annoyed. 'You have more important things to think about.'

'If you had asked me, Andrew, would I have taken any notice?' says Alain Rocard, smiling. 'But who can refuse a beautiful woman?'

When Roger Blake gets back to the Carlton, Esme is putting those extra touches to her portrait that can be accomplished in the sitter's absence. A corner of their room has now been annexed for the project, an intrusion that Roger reluctantly tolerates in anticipation of Andrew Marner's money. His face, stern and unyielding, dominates the picture, but there are some

212

peripheral items on the desk that Esme has imagined to be in front of him that she is adding now.

'It's brilliant,' says Roger, lying on the bed. Midday drinking may be unusually enjoyable, but it doesn't make for a lively afternoon.

'Have you been drinking, lover?' Esme asks.

'Well,' says Roger, 'I had no one to play with.'

'You play, I work. The lot of women through the ages.'

Roger fights sleep on the bed. 'Hey, I met a real-life drug dealer. He tried to flog me some cannabis.'

'Really?' says Esme, pausing in her work. 'How much did you buy?'

'I told him I'd got enough vices already. Also, I was short of money. He had a strange name – what was it? Shaftoe. Anyway, when he asked me where I was staying, he said he'd sold some stuff to a man from the Carlton. Yes, I said, and he's now in the nick. He got caught with it. You've never seen a man disappear so quickly. It was a real Magic Circle job. One minute he was there, and the next he had gone, leaving a full glass of beer.'

'That was him then,' says Esme. 'The man Bruce met. You had a narrow escape there, my boy. You could be in the choky now, pleading for soap.' And she turns back to her painting of an office diary which is on Andrew Marner's desk.

'How much longer is this masterpiece going to take?' asks Roger. 'We used to go out together.'

'I'm trying to finish it by the weekend,' says Esme. 'I want some spending money.'

'Why?' he asks. 'What did you want to buy me?'

'I thought I might get you an aphrodisiac.'

'Ouch,' says Roger. 'Am I losing my touch?'

'No, I'm losing your touch,' says Esme.

'There's a reason for that,' says Roger. 'I've had a traumatic experience. It's quite slowed me down.'

'You don't look traumatised to me,' says Esme. 'Just mildly pissed.'

'Kimberley Neal,' Roger murmurs.

'Old Teeth and Tits?' says Esme. 'What's she been up to now?'

'She claims she had my baby. I'm a father. I have a son.'

Esme puts down her brush and comes over to the bed. 'She said that? And you believe her?'

'Well,' says Roger.

'First she says she met you. Then she says you screwed her. Now she says there was a baby. She'll be claiming you're married next!'

'Perhaps we're divorced,' Roger yawns. 'I'm getting the story a chapter at a time.'

'And this has affected you, has it, this alleged parenthood?'

'Well, it would, wouldn't it? It's not one of those things that you can instantly forget about.'

'She's a lying cow,' says Esme. 'She's trying to pull you.'

'How would that happen?' asks Roger.

'Make you feel close and cosy. And then, if you want to see this boy, if there really is one, she's your only link with him.'

'You never told me women were as artful as that. You said they were nice.'

'Some of them are,' says Esme. 'You have to be selective. But a nice man like you – he's got no chance.'

'Why don't you take me out to dinner tonight as I'm that nice and you're the breadwinner?'

'I think I'd better,' says Esme. 'I didn't realise there was competition.'

15

Saturday morning on the rue Meynadier has the atmosphere of the souk. The long narrow street near the port has not only dozens of shops but stalls in front of the shops, so that everywhere there is the invitation to spend. It is a call that tourists can't resist and they mill around in their hundreds studying watches and cheeses, paintings and cakes, leather goods and toys, as they count money and consult currency charts.

Frances Kerwin is drawn here too, enticed by the prospect of bargains, tempted by the chance of discovering something that it had never occurred to her to buy. She moves through the crowd in search of the unexpected and the unusual, the little trinket that she will forever associate with Cannes. She brings with her the application and single-mindedness of the serious shopper; nobody will be able to surprise *her* with a bargain they found today on the rue Meynadier.

She feels distinctly perky this morning – the unexpected benefit of not having seen Andrew Marner for a couple of days. A regime of fresh air, exercise and early nights has brought her to a peak of vigorous good health that a long evening of sexual athletics would have placed beyond her reach.

Last night, while Andrew addressed a board meeting in Nice, she had paid another visit to Bruce, an almost pointless social engagement, doomed by his uncommunicative misery and her poorly disguised urge to fly. She had wanted to tell him that Andrew had spoken to a man who could, in some sinister way, obtain his release, but she didn't want to raise his hopes when she didn't know how it was going to end. Andrew had assured her that he had given the information to the right person and that it was now just a question of waiting while instructions were passed along from one gendarme to another. Nothing had happened so far but it was too early to accuse Andrew of letting her down. So she talked to Bruce about Marseille and what arrangements she would have to make to visit him there, trying to believe that she would never have to do it.

Her attention is caught by some brown leather skirts which seem to her to be just the raunchy, modish item that she needs. Her new image demands them, her purse can afford them: she goes into the shop. When she comes out ten minutes later she is wearing the skirt, convinced that it has knocked another five years off her age. It is short, tight and sexy and she loves the feel of it against her hips. The white blouse above it has a plunging neckline showing cleavage that is rarely displayed, and she feels quite tarty as she swings down the rue Meynadier and almost bumps into Andrew Marner.

'Wow,' he says. 'How much for a quick jump?'

'A thousand francs should cover it,' says Frances. 'What are you doing here?'

'It's Saturday,' says Andrew. 'I have a morning off. And I remembered you said that you were going to have a look at this street market.'

'Where's Kimberley?'

'Writing her column. She's a busy little girl – scribble, scribble. Can I buy you a coffee?'

'You mean "may I?"' says Frances. 'I thought you were a stickler for words. How did the board meeting go?'

'Who can tell?' says Andrew. 'The Frogs are getting to be as inscrutable as the men in Hong Kong.'

'Okay,' says Frances. 'Hit me with a café au lait.'

They find a bar-restaurant and go in. Impressionist prints festoon the walls. A notice announces that Cannes has won France's *Pavillon Bleu* award for best-kept beaches.

'That's some skirt,' says Andrew, when they have found a table. 'It gives a man ideas.'

'It doesn't take a skirt to give you ideas,' says Frances. 'If the Marner Press goes down the tubes you could earn a living getting stud fees.'

'I've missed you,' says Andrew. 'Two days is a long time between meals when you have an appetite like mine.'

'I'm sorry for you,' Frances whispers, 'in thrall to such a terrible lust.'

'Does that expression of sympathy mean that, should the opportunity present itself, you wouldn't be averse to an impromptu bonk?'

'Sex in the morning?' says Frances. 'How decadent.'

'I don't see why sex should be something that happens at the end of the day, if at all. It's saddled with a valedictory image,' says Andrew. 'Let's bring it into the morning. Let's do it at lunch.'

'I don't see the thousand-franc note,' says Frances.

Andrew Marner this morning is dressed informally – in a brown, short-sleeve shirt and check trousers. But from the top pocket of the shirt he plucks a wad of banknotes and lays a 1000-franc one on the table between their coffees.

'You're not registered for VAT, I hope?' he enquires.

Frances sees that this little joke can be carried further. She picks the note up and puts it into her bag. 'If the skirt turns you on, it's only fair that you should pay for it,' she says. 'My place or my place?'

'Your place,' says Andrew. 'We don't want to disturb the columnist.'

In the solitary gloom of his dusty cell, Bruce Kerwin is devising exercises that he hopes will delay the physical deterioration that must surely follow his present unhealthy existence. He yearns for good food, space and fresh air. Panic-stricken, he feels that he is watching his own decline.

The bed and the chair are the only apparatus available to him and his body straddles the two, his head on one and his feet on the other; his body is a bridge that aches. The aches and the pains he takes to be a normal concomitant of strenuous exercise, but he hopes that the stomach muscles are strengthening as he strives to maintain a rigid position between the two pieces of furniture.

His mind has undergone many changes during his sojourn here. Initial thoughts of a swift release were followed by the acceptance of a trial, and for a few days he pictured the acquittal and the fulsome apologies of the court. But things have moved on now and in the long lonely hours a subdued reality has intruded. Today his thoughts are focused on survival, on getting through whatever the world is going to throw at him. He holds his position for as long as he can until the strain on his stomach causes him to subside slowly to the floor.

He is in this position, red-faced and slightly breathless, when the cell door opens and a grey-haired police officer he has never seen marches in with a thoroughly inappropriate smile on his face. His uniform suggests that he is of a higher rank than the policemen Bruce Kerwin has been dealing with: he is in a jacket, not shirt-sleeves, and there are some silver buttons on his shoulders.

Bruce Kerwin pulls himself off the floor and sits on the bed. This is the move to Marseille that he has been dreading, although, he tells himself, at least it will mean that he can have a bath. He is now so unwashed that he is embarrassed when a policeman comes into the cell.

'Mr Kerwin,' says the policeman in perfect English. 'How are you today?'

Bruce Kerwin looks at him, confused by his manner. 'How the hell do you think I am?' he asks. 'I'm filthy, hungry and bored.'

'We can't have that,' says the policeman. 'We can't have that. Collect your things. You will follow me.'

'Things?' says Bruce. 'I haven't got any things.'

But the policeman is leaving the cell and beckoning Bruce to follow. They turn down an unfamiliar corridor and arrive eventually in a comfortable, well-furnished office with thick carpets, an expensive oak desk and pleasant pictures on the wall. It is quite unlike any other room that Bruce has seen in this grim building. The policeman shows him to an armchair and then sits himself informally on the edge of his desk.

'Would you like coffee?' he asks. 'Biscuits?'

221

'Yes, I would,' says Bruce. 'If you mean proper coffee.'

'It will be excellent coffee, Mr Kerwin.'

He picks up a phone and speaks rapidly in French for some time.

'You have important friends, Mr Kerwin,' he says when he has replaced the phone.

'I have?' Bruce is baffled.

'Indeed. And we are very sorry for what has happened.'

'You are?' says Bruce.

'Very sorry. But today we make up for our mistake. Today you go home.'

Two policemen come in before Bruce can reply to this. One carries a tray with coffee and biscuits on it, the other a cardboard box. When they have gone, the policeman takes the tray across to Bruce who discovers immediately that it is indeed excellent coffee and not at all like the stuff he has been offered during the last week.

'So I can go home?' he asks, barely able to believe it.

'To your hotel. But one thing, Mr Kerwin: we want to hear no more about this. We all pretend it never happened. Documents will be destroyed. This is a very difficult situation, so I want your word.'

Bruce eats a biscuit and drinks his coffee. If all he has to promise to secure his release is a discreet silence, he can't wait to commit himself.

'You have my word of honour,' he says fervently.

'Good,' says the policeman. 'Now, what is in here?'

He empties the cardboard box on his desk. It contains the contents of Bruce's pockets when he was arrested – the hotel key, loose change, a pen, a wallet full of notes, his passport, some credit cards and a street map of Cannes. The cannabis has disappeared.

The notion descends suddenly on Bruce Kerwin that this is all a terrible mistake, a glitch in the police computer, and this idea propels him to his feet. He must get out of here before this nice man discovers that he is releasing the wrong prisoner. He finishes his coffee quickly and stuffs the returned articles into the front and back pockets of his jeans.

The policeman smiles. 'You want to be off, of course. May we give you a lift to the Carlton?'

Bruce Kerwin can think of at least three reasons why he should not accept this offer. In the first place, he needs some exercise and fresh air. Secondly, the police might discover their mistake while he's in their car and radio it to turn back. And, finally, arriving at the Carlton Hotel in a police car might bring a certain opprobrium that would take the shine off things.

'I'd prefer to walk,' he says, finding his first smile for a week. It lodges on his face and requires a conscious effort to dismantle it. 'I need the air.'

'Whatever you say, Mr Kerwin,' says the policeman, standing up. 'Let me show you out.' He leads Bruce out of the office and along many corridors on different floors, some beautifully done up, others disgracefully run down. They soon reach the entrance hall where Bruce had arrived in some confusion two Thursdays ago. The policeman stops, smiles and opens the door as if bidding farewell to a cherished dinner guest.

'Is everything all right, Mr Kerwin?' he asks.

'Fine,' says Bruce, blinking at the sun that is now flooding in.

The policeman extends his hand and Bruce shakes it

gratefully. 'Well, goodbye then. And say hallo to your friend for me.'

'I will,' says Bruce. 'I certainly will.'

His impulse now is to run and hide before the police discover their error, but he gets a grip on himself and turns and walks at a normal pace away from Cannes Central Police Station, out of the Avenue de Grasse and down the rue Buttura towards the town and the sea.

He is conscious of his appearance and watches to see whether the other people in the street are looking at him for too long, picking him out as somebody who doesn't quite belong among all this Saturday morning smartness. His T-shirt is filthy, his jeans are crumpled, his unwashed hair refuses to go where he guides it and he needs a shave. And the public does react, giving him a wider berth as they pass than he has known before. Only the dogs seek proximity, sniffing curiously at someone they evidently suppose to be a friend.

When he reaches the Croisette and sees the sea again, his release becomes real and he can believe that he is out. He is elated and hungry. But before he can eat, before he can mingle again with the human race, he must take a long bath.

There is no one he knows in the vicinity of the Carlton Hotel and he slips in past the two guards who always stand at the door with their security badges, crosses the lobby quickly and gets into the lift. Luckily he has it to himself, although given the expensive aromas, the fragrant scents and perfumes and pomades that emanate like a financial challenge from the other guests, he doubts whether there is any room left in the local nostrils for the stale smell that hangs pervasively around him.

His room is empty, which must mean that Frances

is out spending money, and he goes immediately to the bathroom and turns on the taps. When the bath is almost full he takes off his dirty clothes and climbs in. The feeling, as he sinks into the warm water, is as near to bliss as he has been for some time, and he lies in the bath not wanting to move.

On the floor beside him the jeans and T-shirt stand as testimony to an experiment that has failed. When he gets out of the bath and has shaved and washed his hair, he decides, he will put on a suit.

Frances Kerwin and Andrew Marner reach the room in an unseemly rush. The sexy thoughts and earthy conversation that have carried them along the Croisette and back to the hotel have roused their expectations about the next hour. In less than a minute Andrew has removed his shirt and turned his attention to the delicious task of unfastening Frances' new leather skirt. Shoes fall to the floor, bedsprings creak.

Bruce Kerwin has emerged from the bath, shaved, washed his hair and come out to put on his best grey suit, with white shirt and pale blue tie. He has now gone back into the bathroom to attend to his hair, which he is carefully restoring to the combed-back look he had when he arrived in France. He bears very little resemblance now to the man released from the police station earlier this morning, and he looks at the mirror's image approvingly, liking what he sees.

A noise disturbs him as he puts the final touches to his hair. A door slams and he hears laughter and movement in the bedroom. He pauses, baffled, wondering whether nine days in a cell have affected his memory and he has stupidly returned to the wrong room. But in the silence, he knows it is Frances' voice he hears. It is saying: 'Screw me, baby.'

Bruce Kerwin stands stock-still, worried again that the events of the last week have damaged his mind. He seems to have been pitched into some sort of dream. But the voices continue, and they are real enough. One of them sounds like Andrew Marner's. It is saying: 'Get on the end of this and walk towards me.' His wife's laughter which follows this is too raucous for a dream.

Bruce Kerwin moves swiftly across the bathroom and throws open the door. The sight which meets him stuns him into silence. His wife is naked on the bed, lying on her back and laughing. Andrew Marner is attempting to disentangle his feet from a pair of check trousers that are gripping his ankles.

'Jesus,' says Frances. 'It's Bruce.'

Andrew Marner turns on the bed and looks at the man in the bathroom doorway. 'It doesn't look like Bruce,' he says. 'It's an intruder.' In seconds he has hoisted his trousers back to his waist, zipped his fly, and got off the bed. 'Phone Reception,' he says to Frances. 'We'll have him arrested.'

'What the bloody hell is going on?' asks Bruce.

'You'll find out soon enough,' says Andrew, about to grip his arm. But now that he is nearer he sees that this *is* Bruce Kerwin, or somebody who looks very like him and he backs off uncertainly and picks up his shirt.

'Bruce,' says Frances. 'You're out, thank God.'

But Bruce Kerwin seems to be in a trance. He stares disbelievingly at the two of them and repeats: 'What the bloody hell is going on?'

Frances Kerwin, her heart pounding, is trying to find her hastily discarded clothes. Andrew Marner, unsure what action is required, is buttoning his shirt.

The situation is beyond explaining and he pursues another line.

'I'm glad you're out, Bruce. You have me to thank for that.'

'Yes,' says Frances, grateful for something to say. 'Andrew got you out. He knows a man who knows the Police Chief. If it wasn't for Andrew – '

But Bruce Kerwin has turned away from both of them and headed for the door. He goes out and slams it shut with a bang that echoes down the hotel's corridors.

'Where were we?' says Andrew, unzipping his trousers.

'I don't think so,' says Frances. 'Not now.'

Esme Rutherford walks happily along the Croisette feeling the deep satisfaction of a job well done. Her painting of Andrew Marner, a masterly portrayal of a steely-eyed captain of industry, is complete and ready to be delivered. French francs will soon brim from her purse. In the meantime there is the celebratory drink, the need to savour the moment, and in what is now his favourite bar, Roger Blake is waiting to buy it.

The Croisette is as crowded as ever and she weaves a path between kids and dogs, prams and wheelchairs, and is in sight of the bar when a man who has been sitting on one of the few seats where old folk rest or hide from the sun is suddenly on his feet and blocking her path.

'Esme,' he says. 'It's good to see you.'

For a moment she doesn't recognise him in his smart grey suit and white shirt. His clothes are more suited to a London office than the South of France. But then she realises that this is Bruce Kerwin, or rather a new, refurbished version of the man.

'You're out,' she beams. 'That's wonderful!'

'They let me out this morning and I'm beginning to wish they never had,' he says. 'Can I buy you a drink? I've been thinking about you a lot.'

Esme looks at him, trying to gauge what she is dealing with here. She has seen this look on a man's face before.

'You wish you were still locked up, Bruce? What do you mean?' she says.

'You wouldn't believe me if I told you, Esme. Come and have a drink.'

'I'm just going to have a drink,' says Esme, 'with Roger. Why don't you join us?'

'Ah, Roger,' says Bruce. 'How is he? He's a lucky man.' He falls in beside her and they walk together towards the bar.

'Roger's fine,' says Esme. 'But how about you? You look pale and thin. Was it awful?'

'It wasn't good,' says Bruce.

'You'll soon be okay again with a bit of sun and some good food.'

'No, I won't,' says Bruce. 'I've just had a terrible shock.'

'What was it?' asks Esme. 'What's happened?'

'I don't want to talk about it,' says Bruce. 'I'm beginning to think that I belong to a peculiarly blighted family.'

Roger Blake sits on his usual stool watching the holiday parade. He is beginning to feel like a kid with his nose up against the shop window of life. Money saunters past, drives past, sails by in the bay. The women look wonderful, even if it has taken a rejuvenation course in a Swiss clinic to achieve it. Money again.

228

He sips his Heineken and sees Kimberley Neal coming through the door.

'This is a surprise,' says Roger. 'Have you taken up lunchtime drinking?'

'Kind of you,' says Kimberley. 'I'll have a beer. I've been working all morning and deserve a small reward.'

'How's Andrew?'

'It's always a feast or a fast with that man.'

'Which is it at the moment?'

'A fast.'

Roger orders her a beer. He gets excellent service in this bar now and suspects that the barman, having become used to his face, believes him to be a resident who merits more respect than a here-today-gone-tomorrow tourist.

'I've been thinking about detectives,' says Roger. 'The *Yellow Pages* are full of them. I reckon half the people who are thrown out of work start new careers as private dicks.'

'Detectives?' says Kimberley.

'To find our son.'

'Oh dear, I don't think that's a very good idea,' says Kimberley. 'We don't want to disturb him at this crucial stage of his development.'

'I don't want to disturb him, I want to see him,' says Roger. 'I'm curious, and getting curiouser.'

'You must be patient and control your curiosity,' says Kimberley firmly. 'You could end up doing more harm than good.'

Roger is about to dispute this when Esme comes into the bar with Bruce Kerwin.

'Good God,' says Roger. 'It's the felon.'

'Hallo, everybody,' says Bruce Kerwin, looking miserable.

229

'It worked then,' says Kimberley. 'We got you out.'

'Somebody got me out,' says Bruce gloomily. 'It's all something of a mystery.'

'Andrew knew a man with a bit of influence,' Kimberley tells him.

'I'd rather you didn't mention Andrew,' says Bruce. 'Can I buy drinks?'

'Let me,' offers Roger. 'I'm getting Esme a bottle of champagne and she may share it.'

'I certainly will,' says Esme, kissing Roger's cheek. 'The painting looks fine.'

'Great,' says Roger. 'What a brilliant girl I have.' He orders a bottle of champagne and four glasses. Bruce Kerwin's disappears instantly and Roger refills his glass. 'I suppose you got a little thirsty in there,' he says sympathetically. 'Was it hell?'

'I don't recommend it,' says Bruce.

'It's done wonders for your sartorial tastes,' says Kimberley. 'Why don't you want us to mention Andrew? Not that I want to mention him myself.'

'He's had a shock,' says Esme, 'but he doesn't want to talk about it.'

Everybody looks at Bruce Kerwin. The champagne fizzes in his empty stomach. 'I don't mind talking about it,' he says defiantly. 'I got back to the hotel after nine days in a cell to find Andrew Marner and my wife about to make love.'

'*About* to make love?' Roger looks baffled.

'Well, he was tearing his trousers off and she was stark naked. What do you imagine they were about to do?'

'Play doctors?' says Roger.

'It doesn't sound like whist,' agrees Kimberley. 'I'll spay the bastard!'

'Isn't that a female operation?' asks Esme.

'What the hell,' says Kimberley. 'We can't take any chances.'

'It must have been a terrible surprise for you,' says Esme, who is not at all surprised by Bruce's news. He is holding an empty glass out for Roger to fill. The drink empties the bottle, and Roger orders another.

'I'm astounded,' says Bruce, 'but something had happened to her. She had her hair cut shorter and bought younger clothes. She changed dramatically while I was locked up. Apparently she was doing exercises.'

'That *is* disturbing,' says Roger. 'Perhaps the sun had got to her.'

'Perhaps she went to pieces in your absence,' says Esme hopefully.

'It didn't look as if she'd gone to pieces to me,' says Kimberley, savage now. 'She'd turned into a right little tart.'

'I don't think you should speak about Mrs Kerwin like that,' says Roger. 'At least, not while Mr Kerwin is here. Of course, when Bruce has gone it will be open season and you can lob in your two bits.'

'She's trying to steal my man,' says Kimberley. 'She's screwing my meal ticket. What am I supposed to do?'

'That's all right,' says Bruce. 'It seems a fair description to me. I just can't work out what's got into her.'

'Anyway, Andrew isn't your man,' says Esme. 'Doesn't he have a wife at home?'

'Bertha,' says Kimberley. 'Big Bertha.'

'The man has obviously got the sexual drive of a guillemot.'

'Intermittently,' agrees Kimberley.

Roger holds up the new bottle of champagne and they all offer him their empty glasses. He fills them and then puts his arm round Bruce Kerwin's shoulders.

'Anyway, Bruce, old mate,' he says. 'What are you going to do about it all?'

Bruce removes the refilled glass from his lips. 'Do about it all?' he says. 'I'm going to have a few drinks.'

WEEK 3

The trouble with many travellers is that they take themselves along.

Joseph Prescott *Aphorisms and Other Observations*

16

In a Georgian mansion hidden in the rolling Berkshire countryside, Bertha Marner is making herself a cup of tea – camomile with honey – using her favourite Villeroy & Boch crockery. She is a tall, heavily-built lady who dominates any room she enters, which is useful because she is accustomed to organising things.

On this Sunday morning there is a temporary respite in her busy social calendar and she is relaxing amid the various luxuries that are part of the Marners' endlessly converted home: wood-panelled walls and marble fireplaces; hand-tufted carpets. In the white French stone entrance hall, a quarter-ton crystal chandelier is powered by an electric motor that enables it to be lowered for cleaning.

These things and more have flowed remorselessly from Andrew's success, and Bertha is proud of the part that she has played, advising, comforting, supporting, encouraging, through good moments and bad. And there have been bad moments. Just after the terminal hubris of Mrs Thatcher, his whole enterprise seemed on the verge of collapse but Bertha refused to let it happen. Bank support was obtained, the death rattle turned out to be a cough, and business revived.

She is proud, too, of the way that she has handled their marriage, steering it away from the emotional disturbances and rancorous abuse that seemed to beset less thoughtful liaisons. Bertha is fifty, the same age as her husband, but while she seems older than fifty, he seems younger. She can see now that men should be older than their wives but she has handled the disparity with some skill and the proof of her success is that Andrew is still here, and shows no desire to move out. His frequent absences suit them both: he loves to travel and gets bored at home; she hates abroad and loves golf.

The phone rings as she is drinking her tea in the spacious Marner kitchen. She takes the extension off the wall. Her friend Jane, whose husband is dove shooting in Maryland, wants an afternoon on the golf course, but the kitchen television, left on from an earlier programme, is transmitting a church service which makes Jane difficult to hear.

'Just a minute, my dear,' says Bertha. 'There's some geriatric twerp on the telly giving us some garbage about life after death.'

'A bit of life before death would be more to the point,' says Jane. Bertha thinks that Jane has every chance of receiving the attention that she craves if she can find a half-drunk paratrooper trapped in a blindfold, but she omits to mention this and puts the phone down while she turns off the television.

When her afternoon on the golf course has been arranged and she has finished her tea, she busies herself with the tidying-up that falls to her at weekends when her cleaning lady doesn't appear. The week's post, collected off the mat and left mostly in the kitchen, is rounded up and taken to Andrew's study to be left on his desk. As usual, she flips through the envelopes without opening them to see whether there are any which look urgent or interesting, and one immediately stands out. She holds it for a moment, wondering whether this is a letter that she can justify opening, and then, consumed by curiosity, she does. It is a long time since anything has surprised Bertha Marner, and much longer since she was impressed, but she reads this beautifully typed letter in open-mouthed stupefaction.

Andrew Marner,
Berkeley Stowe,
Near Lambourn,
Berkshire,

    Dear Sir,
I am directed by the Prime Minister to inform you that he proposes on the occasion of the forthcoming New Year Honours List to submit your name to the Queen with a recommendation that the honour of Knight Bachelor be conferred on you.

    I am to request that you will be good enough to inform me as soon as possible whether this honour would be agreeable to you and at the same time furnish me with your full Christian names, surname and permanent address.

    I must further ask you to treat this matter as entirely confidential until such time as the Honours List is published.

                                        I am, Sir,
                                Your obedient servant

Bertha Marner has no time to admire the flamboyant signature of the Prime Minister's obedient servant. She has hurled the letter into the air and released a deep-throated whoop which would have intimidated a professionally-active pitbull terrier. Her mind is racing, and before the letter can float to the floor, she has scooped it up with an athletic gesture which belies her build, and reached with her other hand for the telephone on her husband's desk.

She realises then with a little flutter of frustration that the telephone number that she wants is downstairs, scribbled on one of those loose-leaf wall pads in the kitchen where the week's grocery requirements are dutifully listed. She goes down in a hurry to find it.

It is there, two pages back, superseded now by a need for ground nutmeg, Schwartz lamb seasoning, cocktail onions in vinegar, capers and Camembert. *Carlton Hotel*, it says in Andrew's writing. *58 La Croisette, BP 155, 06406 Cannes Cedex. Telephone: 93 689168. Fax: 93 382090.*

She goes now into the dining room where there is a phone that she can sit down with. Through the windows she can see her beautifully laid out garden which drops gently for more than a hundred yards towards a decorative duck pond. She has forgotten, if she ever knew, the digits that she needs to dial direct and calls instead Directory Enquiries. But as she sits there waiting for a helpful voice she suddenly regrets her impetuosity. She replaces the phone quickly before anybody can speak and gives herself time to think.

This news is much too important to be relayed over a telephone. She needs to be there to celebrate with him. She wants to see his face when he hears the news! She gets up, smiles to herself, and returns to her tidying-up duties.

First thing in the morning she will ring the travel agent.

A discreet silence prevails that morning in the Kerwins' comfortable second-floor room at the Carlton Hotel. The discretion is being exercised by Frances Kerwin, who is cautiously carrying out in silence those little tasks that occupy a person between bed and breakfast. Wardrobe doors are opened, but gently; taps are turned on, but not too much. One function, however, does not permit a diminution of decibels and it is the flushing of the lavatory that eventually stirs the recumbent figure who has shared her bed.

Bruce Kerwin and his wife have not spoken since his abrupt departure from the room. Indeed, they have not seen each other. Bruce, encouraged by midday champagne, went on to try other intoxicating refreshments available for holidaymakers with time on their hands. He sobered himself by enjoying his first proper meal for a week in the middle of the afternoon and then devoted the evening to an unhurried assessment of the local beers. This took him beyond the port and up to the old town, Le Suquet, where, he can quite clearly remember, nobody understood a word that he said. Whether this was because the native tongue was not English, or whether it was due to the extent of the research he had conducted into the local brews, he doesn't know, but what he does know is that the evening thereafter is full of memory gaps. He certainly didn't make a conscious decision to rejoin his wife at the Carlton Hotel. By that time he was on some sort of automatic pilot, operating on instinct, and returning to the bed that he knew.

Frances Kerwin had a miserable day. What should have been a joyful celebration of her husband's release had been destroyed at the moment of his arrival. She spent the day in her room, meals delivered, wrestling with her guilt and wondering what had happened to her husband. At midnight she turned off the television and went to bed; and when she woke up he was beside her.

Now she comes out of the bathroom, dressed and ready for breakfast, and confronts her husband who is lying on his back in bed, his eyes wide open and staring at the ceiling.

'My head says I've been drinking,' he tells her.

'My nose agrees with that,' says Frances. 'How do you feel?'

'I shouldn't be here,' says Bruce. 'I meant to end up somewhere else.'

'That would be rather silly, given the price you are paying for this room,' says Frances. 'You've already wasted nine nights. Why don't you get up and come down to the terrace for some breakfast?'

She is struggling to impose some normality on the scene and is determined not to give way to embarrassment. After all, he was in the wrong before she was, and anyway, it is far too early for serious conversations. Bruce Kerwin, lying in bed with the memories flooding back, is not quite ready for a serious conversation either.

He leaves his bed gingerly and walks slowly to the bathroom where he discovers that he doesn't feel too bad. By the time he has washed, shaved and dressed he is astonished at his own resilience. They take the lift down in silence, and Frances wonders when he will speak. With his suit and tie and brushed-back hair

240

he looks like the husband she used to know. But she, with her short hair and short skirt, knows that she is strange to him. The position of ten days ago has been reversed. She now looks like his daughter.

Morning sun fills the terrace as they sit at a table facing the sea. They order coffee and scrambled eggs and watch a cruise liner on the horizon ploughing an eastward path towards Nice. Early morning promenaders stroll along the Croisette as if not a moment of their holidays can be wasted in the shadows of indoors.

When the food arrives and Bruce Kerwin has drunk some coffee he looks at his wife and says: 'Something has happened to you, Frances, and I don't know what it is.'

'Nothing has happened, Bruce,' says Frances. 'A change of clothes, a change of hairstyle. Women do it every day.'

'A change of man, from what I see of it,' says Bruce. 'I don't know what the mechanics of divorce are but we can find out when we get home.'

'The mechanics of what?' says Frances.

'Divorce,' Bruce repeats. 'The legal dissolution of a marriage.'

'Isn't that a little drastic?' Frances feels mildly alarmed. 'Nothing happened with Andrew Marner. He left the room just after you.'

'What was he doing there in the first place is what I'd like to know,' says Bruce, forking scrambled eggs. Of all the things that he has missed in the last week, a decent breakfast is high on the list.

'He fancies me, Bruce, and I owed him something. He got you out. You would be going off to prison for a couple of years now but for him.'

'Owe him?' says Bruce. 'Is sex the currency we

241

use these days? I go through hell and come out to discover that!'

Backed against the ropes, ostensibly defenceless, Frances feels the need to hit back. The man coming forward presents targets that are easier to reach than those of a man in retreat.

'Don't over-egg the pudding, Bruce. You haven't spent five years chained to a radiator. Nor were you wrongfully locked up. You brought it on yourself, and Andrew saved you. Should I tell him to sod off?'

'Incredible,' says Bruce. 'Incredible. Getting laid is now an expression of gratitude, is it?'

'I didn't get laid,' says Frances. 'Your timely arrival preserved my honour.' She pours herself more coffee and refills Bruce's cup as an afterthought. The talk of divorce has surprised her and she is trying to get used to it. Better a divorce, with its financial compensations, than the prospect that faced her two days ago – a husband in a foreign prison, endless expense and loneliness without freedom. And yet the word unsettles her. She is not sure that she would welcome the upheaval. 'You could see me as a heroine if you weren't so obtuse,' she tells him. 'Prepared to give myself to save my husband. I deserve a medal.'

This flippant approach to a serious matter irritates Bruce Kerwin. 'Jesus,' he says. 'Acclaimed for her adultery: Woman of the Year.'

'There was no adultery, Bruce,' says Frances with such force that she begins to believe it herself. 'Whatever I did it wasn't enough to get me arrested and locked up for a week. If we're talking about crazy behaviour, you want to look at yourself.'

242

'The world might think that having some cannabis in your pocket is more serious than jumping into bed with someone else's husband, but the world, as usual, is wrong,' says Bruce. 'We're talking about loyalty and trust, not some piddling rule about tobacco.'

'It seems to me,' says Frances, pushing back her chair, 'that returning to suits and ties has turned you into a bit of a prig. What happened to the T-shirts and jeans? Where's the medallion?'

'Clearly it was a mistake,' says Bruce. 'I admit mine.' He has finished his breakfast but, despite the conversation, is reluctant to move. Sunshine on the terrace is an almost sensuous pleasure after his surroundings of the last week.

'Well, we can't get the toothpaste back in the tube,' declares Frances, 'so there's no point in sitting here moaning about it.'

'That's all you've got to say, is it?' asks Bruce.

'More or less,' says Frances, standing up. 'I'm going for a walk down to the port now. Apparently you can get a catamaran to Saint-Tropez for a hundred and eighty francs. Fancy it?'

Bruce Kerwin opens his mouth to decline this offer, but he has wanted to go to Saint-Tropez for more than twenty years, an ambition implanted by an early film of Brigitte Bardot's.

'I might as well,' he says.

Esme Rutherford is taking her completed painting from the second floor up to the third. She waits until she can get a lift to herself. The portrait on its frame is awkward to carry and she is scared of damaging it. It's a relief that Andrew Marner is going

243

to have to haul it all the way back to Heathrow and beyond.

He opens the door in his Sunday clothes of short-sleeve shirt and slacks.

'Come in. Bring it in,' he says. 'Let's put it in the light.'

Esme carries the painting across the room and leans it against a chair so that it faces a window. Kimberley Neal rises from a table where she has been trying to write and comes over to have a look. She appears sullen and distracted and can hardly bring herself to say hallo.

'It's quite excellent, Esme,' says Andrew. 'What do you think, Kimberley?'

'It's very good,' says Kimberley. 'Flattering, too.'

'It's not flattering,' says Andrew, winking at Esme. 'I really look as nice as that. Now, what about money? You'll want cash?'

'Please,' says Esme. 'We rather left the fee up for negotiation.'

'Fifteen hundred springs to mind,' says Andrew. 'God knows what that is in francs.'

'It's eight point eight,' says Kimberley. 'Here's a calculator.'

'I'll call it fourteen thousand francs,' says Andrew, ignoring the calculator. 'My money is in a safe deposit box at the cashier's desk downstairs.'

'That's very generous,' says Esme.

'Girl, you've earned it, which isn't always the case these days,' says Andrew. 'Follow me downstairs. I may buy you a drink.'

Esme follows him to the door. He seems very chirpy this morning, considering yesterday's episode with Bruce Kerwin, but obviously people as successful as

Andrew Marner have an enduring capacity to shrug off setbacks and proceed as if they never happened. They operate in a world where embarrassment doesn't exist. He opens the door for her and bows her through it.

When they have gone, Kimberley Neal sighs, counts to ten and then, satisfied that there will be no more interruptions, returns to her novel, which is now called *The Topless Sandwich*. *Belinda was glad to see the back of the treacherous tycoon*, she writes. Real life and fantasy have become so intermingled in her narrative that she can no longer be sure where fact ends and fiction begins. But under its new, more suggestive title, the work has enjoyed a little spurt, an acceleration helped perhaps by its downhill journey into the *demi-monde* of The Black Whores Agency.

Things have not gone well for Belinda. Her secretarial contributions to the agency's success have not been thought to be adequate, and she has been told, in indelicate language, that a girl like her has more tangible things to offer than a pleasant telephone voice. It is a suggestion that demoralises her, and yet she can see its justification. She has studied the agency's accounts and knows that even a bordello is not immune to a recession. For some people, sex is the first economy.

Her troubles began when she took a phone call from a Frenchman called Rocard. He was enquiring about the girls and services provided, but before the conversation was through he had fallen in love with Belinda's husky voice. Soon he was calling the foreign gentleman who presided over this erotic empire, demanding the telephonist and no one else.

Kimberley is blocked here, uncertain how to move the story forward. Belinda's plunge into prostitution might raise questions that she is incapable of answering. She puts her pen down, shuts the world out and tries to concentrate. The telephone rings as her mind gropes towards an answer.

She gets up impatiently and reaches for the receiver. A French voice whispers in her ear directly she says, 'Hallo?'

'Your friend is out,' says Monsieur Rocard. 'The things I do for love.'

'Alain!' says Kimberley, remembering her place. The novel has dragged her away from the world's commercial realities. 'Thank you so much for helping. They let him out yesterday morning and he's pretty grateful.'

'It's not him I want to be grateful,' says Monsieur Rocard. 'How are you, Kimberley?'

'I'm busy as usual,' says Kimberley. 'I'm trying to write a novel, but it isn't easy.' She feels herself erecting barriers.

'Time for a break,' says Monsieur Rocard. 'I should be honoured if you would join me for dinner tomorrow night.'

'Tomorrow night?' Kimberley thinks quickly, but no excuse will come. 'It's possible,' she concedes. Playing for time, she asks: 'How did the board meeting go, Alain? Did Andrew impress your directors?'

'Very much, Kimberley,' Monsieur Rocard says soothingly. 'It looks as if we might well do a deal. Now, what about dinner? I can send a car to your hotel.'

Kimberley Neal feels the ground crumbling beneath her feet, but at the same time she can see her opportunity. If she met Rocard, she could get the credit if the Frenchman agrees to the partnership that Andrew

Marner wants. And another thought drifts into her mind: the problem of Belinda could look a lot easier afterwards. She has a date with a demanding Frenchman called Rocard, too.

17

After a gastronomic breakfast the following morning that has made few noticeable concessions to the champagne of a few hours earlier, Andrew Marner sits in his sunlit room studying the latest issues of his magazines that have been flown here for his carping examination. He comes to *World Review* nervously, partly because of its earlier gaffe, and partly because a sacked editor who has not yet left is a loose cannon on the editorial deck. But the issue is splendid, packed with the serious well-written stuff that he had always intended for it. The mounting slaughter in South Africa, examined from the peaceful ambience of an Oxford study; the resurgence of Communism in Poland, analysed from a bedroom in Hampstead; the work techniques of the Japanese, with company uniforms and early morning callisthenics, discussed by a Labour MP at Westminster; and the struggle to drag Russia into the twentieth century before the rest of us leave for the twenty-first, written by a retired academic in Somerset. Say what you like about Garnett, he certainly knew how to save on air fares. Andrew turns the pages, looking for Kimberley Neal's article on drugs, but it is trailed for next week: *Britain's drugs law farce, by Kimberley Neal.*

She comes out of the bathroom as he is scribbling a few vituperative messages to his understandably paranoid editors, and says: 'What do you think about this Rocard business? Should I meet him?'

Andrew Marner looks up, concerned. 'Of course you must meet him. A lot hangs on it.'

'He'll probably want to go to bed with me,' says Kimberley, as if this is an activity that is alien to her on religious grounds.

'Most men do,' says Andrew, 'but that's your business.'

'He's got a bony face and greasy hair,' Kimberley shudders. 'We're not talking sex symbol here.'

'All I'm concerned about, Kimberley, is that you keep him happy. How you do it is up to you, but I'll just say this: if Rocard goes ahead with the newspaper partnership I shall be a very happy man. You said that what you wanted was an editorship. Well, there's an editor's chair about to become vacant at *World Review.* Do you, as they say these days, catch my drift?'

'Wow,' gulps Kimberley, running her fingers through her hair. 'I think I'll go out and buy some new perfume.'

'Good idea,' says Andrew, getting up. 'I'm just going downstairs to fax some abuse.'

The lift takes him down one floor and then stops. The doors slide open to reveal Frances Kerwin, who is about to go shopping again. She steps in and smiles nervously.

'Hallo, Andrew.'

'Beautiful lady,' says Andrew. 'I wondered where you'd got to.'

'I'm here,' says Frances.

'And Bruce? How is he?'

'Under the moon, I'd say.'

'He wasn't a happy man before they locked him up, he wasn't happy when he was locked up, and he's still not happy now that they've released him. What is it with Bruce?'

'Finding us on the bed together was a bit of a downer.'

'Which reminds me,' says Andrew. 'We have some unfinished business.'

'We have?' says Frances.

'I definitely remember some loose talk about crumpled sheets if I got Brucie out. I also seem to remember handing over a thousand-franc note although, of course, I'm too much of a gentleman to mention it.'

Frances is embarrassed. She remembers throwing out a few unthinking promises in the push to get her husband released, but now that Bruce is back it all looks rather different. The money doesn't worry her.

'I bought a skirt with it, if you remember,' she says. 'I don't do refunds.'

The lift opens on the ground floor and they walk together into the lobby. Andrew decides to try a gentler approach.

'That's quite all right,' he says. 'I don't even want a credit note. But, Frances, this isn't a quick holiday fling. Not where I'm concerned, anyway.'

'It was wonderful, Andrew,' says Frances, 'and don't think that I didn't enjoy it, but I am trying at the moment to soothe an irate husband and I've got to watch my step.'

'Of course, of course,' says Andrew, patting her shoulder. 'I understand. I was glad to be able to help him. But I'd hate to think that I wasn't going to see you again.' He searches for an idea. 'Why don't we take a helicopter to Monte Carlo?'

Behind him, Frances can see Kimberley Neal striding across the lobby and out of the hotel, pausing briefly to give them a quizzical glance. 'Monte Carlo?'

'By helicopter,' says Andrew. 'The view of the coast is wonderful, I hear.'

'Lovely in theory, difficult in practice,' says Frances.

'I don't like to hear this defeatist talk,' says Andrew. 'At the Marner Press we don't allow it.'

'The Marner Press doesn't concern itself with adultery and deception, I imagine.'

'Oh, I don't know,' says Andrew. 'We have our moments.'

'Look,' says Frances, anxious to break off this conversation. 'I've got a bit of shopping to do.'

'Off you go then, beautiful lady,' says Andrew. 'I've got to fax a few messages to London myself. But think about what I said.'

'I will,' says Frances, moving away.

'Think helicopters.'

Frances Kerwin's hunt for new shopping experiences brings her eventually to the French department store, Galeries Lafayette. She has heard of the one in Paris, and has visited the branch in Nice, but didn't know that there was a smaller one here, tucked away in the back streets of Cannes. Her quest this morning is to find a peace offering for her husband, and Galeries Lafayette is a suitable place to conduct it. She is looking for cuff-links with matching tiepin, a present that he might appreciate now that he has abandoned hippiedom and reverted to the ironed shirt and the conventional suit.

Frances Kerwin regards it as a piece of priceless good fortune that she mentioned Saint-Tropez when she did. It was probably the only suggestion that would have kept them together yesterday, and once they had arrived and watched *pétanque* and talked to the artists on the quay, Bruce's displeasure became difficult to maintain. The day was too enjoyable and he was a free man again. By the time they came back on the catamaran things were almost normal between them and it was no longer possible for him to recreate the frigidity of that morning. Once or twice she had even made him laugh. The future is uncertain but she believes that with each day that passes it will become more difficult for him to return to the subject of divorce, a prospect Frances now sees as likely to cause more problems than it solves.

She finds the cuff-links and the tiepin that she wants, has them gift-wrapped, and then embarks on her customary search for the off-beat item that makes shopping so enjoyable for her. She has combed two floors when she sees Kimberley Neal dabbing sample perfumes on her wrist.

'What was Andrew talking about just now?' asks Kimberley. 'Is he still pestering you?'

'Well,' says Frances, surprised to be asked.

'I thought he might lay off now Bruce is out.'

'I think it's because of Bruce that he spoke to me. He thinks I owe him something,' says Frances.

'Oh?' says Kimberley. 'Why would that be?'

'Well, he played a rather important role in getting my husband out. If it wasn't for Andrew, Bruce would be looking forward to two or three years in prison.'

'But that isn't true, Frances,' says Kimberley. 'Andrew played no role at all.'

'He spoke to a man called Rocard, didn't he?'

'Did he hell,' sniffs Kimberley. 'I spoke to Rocard. Andrew wouldn't do it. He was scared of jeopardising his big deal, and I don't think he was that anxious for Bruce to get out anyway.'

'I thought – ' says Frances.

'Let me tell you what happened. Andrew wasn't going to bring it up; he said so himself. And when I raised the subject he was annoyed.'

'He's certainly misled me,' says Frances.

'I'll tell you something else: Rocard said he wouldn't have done it for Andrew anyway. He may have been joking, but he said "I cannot refuse a beautiful woman".'

Kimberley attempts a French accent with this last quotation and they both laugh. But Frances doesn't feel like laughing: she is angry at the thought that Andrew has been deceiving her.

'The lying bastard,' she says thoughtfully. 'I'm not in his debt at all.'

'You can now tell him to piss off with a clear conscience,' says Kimberley. It has been hard work getting the skids under this relationship but at last she feels that she has achieved it.

'I will,' says Frances.

'What do you think of this scent?' says Kimberley, picking up the bottle again. 'I'm meeting Rocard myself tonight. Do you think it will turn him on?'

'An unnecessary expense,' Frances declares. 'Getting scent to arouse a Frenchman is like buying a rapist Ginseng.'

* * *

Some hours later, from a penthouse suite that thrusts into the sky above the hilltop town of Grasse, Kimberley Neal looks down on the reddish stone of the Cathedral of Notre-Dame, surrounded by delightful fountains, arcades and cobbled streets and, beyond, lavender fields and rocky limestone hills. Alain Rocard has brought her inland to his plush eyrie in the hills, a remote residence that is equipped for his secret pleasures, with low lights, two-way mirrors, concealed cameras and constant subliminal music. He has talked of amazing views – 'on a clear day you can see Corsica' – but the view now is of Monsieur Rocard struggling drunkenly with a recalcitrant zip on his moleskin trousers.

Kimberley Neal, not entirely sober herself, has segued into the role of Belinda and, unable to take notes, is trying to remember things that will help her to write her novel. Whether the Monsieur Rocard who Belinda is going to meet would have the luxurious accommodation of her present host is unlikely, but she thinks that she can rewrite him so that the fictional character will come to resemble the real Alain Rocard to such an extent that the two will become indistinguishable. This way, as usual, she will avoid the challenges of invention and imagination that slow up other writers.

Monsieur Rocard slumps back now into a very deep sofa, unsure whether it's his drunkenness or the zip that is preventing the removal of his trousers, an objective to which he attaches great importance. Whichever it is he has postponed the struggle, and gazes up at Kimberley with a satisfied smile on his face as if all passion is already spent.

'You are a beautiful woman, Kimberley,' he says. 'What is the perfume?'

'Coco,' says Kimberley, smiling down at him.

'Coals to Newcastle, as you British say. Grasse is the perfume capital of the world.'

'It should be cheaper here then,' says Kimberley.

'Cheaper? No,' says Monsieur Rocard. 'It takes a ton of petals to produce two pounds of essence. Can you imagine a ton of petals?'

He closes his eyes as if to visualise this extravagant spectacle and Kimberley squats at his feet. The transition to vamp has not been accomplished as easily as she had hoped; indeed, she is not sure that it has been accomplished at all. This has come as somewhat of a surprise to her. Attracting and seducing men was a talent that she had effortlessly mastered before she was eighteen. She looks at Monsieur Rocard's untidy face and realises what the problem is. She has only ever seduced men that she fancied: the missing ingredient here is an initial sexual attraction.

This makes the problem of Belinda difficult to handle. Belinda, with the folding money already on the bed, would be required to attract and seduce without the stimulus of mutual attraction. Kimberley takes Monsieur Rocard's hand and tries to see the situation through the eyes of Belinda, but as she does so she realises that the eyes of the Frenchman have not opened since the conversation about the perfume and he is, in fact, deeply asleep.

They had eaten at the Chantecler at the Hotel Negresco on the promenade des Anglais where Monsieur Rocard introduced her to a new wine that he had discovered, produced locally only three kilometres from Nice. The wine was pleasant enough but Kimberley drank sparingly. She didn't have the capacity of a man and thought of herself, anyway, as being on duty. She drank enough to get pleasantly buzzed, but three or possibly four bottles passed across the table and she was fairly confident that the waiter wasn't drinking any. She reckoned that Alain Rocard had drunk the best part of three bottles himself as he discussed enthusiastically the beautiful love they would make in his 'flat in Grasse' and the tremendous success that he was going to have with Andrew Marner when they launched a new national newspaper in Britain. His eagerness and high expectations about these two projects seemed to create a thirst that was a challenge to the French wine industry, and when they walked from the Chantecler to Alain Rocard's chauffeur-driven Citroën, Kimberley thought that a younger man would by now be under the table.

Rocard, however, was the veteran of a thousand lunch-dates and God knows how many evening assignations, and he conducted himself perfectly. He had no need to grope her in the car; more felicitous surroundings would soon be available.

But he had underestimated the potency of his newly-discovered wine. Deterioration set in soon after they left the restaurant and was well-established by the time they reached his apartment. Unconsciousness loomed as the advertised prospect of unbridled sex receded.

Kimberley Neal, realising his condition with relief, abandons her submissive position on the floor and jumps purposefully to her feet. She tears a sheet from the notebook in her bag and looks for her pen. The important thing, she decides, is not that she goes to bed with Alain Rocard, but that he believes that she did. *Alain*, she writes, *you were wonderful in bed. Love, Kimberley.*

To add some verisimilitude to this, she masters the zip that had defeated him and removes his trousers and underpants. As a final telling touch she takes off her pants and drops them on the floor, too. She leaves the note by his side, slips out of the apartment, gets the lift to the ground floor and with the wind blowing round her bare buttocks, begins the long search for a taxi.

18

‘A history lesson,’ says Andrew Marner as he carelessly fills six champagne glasses and beams round the table.

'Between 1940 and 1944, this hotel was the favourite meeting place for spies and secret agents from both sides of the great unpleasantness. By 1944, the plotting and the conspiring were getting out of hand and the management were so anxious to stay out of trouble that they decided to shut up shop. They locked the hotel in June, and the beach, where you've all been lying in the sun, was sealed off and mined. Luckily, this only lasted two months. In August of that year, American troops arrived in Saint-Raphaël, and the hotel re-opened to welcome its liberators. Two floors were requisitioned for the officers of the American general staff. Parties and shows were organised to help them forget the war and relax. Maurice Chevalier appeared in a monthly revue, Mistinguett performed in the lobby. August 24 has been a special day in Cannes ever since. As the more observant among you will have noticed, there's even a street named *rue 24 Août*.'

'And that's why we're going to watch fireworks tonight?' says Roger Blake. 'What fun.'

'They do it every year,' says Andrew. 'The best bloody firework display you'll ever see, apparently.'

He sits back happily and smiles at his guests. He has invited Roger Blake and Esme, and Bruce and Frances Kerwin, to join him and Kimberley for dinner on the terrace to watch the firework display that will take place this evening, but his celebratory mood has nothing to do with fireworks or the liberation of Cannes: Alain Rocard has come across. His board have endorsed his decision to form a partnership with the Marner Press, with the intention of launching a new national newspaper in Britain, and tomorrow in Nice Andrew and Rocard will sign a formal agreement.

Andrew Marner isn't sure how much he owes to Kimberley Neal for this sudden, dramatic conclusion to his tortured negotiations, but Rocard has assured him over the phone that she is 'very sexy'. Whatever her role, the future which now confronts Andrew Marner glitters with promise. Fame, prestige and influence, the natural accessories to owning a national newspaper, await him; the influx of French francs removes the worry over Garnett's absurd libel; and perhaps best of all, the news makes the knighthood a certainty. He can afford to be generous tonight.

'I read that the Americans brought some lasting fashions with them,' says Esme, who has studied far more local history than Andrew during this holiday. 'Bikinis, chewing gum, sunbathing, whisky, Coca-Cola and cocktails. Tick the harmful ones.'

'They all sound good to me,' says Roger, 'but I'm a child of the American age.'

'Even if you've never been there,' says Esme.

'He doesn't need to go there,' says Frances. 'He's got a television set.'

'Travel broadens the mind, television broadens the arse,' says Esme.

She is striking a slightly churlish note this evening, she realises, and wonders why. Certainly she is not in quite the lighthearted mood that the occasion requires. A trip with Roger that afternoon to the Matisse Museum at Cimiez has tired her more than she expected, and there are other physical signals that are not conducive to good humour. She has felt tired and slightly sick for two or three days, her breasts are sore and she has missed a period. She can see where this leads and she can scarcely believe it, but she remembers a spell in the spring when she was on antibiotics and didn't take the Pill. Perhaps tomorrow she will try to find one of those do-it-yourself pregnancy tests in a *pharmacie*.

Printed menus for *dîner du 24 août* are passed round the table. Bruce Kerwin takes his and reads *Chartreuse de légumes et saumon frais aux capres, huile d'olive du moulin*. As the menus in London are in French he feels that it would be only equitable for them to be in English here. He has come to this table with some reluctance, but has capitulated to his wife's wishes.

'Forget Andrew. It will be a wonderful evening and we don't have to pay,' Frances pleaded. 'It would be stupid of us to miss it.'

So Bruce has dressed up smartly in his best suit, new shirt and new tiepin and cuff-links, and is trying tonight to reveal a more congenial side of his nature.

261

After all, he tells himself, I have got Frances and Andrew Marner hasn't.

It is a thought that has crossed Andrew Marner's mind too, along with the fact that in a few days they are all due to go home and Frances Kerwin will become difficult to find. Andrew Marner has a plan to deal with this problem, as with most others.

Beside him, Kimberley Neal, having largely shunned the alcohol last night, sees no reason to hold back now. Everything is falling into place and it has required remarkably little effort from her. She had a nasty moment earlier when she suddenly remembered the expensive camera equipment that was concealed not very efficiently on the walls of Alain Rocard's apartment. The thought of him returning sober today to watch hours of video recordings that would reveal the shocking innocence of their encounter gave her palpitations, but then she remembered that he was too drunk when they arrived to switch them on. She refills her champagne glass and hiccups gaily.

'In two days' time there's a firework display at Juan-les-Pins which presumably means that the Americans took two days to get from here to there,' she tells everybody. 'They must have been having a good time in Cannes.'

'Who doesn't?' says Roger, as their food arrives. He has relaxed for the first time in his life and doesn't want the holiday to end. The thought that this pleasurable stay in the sun is about to be followed by an English winter with six hours of daylight and eighteen of darkness is one that he tries to push from his mind.

A man is talking into a microphone on the other side of the Croisette, and a waiter tells them that he is the Mayor of Cannes, paying tribute to the Americans who liberated the town. When he has finished, the lights go out and they are all sitting in darkness. Suddenly the fireworks begin. Rockets, or fireworks that behave like rockets, soar into the sky from boats in the bay. They rise not in twos or threes but in tens or twelves, exploding in a shower of iridescent lights that must surely be visible in Italy and Toulon. They fall gracefully like spring rain while the rockets themselves plummet seaward trailing fire. Most of the hotel's clientèle, boosted today by a convention of cardiologists, have come out to the front to watch these pyrotechnics. Huge bangs resound along the street, creating an impression of seafront warfare that reminds people of Beirut, and in the sky there are always different colours, different patterns that light up the whole Croisette and pick out the black silhouette of the palm trees in the middle of the road. It is a firework display that only a city could afford, and people watch fascinated, never having seen money burnt on this scale.

The concentration that the show demands enables Andrew to whisper unseen to Frances: 'Do you think Bruce would come and work for me? The Marner Press is about to expand in a very big way.'

'So that we could continue to see each other?' says Frances. 'I shouldn't think so.'

'I thought he lost his job,' says Andrew. 'Well, I'm going to have plenty of jobs.'

'Tell me something,' says Frances. They are eating now by the light of the fireworks. 'Who got Bruce out – you, or Kimberley?'

'Well, it was my contact,' Andrew hedges.

'But Kimberley asked him?'

'I believe she did.'

'You haven't been quite honest with me, Andrew,'

says Frances. 'You led me to believe that you were responsible for his release.'

Andrew smiles innocently. 'That's because I yearn for you, Frances. I crave you with a desire that makes me feel quite ill.'

'Terrific,' says Frances.

'A man in the grip of a terrible passion is capable of doing foolish things.'

'I'm surrounded by men who do foolish things,' Frances tells him. 'I'm getting tired of it.'

Andrew takes this rebuff with a tolerant smile. He has to allow women their little displays of petulance; it gives them satisfaction and is only a pinprick to him. Anyway, he decides, plotting and planning, he can circumvent the indignation of Frances by approaching Bruce direct.

Fireworks still illuminate the night sky and people are reluctant to turn their eyes away in case they miss a four-second spectacle costing hundreds of pounds that will not be repeated. It is hard to see how many people and boats out there in the dark are responsible for the display, but the organisation is breathtaking – one star-spangled explosion follows another with hardly a gap.

'It makes my Catherine wheels look pretty poxy,' says Roger. 'Guy Fawkes night will never be the same.'

'The colour kaleidoscope is extraordinary,' says Esme. 'I'm going to try to paint it.'

'Hey, Bruce,' says Andrew. 'Do you want a job?'

'Why would I want a job?' asks Bruce. 'I've got all that redundancy money to spend.'

The waiters are taking a break during the fireworks. It is too dark for them to collect crockery, take orders and deliver fresh courses, and so they wait in the shadows leaving guests with their empty plates.

'What did Bruce say?' asks Frances. The little booms and the big bangs have left a ringing in her ears. The milder bursts have sounded like the limited explosions that blow a door in, but the bigger ones are like a terrorist outrage that devastates a street.

'He says he doesn't need a job.' Andrew looks hurt. 'He has enough money already, lucky man.'

'It would be a bizarre thing if he went to work for a man he found in bed with his wife,' says Frances. 'You expect a lot of him.'

'Most people would forget that for fifty grand a year,' says Andrew.

'How many grand?' says Frances.

'Fifty,' says Andrew. 'Plus a car.'

'You pay peanuts, you get monkeys,' says Frances for a joke. She waits to see whether an improved offer will arrive but suddenly the lights are switched on again and people can be seen. The fireworks are over.

Andrew, a busy host and master of sociability now, beckons waiters, distributes menus, orders more champagne. At the corner of the terrace three musicians are assembling their equipment: a middle-aged lady is going to sing.

'I'll have *sorbet au jasmin*,' says Esme, who still feels a little sick. 'Have you got any more jobs going, Andrew, at fifty grand a year? Roger is embarrassingly available.'

'What is his expertise?' asks Andrew.

'Well,' says Esme. 'He's good in bed.'

'We already have people who can handle that,' says Andrew.

'You?' says Esme.

'I take a personal interest in that side of things,' says Andrew. 'Yes.'

The lady on a rostrum in the corner launches herself into an old Lorenz Hart number as various puddings arrive. Looking around the terrace, Roger decides that the Carlton Hotel should have a Joan Collins lookalike competition in the same way that more downmarket establishments have wet T-shirt contests. He notices something else: rich customers leave their drinks in a way that the poor would never do. He finishes his and Andrew promptly refills it.

'What's this all about, Andrew?' he asks. 'Some scheme in the offing to make you even richer?'

'Richer and more powerful, Roger,' Andrew says. 'One day you will tell people that Sir Andrew Marner once bought you dinner.'

'Blimey,' says Roger. 'What are you going to do? Open a dirty video shop?'

'A video shop?' says Andrew, perplexed. 'No. Tomorrow in Nice I'm going to sign a contract with a French publisher and then, one fine morning, you will wake up to discover that Britain has a new daily newspaper, a newspaper for the twenty-first century, a paper that doesn't believe that its readers are morons, bores or snobs.'

'How interesting,' says Esme. 'And where will this newspaper stand, politically?'

'We're going to fly by the seat of our pants,' says Andrew. 'We'll find out where public opinion is going and squat down in the middle of it.'

'Brave stuff,' says Esme. 'Not stand up to be counted, more lie down and count them.'

'No point in alienating half the electorate,' Andrew tells her sagely. 'We need readers, not enemies.'

266

'What do you make of him, Frances?' asks Esme.

'Andrew?' says Frances. 'He's a rogue. I suppose his heart is in the right place: it's the whereabouts of his trousers that causes scandal and concern.'

'And you reckon this little venture is going to make you a knight?' asks Roger.

'When this newspaper gets going I'll probably be offered a peerage,' says Andrew. 'It goes with the territory.'

'Lord Libertine of Leg-over,' says Frances to Esme. 'A new virile image for the Upper House.'

'You'd better give me your phone number, Roger,' says Andrew, ignoring them. 'There'll be new premises and much work to do. I seem to remember that you are in the business of providing teams of reliable men?'

'Builders, painters, carpenters, joiners,' says Roger. It seems a long time since he organised anybody.

'That's what I'll need,' says Andrew. 'The future starts now.'

In the corner the singer is telling them why the lady is a tramp, and part of the terrace has been given over to dancing. Couples move sedately through the hot evening air, as waiters struggle to deliver coffee.

Kimberley Neal turns to Bruce Kerwin, who seems to have said so little this evening. 'You've changed, Bruce,' she tells him. 'Captivity has matured you.' She wonders whether he realises how many women got laid, or nearly got laid, in the noble cause of obtaining his freedom.

'I was only an old man with go-faster stripes,' says Bruce. 'I'm learning to act my age.'

The irony, thinks Kimberley, is that the only person not to benefit in the sexual stock exchange was Bruce himself, but he looks like a man who has spent his life relentlessly preoccupied with matters of no importance while everybody else was queueing up for the world's pleasures. To Kimberley he seems a somewhat irascible person, dazed by failure, but she feels no wave of sympathy. She believes that, one way or another, you make your own luck.

'What are you going to do about work when you get home?' she asks.

'I'll get a job,' says Bruce. 'Recessions end. All the firms who were ruthlessly laying off people a year or so ago will soon be looking for staff. It's happening in the City already.'

'You should have taken up Andrew's kind offer,' says Kimberley. 'Mr Marner is going places.'

'I'd sooner stand on my head in a bucket of cow dung,' says Bruce. 'The last thing I want on this earth is that man for a boss.'

'Well,' says Kimberley, surprised at the venom, 'his pay is good.'

'I don't want his pay,' says Bruce. 'All I want where Andrew Marner is concerned is revenge. It wasn't even him, apparently, who got me out of that cell. It was you, wasn't it?'

'It was, Bruce,' says Kimberley.

'I'm very grateful. What can I buy you?'

'A Roller?' says Kimberley. 'A Picasso? How are you going to get your revenge on poor old Andrew then? Do tell!'

'I don't know,' says Bruce, 'but something will turn up.'

19

A broad has never held much interest for Bertha Marner but she feels a mild exhilaration as her British Airways Airbus bounces on to the runway at Nice. The news that she is bringing will make this journey memorable and easily justify the hours that she is losing on the golf course. It will certainly produce a celebration that she couldn't miss.

She comes out of the airport building with one large suitcase and finds a queue of taxis waiting impatiently for business. Soon she is hurtling west on roads that seem dangerously fast, but Bertha Marner is a stoic and she shuts her mind to the palpable hazards that surround her and tries to imagine how Andrew will react to the wonderful letter in her handbag.

He is not a man given to demonstrative behaviour; he doesn't shout and dance. Emotionally he is locked to the Marner Press and its setbacks and successes. It was probably just as well that they never had children; she fears that, obsessive worker that he is, he would have been an absentee father. She thinks too, that the little ones might have irritated her quite quickly, interfering with her busy social schedule and curbing her bridge parties and golf. In retrospect, the non-appearance of children has suited them both.

More surprising, perhaps, is his disinterest in sex. She can understand that he doesn't find her as attractive as she once was, but she is quietly mystified that he hasn't taken another woman into his life on a part-time basis. Over the years there has never been a rumour or a hint, and she has watched for the signs with gimlet eyes. Looking back on it all, her husband has been a gem – faithful, hard-working and a marvellous provider of the material things that have become so difficult for many people to afford in the depressed decade that is carrying them all to the millennium. A knighthood is the least he deserves.

Her taxi has abandoned the crowded highway and nose-dived down a slip road that has taken her into various junctions and on to a long straight road that heads south to the sea. Bertha Marner perks up, studying architecture and shops, and then they are on the front with the sea glistening in the sun on their left. The crowds basking in the summer's heat evoke no envy: she prefers the windy challenge of eighteen holes at the East Berks.

The taxi turns into the shadows of a huge white building and comes to a halt beneath white columns and palm trees. This is clearly the grand entrance to the hotel and she gets out and pays the driver. It has been a trouble-free journey during which nothing has gone wrong; but from this moment nothing goes right.

The man on duty at the reception desk, a polite and charming young Frenchman, explains that it is not possible to book into a room that already has a resident unless that resident appears at Reception to make the arrangement himself.

'Residents would come back and find people in their rooms,' he says with an uneasy laugh.

'Get him on the phone,' says Bertha Marner. 'I'm his wife, you stupid man.'

The man turns and calls a number on the desk phone and then stands there patiently with the receiver at his ear.

'There is no reply,' he says. 'Mr Marner must be out.'

'And what am I supposed to do?' asks Bertha Marner. 'Stand here all day?'

'Madam, I suggest you sit down over there,' says the receptionist, pointing at dozens of expensive sofas that are placed on carpeted squares throughout the hall.

Bertha Marner picks up her case, stomps twenty yards to the nearest seat and then sits down angrily and prepares to wait.

In a spotless *pharmacie* on the rue d'Antibes, Esme Rutherford picks her way nervously through sun creams and corn plasters, laxatives and lozenges, eye drops and insect repellent, in search of a discreet pregnancy test that can be conducted in the privacy of her hotel bedroom. She has looked up 'pregnant' in her French dictionary and found *enceinte* – a word that she thought was English anyway. 'Test' she can't find, but 'testament' is *testament*, 'testicle' is *testicule* and 'textile' is *textile*. It is difficult to see what the language problem is.

The room is blindingly white and the sun dips in to dazzle her as it shimmers off the white floor, white walls and white chairs which this chemist has thoughtfully provided on the assumption that his customers are less healthy than most. She picks up what appears to be a pregnancy test and reads the instructions in French. Babies and childbirth are so far removed from her primary interests that she would have difficulty in following the message if it was in English.

She moves towards the French girl behind the counter, seeking help and enlightenment, but is stopped by the groan of a woman behind her.

'Get me some headache pills,' says Kimberley Neal. 'I'm dying.'

'Did we overdo it last night?' asks Esme.

'I think we might have had rather more than was good for us,' says Kimberley, 'and then I woke up in the night with a splitting head and found I was out of Veganin. But it was a great evening, wasn't it? The trouble is, I've got to go off drinking again in a minute. Andrew's signing his big deal, after which we plan to get smashed.'

'Lovely,' says Esme doubtfully. The eternal appeal of alcohol as the companion for every celebration has always been a mystery to her. 'Couldn't you celebrate with tomato juice?'

'Tomato juice doesn't seem to do it somehow,' sighs Kimberley. 'What's that you're buying?'

'I'm hoping it's a pregnancy test,' says Esme. 'On the other hand, it could be a device for removing calluses and extraneous tissue.'

'A pregnancy test?' says Kimberley. 'You're not pregnant, Esme, are you?'

'I don't know that, do I, Kimberley? It explains, if you think about it, why I'm buying a test.'

'My God, sooner you than me,' shudders Kimberley. 'I just can't imagine having some little bastard inside kicking me around.'

'You can't imagine?' says Esme. 'Have you never had a child?'

'No, and I never will,' says Kimberley. 'I've got enough to do with my life without trying to make time for some demanding little brat.'

'But I thought you had a son,' says Esme. 'Roger thinks you have a son.'

'Oh, that!' says Kimberley, remembering. She laughs but isn't really embarrassed. 'It's a little difficult to explain.'

'Have a go,' says Esme.

'Well,' says Kimberley, 'I've been writing a novel and the things I told Roger were what was happening in the book. When I got his reaction, I wrote it into the novel. That way, what I put into the story was real and had an authentic ring. It was, after all, the way that a man would really react to the news of a baby.'

'I always thought writers had to imagine these things,' says Esme. 'Silly me.'

'It's a lot easier if you don't. And best of all, you know you've got it right because you've watched it take place in front of you.'

'So you make things happen to fit the demands of your narrative,' says Esme.

'It's called research,' says Kimberley. 'At least, that's what I call it.' She looks at the goods displayed on the counter. 'What's French for headache?'

'*Mal de tête*,' says Esme, walking over to the assistant.

She is meeting Roger for a coffee in the port, and then they are going to take a boat trip. Most of this holiday has now slipped by without their managing to get on the water. He is sitting as arranged in the Cristal Bar, reading an English newspaper. For half an

273

hour he has walked round the port, feeling that he is saying goodbye to it and wondering if he will ever get down here again.

On the Quai Saint Pierre, which runs along one side of the port, the influence is uniformly nautical, with shops that sell inflatable dinghies and offices that specialise in yacht charters. It is the sea connection, Roger thinks now, that gives the place its magic, bestowing qualities of air and space that are not to be found in a land-locked city that has never heard the plaintive boom of a ship's horn.

'Things are as bad as ever at home,' he says, putting down his newspaper. 'We'd better stay here.'

'I could handle that,' says Esme, 'but what do we use for francs?'

He gets up and fetches her a coffee.

'Do you want the good news or the bad news?' she asks when he sits down.

'Confine yourself to the good news,' says Roger. 'I feel a little fragile this morning.'

'I bumped into your old friend Kimberley Neal in the chemist. We had a little chat.'

'That's nice,' says Roger.

'She's never had a baby in her life. You are not a father.'

'That's not good news, it's bad news.'

'I, on the other hand, am almost certainly pregnant. I've just bought a test that I'm sure will confirm it.'

'That's not bad news, that's good news,' says Roger.

'I'm glad you think so.'

'What was Kimberley playing at, then?'

'You were a guinea pig in her drive for literary veracity,' says Esme. 'She wrote your reaction into some novel she's writing.'

'The lying cow,' says Roger. 'I feel used.'

'Used and discarded like an old sock,' sighs Esme. 'But you could end up as a footnote in some future literary encyclopaedia. Are you ready for immortality?'

'I'm ready for fatherhood,' says Roger. 'At least she's prepared me for that.'

'I'm glad to hear it,' says Esme. 'How are you with nappies?'

'I'll learn,' says Roger. 'When is this little treasure due?'

'I've no idea,' says Esme, 'but I've got an awful feeling that I am more pregnant than most women are when they first discover it. It just never occurred to me.'

'April!' Roger exclaims. 'You conceived in April. We're looking at a New Year baby here.'

'You suddenly know an awful lot.'

'I was there,' says Roger. 'I participated. I participated myself stupid, I seem to remember. What happened to the magic of the Pill?'

'I stopped it for a while when I was on antibiotics.'

'It was April then,' says Roger. 'I was right.'

They go out of the Cristal Bar and head for the boats. Esme, relieved at Roger's reaction, takes his hand. He is undergoing an intensive period of adjustment as he quietly forgets the son that he has been thinking about and starts instead to imagine spending time with a child who has not yet arrived. The prospect invigorates him and helps to ease the black mood that has begun to descend as the time approaches for him to return home. The future holds something, even if it isn't the limitless wealth he keeps dreaming about. He has something to look forward to.

*　　*　　*

275

Dreams are rampant in the chauffeur-driven Daimler that brings Andrew Marner and Kimberley Neal back from Nice. In this company, stars are there to be reached, targets are made to be hit and fortunes are out there to be made. For once the ecstasy radiated by this pair as they swoop through Antibes owes nothing to physical juxtaposition. It is rooted chastely in Andrew Marner's briefcase, which now holds priceless documents that are prettily beribboned and covered with seals, stamps and signatures.

The mutual joy in the Daimler owes something, too, to champagne, large quantities of which have accompanied the formal proceedings in Alain Rocard's lawyer's office. Every speech, every promise, every signature seemed to require a toast, and Andrew Marner and Kimberley Neal are now such boisterous company that their driver has felt obliged to slide shut the window between them.

'When I was twenty and full of tomorrow,' says Andrew far too loudly.

'As opposed to fifty and full of yesterday,' says Kimberley, burping and laughing.

'I could not have dreamed that things would fall this way. But determination and dedication kicks the doors open, plus a bit of luck and a lot of seven-day weeks. And so now – to the productive come the prizes. For myself, for dealing so patiently with the serpentine mind of Alain Rocard, a knighthood at the very least. And for Kimberley Neal – '

'Whose tireless energy, loyalty and superb support have helped to make the Marner Press what it is – '

'The coveted and prestigious editorship of *World Review*. A stepping stone, we all believe, to greater things.'

'Oh, Andrew,' says Kimberley, 'do you really mean it?'

'I mean it,' says Andrew. 'I shall fax the news to London today.'

Kimberley Neal falls across him in the back of the Daimler and kisses his neck, his face, his mouth. 'I've an idea,' she whispers.

'That's what you're paid for, Miss Neal.'

'Why don't we go to bed?'

'That is a concept of the highest quality,' says Andrew. 'Driver, hit that horse.'

The mood is quite different on the beach where Bruce and Frances Kerwin lie on adjacent sunbeds in uneasy peace. They are sadly aware that they are not going to see much sun in the next few months and feel that they should not waste what is available here today, but as they lie on their backs with their eyes closed and various creams and ointments smeared over their faces and bodies, they find little to say to each other. There is much healing to be done in this relationship and healing takes time.

Frances is very brown now, but her husband, who has unfortunately missed quite a lot of the sun's attention, is appreciably paler. He lies there hoping to reduce the gap so that he won't be asked to explain when they get home why he is so white when his wife is so tanned.

His sense of grievance, the freight he always carries with him, shows no sign of abating now that he is free. Griefs and gripes, trials, troubles and tribulations, seem to follow one another in his long journey towards old age, leaving no gap for the gaiety which sustains others. Today's bout of melancholy has been provoked by the sight last night of Andrew Marner dispensing food, drinks and jokes to his captive audience, bought by his money and compromised by his endless generosity. The Andrew Marners of this world ignore the feelings of ordinary people, take what they want – *and then behave as if they haven't taken it!* People are left in their wake, humiliated and confused, while the Andrew Marners stride on, with an indifferent smile, as they close tenaciously on some elusive goal.

It is difficult for Bruce Kerwin to relax with thoughts like this surging through his head, and he sits up and gazes round the beach. A family plays in the shallow water a few feet in front of him, and beyond them, water skiers are plunging precariously over the placid sea. The people around him on the sunbeds on the beach have found a peace that continues to elude him. Frances, for one, is obviously asleep, and he wonders as he looks at her whether she went to bed with Andrew Marner while he was locked up.

He doesn't dare to ask. He doesn't want to know. The truth could be one more obstacle to his contentment.

He slips on his trousers and shoes and reaches for an old Marks and Spencer shirt that he has worn to the beach. His mind won't allow him to sleep and a little exercise will do him good. His movements wake Frances.

'Can't you relax?' she asks.

'Oddly, no,' says Bruce. 'I'm going for a walk along the front. I'll see you back in the hotel.'

'Don't talk to any strange men,' says Frances, 'particularly if they're bearing gifts.'

'That's very whimsical, Frances,' says Bruce. 'You ignore the men as well, strange or otherwise.'

He climbs the steps that lead up from the beach and sets off along the Croisette. Perhaps the use of a little energy will jolt his brain and change his thoughts. Perhaps the view from the Croisette of sea, sand and beautiful women will arrest the gnawing exasperation that eats into him.

And for a while it works. The children on the beach with their kites, the wonderful girls on the sunbeds, the sun in the palm trees, all bring home to him that he is here on holiday and is supposed to be enjoying himself. He walks as far as the port and then turns and heads back for the Carlton Hotel when the trick begins to fail and his thoughts return to Andrew Marner. It generates considerable pique in his brain and he reaches the hotel in a bad mood.

He walks through the lobby wondering whether a few lengths in the pool would help to dispel his ill-humour, when his path is blocked by a very solid woman of about fifty who is wearing an expensive suede jacket that is inappropriate for this heat, and a voluminous jonquil skirt. She has a large face, big hips and solid ankles. He goes to sidestep her as he has seen footballers do, but it is clear that it is him she wants. His impression now is that she was sitting here when he came in and has risen to intercept him.

'I'm looking for somebody who is English,' she says in a deep, confident voice.

'And you picked me out, did you?' says Bruce resentfully. He still hoped, despite the image changes, that he appeared a more cosmopolitan figure.

'In that Marks and Spencer shirt? I should think so,' says the woman with a smile. 'I'm trying to find a man called Andrew Marner, and I wondered if you knew him, or knew where he might be?'

'You'd better get in the queue, madam,' says Bruce, 'although I fear that you're a little old for him.'

279

'Andrew Marner?' says Bertha Marner. 'Are we talk-ing about the same Andrew Marner?'

'He owns magazines,' says Bruce. 'He's staying here with a blonde tart called Kimberley.'

'Oh, I don't think so,' says Bertha Marner. 'Why do you talk about him like this? Don't you like him or something?'

'He's not my favourite person,' Bruce agrees. 'But as I found him in bed with my wife last week it's hardly surprising.'

'Andrew?' says Bertha. 'In bed with your wife?'

'He's a one-man sex orgy,' says Bruce, delighted to be spreading the news. 'The dogs bolt when he shows up, even the male ones.'

Bertha Marner stares at him and wonders whether she is hearing things. 'He's staying here with a girl, you say?'

'Kimberley Neal.'

'I've heard of her. She writes in one of his maga-zines.'

'Tall, sexy blonde,' says Bruce. 'But not even she can satisfy his appetite. When I was away for a few days last week I came back to find him in bed with my wife. The man is a menace, I'm afraid.'

The big woman he is talking to had looked indestruct-ible when she blocked his path, but she has wilted visibly now.

'The astonishing thing is,' says Bruce, for whom this conversation is beginning to assume cathartic qualities, 'the man has actually got a wife somewhere, poor bitch.'

'I am that wife,' says Bertha Marner, sitting down suddenly.

'Oh God, I'm sorry,' says Bruce, sitting down beside her. 'I never knew.'

'I'm the poor bitch,' says Bertha Marner, and there are signs of tears in her eyes. 'Is everything you've told me true?'

'I'm afraid it is,' says Bruce, 'although I wouldn't have sprung it on you like that if I'd known who you were. Can I get you a drink?'

'No, thank you,' says Bertha Marner. 'I'll just sit here for a little while and think.' She pauses and stares thoughtfully into her lap. 'This Kimberley Neal,' she says, 'is she an attractive woman?'

'She'd be more than enough for a normal man,' says Bruce, 'but not enough apparently for your husband.' He searches his mind for something disparaging and damaging that he can throw into this pot which is starting to bubble nicely. 'He should bequeath his libido to the Harvard Medical School for research. They've probably never seen anything like it outside a zoo.'

This seems to be one remark too many for the demoralised matron beside him. She braces her shoulders, as if warding off a blow, and then she relaxes and looks at him with a hard, cool stare.

'Do you know,' she says as she gets a grip on herself, 'I think I've heard enough.'

The woman has an authoritative manner and there is something dismissive about her tone. Bruce Kerwin stands up reluctantly. There were a few more observations that he would have liked to offer, but it is clear that the woman no longer needs his help.

'Well, goodbye then,' he says. 'You have my sympathy.' He turns and walks towards the lift feeling a deep sense of satisfaction that he hasn't known for months.

Bertha Marner remains on the sofa in a state of shock and it is some time before she can collect her thoughts.

When she feels the beginning of a recovery she turns over the conversation in her mind. What she has heard is so at odds with the truth as she knew it that she wonders whether she has just intercepted a madman, disseminating lies and mischief. He was plausible, but that is the insidious characteristic of madmen. She comforts herself with this idea for a few minutes, but then she remembers Kimberley Neal. How would the madman have known her name if she wasn't here? And his description of her fitted the pictures that have appeared with her column in the magazine.

And then she sees them. Arm in arm, clearly drunk, they come rolling through the door of the hotel, clutching each other and laughing. They are far too preoccupied with themselves to notice her, sitting quietly on a sofa twenty yards away. The girl's skirt is riding up her thighs, helped by her husband's hand which is drunkenly fondling her bottom. They cross the hall noisily and vanish into a lift.

Bertha Marner, hurt in a way that she has never been hurt before, sits on the sofa for a long time, wondering what to do. The idea of following them and confronting them is contemplated and rejected. What would it achieve? The fallout would probably destroy her marriage, lose her marvellous home, and severely affect a lifestyle to which she is addicted.

She sits there considering alternative retribution and then she sees what she must do. She pulls the magical letter from her handbag, finds her pen and writes six words in capital letters across the bottom. Then she gets up and goes across to the reception desk where she asks for an envelope and buys a stamp. She goes back to her seat, deciphers the extravagant signature at the foot of the letter and addresses the envelope to him at 10 Downing Street. She has got to do this now, she tells herself, before she changes her mind. She seals and stamps the envelope, gets up and drops it in the hotel's postbox. Then she orders a taxi, which arrives with surprising speed.

As she is hurried back in the direction of Nice Airport, Bertha Marner grimly mutters to herself the six-word message that she has scribbled at the bottom of the letter: STUFF YOUR TRINKETS UP YOUR ARSE.

20

On Saturday morning Roger Blake stands in his room surrounded by clothes, shoes, guidebooks, maps, boxes of chocolates, bottles of wine, presents for friends, museum artefacts collected by Esme, postcards that were never sent, shavers, razors, brushes and boxes.

'The great thing about driving to a holiday is that you don't have to pack,' he says. 'You just lob everything in the car.'

'We'll pack what we can and lob what we can't,' says Esme, folding dresses and putting them in a case. 'We don't want the car to look like a skip. When do you think we'll be home?'

'Ah,' says Roger. 'There's been a change of plan. We're going to stop in Paris to celebrate our news.'

The previous day Esme emerged solemnly from the bathroom to confront him with the result of her pregnancy test. 'The powder has turned pink,' she announced.

'Is that good?' Roger asked. 'Is that what we wanted to happen?'

'It depends how you feel about population increases, Daddy.'

'That's the way it is,' said Roger. 'Well, I'm delighted.'

'If you're delighted, I'm delighted,' said Esme. 'I just hope my mother is delighted.'

'Your mother will be thrilled,' said Roger, kissing her. 'Let's hope the baby looks like you.'

The news could not have arrived for him at a better time. His picture of a deserted son, growing up somewhere in Scotland, had become vivid and was difficult to relinquish. He can let go of it now, forget the imaginary progeny of Kimberley Neal and prepare for something real.

'Paris?' says Esme. 'That would be nice.'

'The Left Bank, Montmartre, the Moulin Rouge!'

'The Louvre,' adds Esme. 'The Mona Lisa, the Venus de Milo.'

'A couple of nights,' decides Roger. 'We'll get a ferry home on Monday evening.'

Esme returns to her packing with renewed vigour. 'In that case,' she says, 'let's hit the road.'

In a suite on the floor above their heads, Kimberley Neal is tearing up her novel which is now called *Loose Screws*. The new title, which was intended to bring her salacious material into a sharper focus for both the writer and the reader, has arrived too late to save the sad story of Belinda from the refuse collectors of Cannes. Kimberley Neal has more exciting objectives to think about, bigger ambitions to fulfil.

The editorship of *World Review* will sweep her into an élite world of pundits and poseurs where surprising invitations arrive in every post. Some of them will come from television producers, and if she isn't summoned to their studios to discuss the Chancellor's handling of the economy, she will certainly be called in to join grinning panels of gabby extroverts who try to guess which celebrity drives this car or what colour knickers the Queen wears.

The future is full of thrilling prospects like this and she rips up the pages of her manuscript without a tinge of regret. She stuffs the pieces into the bin in the bathroom and returns to the more serious business of packing. Her suitcases groan at her wardrobe, miraculously enlarged by the best shops in Cannes, and she sits on lids and wrestles with catches as she tries to get the cases shut.

Andrew Marner, a seasoned traveller, has already packed. His cases wait by the door for a porter's trolley, and he sits at the window reading the *International Herald Tribune* which carries a mournful appraisal of the world's financial expectations in the second half of the 1990s.

'What time is the flight?' he asks.

'Noon,' says Kimberley. 'Unless you want to stay?'

'I do,' says Andrew, 'but my loving wife expects me home.'

'She'll be pleased to see you, will she?'

'Bertha is always pleased to see me,' says Andrew. 'That's what marriage is about.'

Kimberley Neal doesn't want to pursue this and she is saved from doing so by a knock on the door. She abandons the cases and crosses the room to open it.

Bruce Kerwin stands there in grey suit, white shirt, blue tie. He is clutching a small package which, as the door opens, he pushes into Kimberley's hands.

'It's a small thank-you present,' he says, 'for getting me out.'

'Bruce, how kind,' says Kimberley, wondering what so small a parcel could contain.

'I hope you like it,' says Bruce. 'Frances chose it, actually.'

He can sense the possibility that he will be invited in, but through the door he can see Andrew Marner reading a newspaper and he doesn't know whether he is aware of the frank conversation that Bruce has had with his wife.

'I wonder what it is?' says Kimberley, looking at her little packet.

'It's a brooch,' says Bruce. 'My wife tells me it's elegant.'

'Well, that's very kind,' says Kimberley. 'Are you coming in?'

'No, no,' says Bruce, retreating. 'We're still packing. Our flight's at twelve.'

'We're on the same one,' says Kimberley.

'But you'll be at the front and we'll be at the back. Still, I expect we'll see you later.'

He turns and walks down the corridor and Kimberley shuts the door.

'If I was a graffiti merchant I'd spray the walls of this hotel with a message about that little turd,' says Andrew. 'Do you know what it would say?'

'What?' asks Kimberley.

'Killjoy was here.'

'That's very witty, Andrew,' says Kimberley. 'Now can you help me with these bloody cases?'

'Did she open it?' asks Frances Kerwin.

'Not while I was there,' says Bruce.

'Sit down, dear,' says Frances. 'I fetched the bill.'

She is holding a sheaf of blue sheets that are stapled

together in one corner; at the top of each one it says *Facture/Invoice*. Bruce accepts this gift reluctantly and begins to read.

'What's *plage balnéaire, 300 francs*?' he asks. 'It appears a lot.'

'Sunbeds on the beach,' says Frances.

'What's *plage déjeuner, 66 francs*?' asks Bruce.

'Drinks on the beach,' says Frances.

'Health Centre, mini-bar, room service,' says Bruce. 'It certainly pushes the price up.'

'The hotel's slogan is "tradition meets excellence",' says Frances. 'They are the sort of things you have to pay for.'

'Was it worth it?' asks Bruce.

'It certainly was,' Frances assures him. 'It's been a memorable holiday. Thank God we got out of that dump in Nice.'

'There were times when I yearned for that dump in Nice,' says Bruce. 'You won't find Cannes police station in the tourists' guides.'

Frances Kerwin feels that this subject has caused enough pain already and returns to the difficult task of packing. She, too, is finding that the space available for her clothes has failed to keep pace with the booty that she has accrued on the rue d'Antibes, and she is soon engaged in a crushing and cramming exercise, the effects of which will only be repaired by a dry cleaner. Her more exotic purchases are buried deep in her suitcases for she is travelling today in clothes that she brought with her. Apart from the hair trim, she now looks exactly as she did when she arrived three weeks ago.

Bruce Kerwin notices this image shift with approval. After his own ineffectual gropings towards a new persona he doesn't like to mention it, but he wasn't looking forward to the barbed comments of neighbours when his wife reached home looking like a girl of twenty-eight. He puts the bill down and gets up to help her shut the cases.

'I don't know about holidays,' he says. 'They certainly disrupt your life.'

'Of course, not everybody has holidays packed with such drama,' says Frances, 'unless they're skateboarding up the Matterhorn.'

'I know,' says Bruce. 'It's strange. We only came here for a bit of peace.'

In the lobby downstairs they pay their bill with a mixture of Eurocheques, credit cards and real French money. Then they sit down and wait for the porter to catch them up with their luggage before they order a taxi to the airport.

People are leaving, others arriving with pale faces, high hopes and suitcases that carry the baggage stickers of a dozen different airlines. They stumble into the Carlton Hotel and gaze in awe at its marble columns and frescoed ceilings before waiting to be assigned a room.

Roger Blake and Esme Rutherford appear from the lift, laden with flimsy supermarket bags that are full of their belongings. They come over.

'Are you going home today as well?' asks Frances.

'Not exactly,' says Roger. 'We're going to Paris for a couple of days. We car drivers have more flexibility. We're not tied to the schedules and routes of our great national airlines.'

'We're on a little celebration,' says Esme. 'It turns out that I'm expecting a baby.'

'Really?' says Bruce Kerwin, looking sad. 'How wonderful.'

'A baby?' says Frances. 'Are you getting married then?'

'One step at a time, Frances,' says Roger. 'She hasn't asked me yet.'

He goes across to the reception desk to pay the remainder of his bill with money that Esme has earned from her painting. Scared of a spiralling debt, he has been paying the hotel weekly. He is relieved to see when he has settled up that there is enough left to pay for a couple of nights in Paris. He gives the receptionist details about his car which has been spirited away to the Carlton Hotel's concealed car park, and is glad that the task of starting it after all this time won't fall to him. When he returns to the others they are exchanging addresses the way people do at the end of holidays with the promises of Christmas cards, invitations and family news that are rarely fulfilled or even remembered.

'I'm going to knit something for your baby,' Frances tells him.

'That's kind,' says Roger. 'Can you knit banknotes?'

'Fancy you two expecting a baby!' says Bruce.

'I know,' says Roger. 'Mind you, I think sexual intercourse had a lot to do with it.'

A trolley has appeared now with Esme's suitcases, and another arrives with the Kerwins' luggage. At the same moment Andrew Marner and Kimberley Neal come out of the lift carrying Esme's painting which has been carefully packed in a huge blue plastic bag. It is clear that getting this back to London will not be easy, and Andrew leans it with relief against one of the marble columns in the lobby.

'Hallo everybody,' he says. 'Or, rather, goodbye.'

Kimberley Neal – Kimberley, with her shredded novel

291

and her dazzling future – stands beside him beaming at them all.

Roger Blake produces a sheet of paper on which he has written his name, address and telephone number. 'Here you are, Andrew,' he says, handing it to him. 'Any work you want done, any work at all, get in touch.'

'I will,' says Andrew, folding the sheet carefully and putting it in his wallet. 'Have a couple of dozen good men standing by.'

'And you, Esme,' says Kimberley Neal. 'I'm wondering if *World Review* might be able to use your artistic talents. Can you do caricatures?'

'Caricatures, cartoons, collage, posters, portraits, landscapes,' recites Esme. 'What have you got to do with *World Review*?'

'I'm the new editor,' says Kimberley, 'and I'm looking for an infusion of talent. I thought you might be able to do a little work for me at home.'

'Lovely,' says Esme. 'And congratulations. Andrew has my address.'

'I'll contact you,' says Kimberley. 'Between ourselves, women are about to get a look-in in a big way.'

'Oh well,' says Andrew, glancing round the hotel lobby, 'all good things come to an end.'

'The trouble is,' says Bruce Kerwin, 'the end that the good things come to is usually yours. I'm going to order a taxi.'

'Can you order two?' asks Kimberley, as Bruce sets off for the reception desk.

'Still grumpy, is he?' says Andrew to Frances.

'Just a bit,' says Frances. 'But he's getting better.'

Andrew bends down towards her. 'I've something to tell you,' he says.

'I bet you have,' says Frances. 'What is it, Andrew?'

'Kitty Kallen.'

'Kitty Kallen?'

'It's the answer to the question. I faxed my people in London.'

'If Kitty Kallen is the answer, what's the question?'

'Who recorded "Little Things Mean A Lot"?'

'So it is!' says Frances. 'Kitty bloody Kallen. It took you long enough.'

'Well,' says Andrew, 'I've been very busy.'

'Your busyness has impressed us all,' says Frances. 'Now we're going home for a rest.'

Roger is talking to Kimberley Neal.

'No baby then?'

'Sorry about that,' says Kimberley. 'To be honest, if I'd had one I wouldn't have known who the father was.'

'Well, I'm glad I was able to help you with your novel. How is it coming along?'

'It's not coming along at all,' says Kimberley. 'I've torn it up.'

'Life is full of false starts,' says Roger.

'For some people it's the only kind of start they make,' says Kimberley. 'But I know where I'm going now.'

'So do I,' says Roger. 'Paris. And here's my car.'

The grimy Ford Granada has been delivered to the hotel's entrance. It is easily the least impressive vehicle they have seen draw up there during the last three weeks.

'We'd better get moving,' says Esme. 'We don't want to destroy the Carlton's reputation.'

Suddenly the holiday is over and they disperse in confusion. Andrew is paying his bill at the desk with money that he has left in the hotel's safe. Bruce Kerwin is trying to get his bulging luggage into the back of a

293

small taxi. Roger Blake is throwing bags on to the rear seat of the Ford Granada; its boot is already filled by his tent.

'Back to the real world!' shouts Frances, but her rallying cry goes unheard by the others, who are busily preparing for that unwelcome journey.